EVEN IN PARADISE

ELIZABETH NUNEZ

AKASHIC BOOKS

Published by Akashic Books
©2016 Elizabeth Nunez

Hardcover ISBN-13: 978-1-61775-439-5
Paperback ISBN-13: 978-1-61775-440-1
Library of Congress Control Number: 2015954056

Akashic Books
Twitter: @AkashicBooks
Facebook: AkashicBooks
E-mail: info@akashicbooks.com
Website: www.akashicbooks.com

For my granddaughters, Jordan and Savannah Nunez Harrell

Acknowledgments

Once again I am indebted to Johnny Temple, the indefatigable publisher of Akashic Books, and to Ibrahim Ahmad, his intrepid senior editor, both brilliant men who guided me through multiple revisions of this novel. My good friends and sharp literary critics Anne-Marie Stewart and Patricia Ramdeen Anderson were invaluable readers. My deepest gratitude to them.

My sister Judith Veira probably will not remember this, but she was the one who fired my imagination when she took me up a hill in Barbados to meet an aging white Barbadian man whose family had lived for generations in their magnificent house with a miraculous view of a rolling green valley, once a sugarcane plantation, edged by the glistening blue Caribbean Sea. This story, however, is not about him.

Do I dare thank William Shakespeare too for his exquisite verses, his memorable lines, his spellbinding plays, and his profound insights into human nature? Four hundred years have passed since his death in April 1616 and we remain in awe, inspired by the possibility of words to enchant, to show us our worst and best selves.

I thank my son, Jason Harrell, and his wife, Denise Woods Harrell, for their love and support.

Think'st thou that duty shall have dread to speak
When power to flattery bows?
                                                —King Lear

I

I met Corinne Ducksworth when she was a young girl, just turned twelve. There was nothing about her or about the day I first saw her to give me the slightest warning that years later I would fall hopelessly in love with her. At sixteen, I considered myself already a man, and Corinne, to my mind, was still a child.

She had come with her father, Peter Ducksworth, to the racetracks at the Queen's Park Savannah, in the heart of Port of Spain, Trinidad's capital, and I had come with mine. My father, being a stickler for punctuality, had insisted we arrive some fifteen minutes early and I was forced to wait on one of the green wood benches that lined the sidewalk around the Savannah while my father paced, glancing back and forth from the racetracks to the street, checking his watch and mumbling under his breath about inconsiderate people who think nothing about wasting other people's time. He was facing the opposite direction when I saw the Ducksworths coming toward us, the daughter skipping ahead, two thick plaits swinging across her face, legs long and gangly like a young colt's, girlish knobby knees, the father trailing behind her, red-faced, huffing and puffing.

"Sorry, old man." He extended a thick, sweaty hand to my father. "Had to wait for her."

He tossed his head in his daughter's direction and pursed his lips as if he were angry with her, but I could tell he was pretending for I did not miss the gleam in his eyes. I had already been told that Corinne Ducksworth was Peter Ducksworth's favorite child, the youngest of his three daughters, the apple of his eye.

"Oh, Daddy." Corinne raised herself on her tiptoes and kissed her father on the cheek, disarming him completely. The lips softened, the gleam intensified, proving the rumors not unfounded. "You know I was the one waiting for you," she said gaily.

"Had to have my coffee." Peter Ducksworth grinned sheepishly at my father. "Keeps me alert this early in the morning."

My father shook his hand and then glanced again at his watch. The Ducksworths were five minutes late, an eternity for my father. "Sun will be up soon," he grunted.

It was dark, not quite dawn, the stars still visible, shining like diamonds in the navy-blue sky. Dew beaded the grass in the Savannah, skirting above the cool damp earth and signaling the first hints of the coming heat. It had rained all week and the ground was sodden beneath our feet. Along the path to the racetracks and some distance beyond, the Savannah was potholed with pools of thick mud that clung to clumps of grass, making it seem as though tiny brown and green bouquets tied with string had been deliberately planted there.

Corinne was far ahead of us, skipping happily again, a silhouette of arms and legs flung backward and forward until she slipped and I saw her go down, sliding across the wet grass. Peter Ducksworth roared with laughter and quickened his pace toward her. "Well, you wanted to come with me," he said, stretching out his hand to help her up. "I told you it would be messy here."

She screwed up her face, lips and nose twisted comically, turned away from him, and tried to brace herself up on the palms of her hands. Feisty, I thought, but she slipped again and this time I rushed to help her. Her hands were clotted with mud that spread over mine when I pulled her up and for a split second our eyes met. Was that the moment she pierced my heart?

"Don't know why they call this a savannah," Ducksworth said, casting a disapproving eye at me before turning back to his daughter. "Look at your shorts. They're covered in mud." He fished out a handkerchief from his pants pocket and handed it to her. From where I stood, I could see there were brownish stains on it.

"Daddy!" she cried, and pushed away the handkerchief. "It's filthy. I told you I'll wash your clothes if you put them in the hamper."

"Use it anyhow." He waved the dirty handkerchief at her.

"Put it away." She wiped her hands on her shorts, spreading the mud even farther across the back and front.

My father's head jerked backward involuntarily and his mouth fell open. But if he were shocked by Corinne's defiance (I had never dared to defy him so openly), he said nothing, though I had not failed to notice the tightening of the muscles in his jaw when he closed his mouth.

"My daughter," Ducksworth said, balling up the handkerchief and shoving it in his pocket, "she has her own mind. But she looks after me. Right, Corinne?" He winked at her.

"When you let me, Daddy," she said.

"It's this place," Ducksworth grumbled. "Always muddy. Queen's Park Savannah, hah! No more park than a savannah."

And strictly speaking, he was right, for the Queen's Park Savannah—we referred to it simply as The Savannah—was neither a savannah nor a park, though indeed, in the hundred and sixty-five years before we gained our independence, it was once the property of the reigning British monarch since Trinidad was among the chain of islands in the Caribbean that belonged to England after she won her battles with Spain in 1797.

Enslaved Africans, driven mercilessly under a broiling sun, had planted sugarcane here, where we now stood—Peter Ducksworth and his daughter, my father and I—turning what had been a rainforest thick with massive trees and bushes into a thriving sugarcane plantation so that the English could have proper parks in the motherland: Pemberley, where the dashing Mr. Darcy romanced the beautiful Elizabeth Bennet; Mansfield Park, where poor, innocent Fanny Price was cowed into silence when she dared to ask Sir Thomas Bertram what business he had in Antigua that had kept him away from his home for so many long months.

When the horrors of slave labor ended in the British West Indies, Queen's Park Savannah became a cattle pasture, and I suppose that is how it got its reputation as a savannah, for it resembled one: wide swaths of grassy flatland surrounded by big trees that had survived the deforestation, the ground cleared to plant sugarcane. Then someone had the idea that the area could indeed be a sort of park—a park for sports, that is. A cricket mound was erected, a rugby field too, and, of course, a racetrack, where my father, who had a distaste for the slightest whiff of gambling, had been persuaded to accompany Peter Ducksworth, who had come to say goodbye to the last of his racehorses, the ones still remaining in the stables after the races had moved east, to Arima. He needed a friend at his side, Peter Ducksworth said to my father. "Who knows if I could have a relapse?"

My father, John Baxter, was not Peter Ducksworth's friend. He was his doctor, the most prominent surgeon on the island, an important and highly regarded man. And he looked the part: tall, erect, and formidable in his three-piece dark suits, always clean-shaven but with a meticulously trimmed mustache that shadowed what would have been attractive lips—the bottom lip slightly fuller than the top—had he smiled more often. By most standards he would have been considered a handsome man—skin the color of warm caramel, clear brown eyes, an impressive square jaw, his height the envy of most men. But though generally people are drawn to handsome men, my father had such a serious air about him that he intimidated even his colleagues, so it seemed odd to me that Peter Ducksworth would refer to him as a friend.

Ordinarily my father did not attend to patients in their homes. Peter Ducksworth, however, was a cousin of the minister of health, who controlled the purse that financed the efficient running of the hospital. When the minister asked my father as a special favor to take care of Ducksworth in his home, my father obliged.

Ducksworth had inherited five racehorses from his father, who was at heart an inveterate gambler. Yet Peter Ducksworth had no stomach for the roller-coaster world of horseracing. Still, he liked the horses and long after his father died he kept them—until he was bitten by a mosquito in the Caroni Swamp and would have died from a severe bout of the West Nile virus had my father not saved him.

Mosquitoes, it is often said, can be discriminating. They like fresh blood, foreign blood. Peter Ducksworth was not a foreigner even though without any mixing of the bloods he could trace his family back to the mother country. As Jean Rhys's Rochester observed of his West

Indian wife, "Creole of pure English descent she may be, but they are not English or European either." And Peter Ducksworth was not English or European either, though his hair was sandy brown, his eyes blue, and his skin, weathered by the sun, would have been pale as the insides of an almond had he lived in the cold climes of the northern countries.

Peter Ducksworth was Trinidadian; he considered himself a Trinidadian, a Caribbean man, someone who could be completely at home in any of the English-speaking Caribbean islands. Like the English families who had made the islands their home for generations, he spoke with his whole body, with his head, his shoulders, his hands—very un-English expressive movements punctuating the rise and fall of his Trinidadian lilt. He danced like a Trinidadian too, with his hips, not just his legs. Years later, when I saw him dance, it was hard to keep from laughing for he was a solid man. He carried his weight in his broad shoulders, wide chest, and ballooning belly, but his legs were thin and when he danced he looked as if he were balancing a colossus on sticks.

Ducksworth loved calypso and steelpan. Carnival was his favorite festival and it was a source of pride for him that one of his own, Peter Minshall, a descendant too from the English, was for years the owner and costume designer of the best Carnival band in Trinidad. And so, as a true Trini man, Peter Ducksworth didn't hesitate to join his Trinidadian friends—the dark-skinned ones—on a trip down the Caroni Swamp to watch the scarlet ibis return from their feeding grounds in Venezuela to roost on the mangrove trees.

"You have to watch out for the mosquitoes, though," his friend George had warned him.

"Just me, or you too?"

The others laughed. "They don't like peppery blood," one scoffed.

Ducksworth knew of course what they were talking about. He was not dark skinned like they were, but, as most Trinidadians, he liked his food spicy and would complain if his cook did not put enough pepper in it. Rumor had it that once, when a whole pepper in his pelau burst, he continued eating without even stopping to cool his tongue with water.

"We'll see who they bite first," he challenged them.

They lost their way in a turn in the swamp, blind-sided by the low-hanging branches of the mangroves that crisscrossed each other from one side of the narrow river swamp to the other, making it difficult to see in front of them. Without warning, their pirogue hit a buzz saw of mosquitoes. They were all bitten; only Peter Ducksworth got infected with the parasite.

For days he lay in a delirium, hallucinating and burning up with fever, unable to hold down solids or liquids. My father was called to attend to him. I don't think my father administered more than the usual treatment—intravenous liquids to keep him hydrated—but when Ducksworth recovered, he announced that my father was a miracle worker who had not only rescued him from the jaws of death, but had given him a new lease on life. He would no longer put off for tomorrow what he wanted to do today. And what he wanted to do, had always wanted to do for years now, was to live in Barbados. He loved the sea, but the sea in Trinidad was either brown on one side or rough on the other: to the west and south, laden with silt draining from the Orinoco River; to the east, buffeted by the relentless trade winds that eroded the roots of coconut trees; and on the north, except for a smattering of coves where there were wide sandy beaches, was the Atlantic Ocean, big and powerful, slapping huge waves against gigantic black rocks stranded from the shore.

Paradise, Ducksworth called Barbados. The sea there was as blue as the sky, the beaches long and wide, and the sand sparkling white. If he were in Barbados, he could swim in the sea every day, and every day the sea would be blue and clear as glass wherever he went. His wife was dead now many years. His eldest daughter Glynis was sixteen. At the end of the year she would sit for the CXC exam that had replaced the Cambridge O-level exam from colonial times. It would be easy to get her into a good school in Barbados the following year where she could take the CAPE exam, the equivalent of the British A-level exam, which like the CXC was set by the Caribbean Examination Council for the English-speaking Commonwealth Caribbean countries and was required for entry into the University of the West Indies. Rebecca, the middle girl, was one year younger than Glynis, and he worried that changing schools in the year before her CXC exams would put her at a disadvantage. He thought about boarding her at the convent school in Trinidad, but he knew that Rebecca would never agree. She was attached to Glynis. "Like a lost puppy," he said. "She wouldn't know what to do if Glynis wasn't there to tell her." Corinne was twelve. She would begin secondary school that September and would have to go to a different school anyhow. But it had never entered Peter Ducksworth's mind to be separated from his youngest daughter, his joy. This was his chance, he told my father, to have the life he always wanted. He had stayed in Trinidad for his wife's sake, but the miracle that my father had wrought for him was a sure sign that the time was right to make his move. He would sell his assets and relocate. The racehorses were part of his assets.

We were on our way to the racetracks when my father told me this. He said Ducksworth had sold all his horses except one, which was especially hard for him to give up. "When he was in his delirium, Mr. Ducksworth kept mumbling two names, Corinne and Raven," he said. "Of course, I knew Corinne is his youngest daughter, but I didn't know who Raven was until he told me it was his father's old horse. I suppose I felt sorry for him. He must have known, as I did, that the only reason someone's going to pay him for an old horse is to slaughter it for its meat and use the bones and tissues for glue."

I had not thought my father so caring, but then there was a lot I did not know about him, as he did not know about me. He did not know that I had been to the racetracks many times, and though this was the first time I had seen Corinne, I had already met her father.

Ducksworth too had not known I was John Baxter's son. He was still grumbling about his daughter's stubbornness— "I told her the tracks would be muddy, but she wouldn't listen"—when suddenly he turned to me. "You stay behind and watch that she doesn't fall again while I go with Dr. Baxter to negotiate a price for my horse. I'll give you two dollars for your trouble."

My father may have been surprised by his manner of speaking to me, but he gave no indication. He simply informed Ducksworth that it would not be necessary to pay me to look after his daughter. "Émile doesn't need the money," he said.

"I don't think Trevor makes that much at the tracks," Ducksworth countered, "especially now that there are no more races in the Savannah."

"Trevor?" My father arched his eyebrows.

"He's the best groom in Trinidad. Not so, Émile?" Ducksworth slapped me on the back.

I cast my eyes downward and slid my feet on the grass, pretending I was wiping off the mud on the bottom of my shoes.

"Isn't that right, young man?" Ducksworth insisted.

"I suppose so," I mumbled, feeling the heat of my father's eyes on me.

"Don't be shy," Ducksworth said. "You should be proud of your father."

"His father?" Reproof dripped from the upward tilt of my father's voice and I cringed.

"Comes here with him," Ducksworth said. "But not often enough though. You could learn a thing or two if you came with him more often, Émile. Like I said, Trevor's the best in the business."

"Émile?" My father had not taken his eyes off me; he was waiting for my explanation.

"He's not my father, Mr. Ducksworth," I said, finally looking up.

"Not your father?"

"Dr. Baxter is my father."

My father held my eyes a second longer before he released me from the cold grip of his stare. "Trevor is my housekeeper's common-law husband," he said to Ducksworth. The creases in his brow disappeared. "Émile is my son." No questions for me. No apparent curiosity about why Ducksworth should think I was his housekeeper's son.

Ducksworth narrowed his eyes, swiveled his head from me to my father, cleared his throat, and then noticing, as I did, the tight line my father had drawn across his mouth, he shrugged his shoulders and apologized. "Sorry, old man. Hope I didn't offend."

"No offense taken," my father replied.

And concluding correctly that my father wished to put an end to any further discussion about why I had been mistaken for Trevor's son, Ducksworth turned his attentions back to the mud on his daughter's legs. "I knew I shouldn't have agreed to bring her," he said. "You don't mind staying back with her, do you, Émile? There's mud here, but horse crap on the racetracks."

Corinne giggled. "You can say *shit*, Daddy." Her eyes twinkled mischievously and she looked across at me. "Daddy doesn't want me to get horse shit on my sneakers."

"What a mouth my daughter has!" Ducksworth tugged his daughter's plaits. "She has me all twisted around her little finger, you see, Dr. Baxter."

Corinne giggled again, though this time she blushed.

"And what a pretty face. Can't deny her anything when she smiles. She has me too-tool-bay." Ducksworth pecked his daughter on her cheek.

Too-tool-bay. A quintessential Trini expression. He would be willing to be a fool for her, his youngest daughter. She had him in her hands, his mind turned upside down by his love for her. In spite of the story my father had told me about Ducksworth's long family history in Trinidad, it surprised me that a man who looked like an Englishman, a very tanned one to be sure, would use that common Trinidadian expression.

My father seemed a bit disconcerted too by Ducksworth's casual use of the term. *Mout' open, 'tory jump out.* There was much truth in this country saying. From the way a man speaks you can tell his background, his education, his class, his story. Dark-skinned men in important positions, men like my father, were careful to speak the Queen's English. They didn't say *too-tool-bay*. But Ducksworth could, and no one would doubt his story. He was white; there would be no question that he definitely belonged to Trinidad's upper class.

My father grimaced and said gruffly, "We better get going along, Mr. Ducksworth. I have to be in the office soon."

I wanted to go with them. I wanted to see what help my father would be to Ducksworth. I couldn't imagine my father sympathizing with him. What words of consolation would he give him, he who took care of me certainly when I got ill, when I had a cold or a fever, but offered me little else? He gave me medicine and I felt better, but there was no coddling, no hugging, no sympathizing when I vomited my insides or when my body shook with ague. Corinne, though, wanted to stay. She would not admit it, but I think she was repelled by the possibility that horse crap, or shit, as she brazenly said, could get smeared along her bare legs. She flashed me that same smile her father had found irresistible, and caught too in its spell, I said to Mr. Ducksworth that it wouldn't be a problem for me to wait with his daughter until he and my father returned.

The sun was beginning to cast its first light across the horizon, lining the edge of the dark blue sky with gold, tinged with pink and gleaming silver, throwing off enough light to set aglow the wisps of hair loosened from the thick mane of dark brown hair corralled into two long plaits falling past Corinne's shoulders. Sparse, weightless as gossamer, the wisps swirled around her forehead. An innocent girl at play, and yet I saw intimations of a woman secure in her own skin in the way she ran her fingers through those loosened strands, not putting them back in place on her head, but letting them fall again, skimming the surface of her skin, touching and then not touching her forehead. She would be a beauty when she grew up, when her figure blossomed. That hair, those long coltish legs, would turn many a man's head. But what I noticed most about her were her eyes. They were full of light and life as if she knew that the world ahead of her held promises of a future full of all the happiness she could hope for.

"What do you think about moving to Barbados?" I asked her, and she replied, bubbling over with joyful optimism, "My father said it's paradise."

2

I was home from boarding school for the weekend when my father asked me to come along with him to the racetracks. We had not seen each other since Christmas, four months earlier, and after the usual formal inquires—How was school? How are your grades? Do you get enough to eat? Have you made friends?—and my equally formal responses—School is fine. My grades are good. I get enough to eat. I've made good friends—we drifted into a deadening silence, having nothing left to talk about. When Mr. Ducksworth asked my father to accompany him to the racetracks, my father jumped at the chance to include me, relieved to break the tension thrumming between us.

"The tracks will be muddy," he cautioned me.

"That's okay," I said, anxious as he was to find some common ground where we could pretend that the dark cloud looming over us had dissipated.

"We'll have to leave when it's still dark. Four, if we are to be on time. I told Mr. Ducksworth I'll meet him at five."

"I'll be ready," I said.

I did not tell him I had been to the racetracks, that I had woken up earlier than four o'clock many times, or that it would take us only twenty minutes to get to the Savannah—four o'clock was too early—or that I had already met Mr. Ducksworth.

I was my father's only child, having made him a widower at my birth when I killed my mother. *Killed* was not my father's word. He had never used that word, never said I killed my mother. *Killed* was the word that haunted my dreams when I was a child, that woke me up at night, searching the dark. For what? A ghost? For surely that was what my mother was now.

She never appeared—not to console me, not to ease my guilt, not to comfort me. And why should she? I was the one who had turned her into a ghost.

My name: it was all she left for me. Her family had come from France. They were slave owners in Martinique, but one repented. He freed his slaves and brought them with him to Trinidad. There was some mixing of bloods; my mother was not white though she was very fair-skinned. Still, she honored her white ancestor who had been kind to the Africans. Émile. She gave me his name.

My father never blamed me for her death, not directly, but I was keenly aware that my mere physical presence was painful to him, and when I learned that my mother had bled to death within hours of my birth, I too kept a wide path between us. I no more wanted to be a reminder to him of his pain and loss than to see his shoulders and back stiffen in that quick second before he regained his composure, and know he had barely managed to control his disdain for me.

My father had waited years to get married. At sixty he had already had his biblical three score, and surmising that ten more might be possible barring serious illness and death, he began to look around for a bride. He was not expecting love; he simply wanted a woman of childbearing age, someone to extend his lineage. He preferred a son, but he was willing to make peace with a daughter, assuming she would get married and there would be children who would share his bloodline.

He was fortunate on two counts and unfortunate on one. He had caught the attentions of a beautiful young woman, and as unlikely as it seemed—at least to him—she had fallen in love with him and he with her, though it had never been his intention to complicate his life with love. And he had a son, his second stroke of luck. But then it was because of that son he lost the woman, who, against all odds, had melted the frozen carapace that had enclosed his heart.

My relationship with my father was always cordial. No word of anger passed between us, no hint of recrimination on his part nor blame on mine for his coolness toward me. He hired a nanny to raise me—Henrietta was her name—and when I was nine, he shipped me off to a boarding school on the island. We never kissed; I don't remember my father ever kissing me, even when I was a very young child. After our brief formalities, he retired to his room, or rather his suite of rooms that included his study, a bedroom, and a bathroom, and which was closed off from the rest of the house by a heavy mahogany door, which he kept locked. I went to mine, a simple bedroom at the back of the house, with a rather large bed, the first and only one I had after I was removed from my crib, my father anticipating my lengthening limbs. There was also a dresser for my clothes, and a desk and chair where I did my homework.

My father and I had our meals in a darkened dining room. It seems odd to say the dining room was dark, for we lived in the tropics, and if not every day, most days the sun spilled rays out of the sky with such ferocity that even the wide spreading trees could not protect the delicate shoots of new grass from withering beneath them. The sun would have found its way through our windows too if they were not covered with heavy dark drapes, the ends taped to the walls. What light there was in the house came from dimly lit lamps on the scattering of small tables in the living room or from electric lightbulbs overhead, their wattage so low that though my father had Henrietta bring the newspaper to him every morning with his breakfast, he could barely read the print. He would snap the newspaper open, squint his eyes up and down the page, and then snap the newspaper closed again, taking it back with him after breakfast to his rooms where he kept a reading lamp on his desk.

I don't remember how old I was or if anyone had told me, but I understood at an early age that because my father was in mourning, the house was in mourning, and so I never tried to open the drapes, at least not in my father's presence, and I never suggested that he get brighter bulbs for the fixtures on the ceiling.

The kitchen, though, was brightly lit, for Henrietta, who remained in my father's employ as his housekeeper after I no longer needed her to feed and dress me, refused to abide by his funereal behavior. "If he wants to live in a tomb, that's his business," she said to me. "But I'm alive. There'll be time enough for me to go in the dark when they put me six feet under." So Henrietta kept all the windows in the kitchen wide open, no curtains, no shades, shutting them only when rain fell. Even the backdoor was left open. When my father protested—stray dogs often found their way to the backdoor—she threatened to quit. But Henrietta had become indispensable to my father. She cooked his meals according to his taste, washed and ironed his clothes, kept his house clean. She never pried into his comings and goings and she never gossiped. If she had opinions of her own beyond her notion that it made no sense rushing the dark—"The dark will come when it will come.

It don't need your help," she told him many times—she kept her thoughts to herself. She rarely spoke to my father unless to answer a question he asked her, but I think the real reason he tolerated Henrietta's refusal to keep the backdoor closed and her insistence on having the kitchen flooded with light was that she took me off his hands.

I loved her. She had an aura about her. I don't mean there was a halo over her head; I mean she glowed. Her face, arms, and legs shone like a newly minted penny. And she was that color too—penny-colored brown, not bronze. Once when I remarked on the sheen of her skin, she laughed and told me that if I used Vaseline I would shine like her too. But it was her goodness that made her shine, her kindness that poured out of every word she said to me and all the things she did for me.

My world was centered in the bright light of Henrietta's kitchen and it was through her backdoor that I walked to school and back, that I left to play with my friends, and it was there that a little snoop, a neighbor's daughter, saw me with my head between Henrietta's breasts and taunted me. "Émile still nursing!" She wagged her finger wickedly at me. "Come, everybody see!" I was nine years old. It was of course the last time I let Henrietta embrace me this way, and coincidence or not, it was the year I was shipped off to boarding school.

My father rarely came into the kitchen so it was not surprising then that he did not know I was an early riser, or that on most Saturdays I left the house much earlier than four in the morning, when it was so dark I could barely see the outlines of the trees, and except for the occasional drone of a car or truck, the driver returning from a night-time shift, no manmade sounds disturbed the predawn quiet. I could have been in the countryside and not close to the heart of the city, so clearly did I hear the rustle of leaves through the trees and the flapping of wings, birds stirring in their roosts.

Trevor, Henrietta's common-law husband, introduced me to Peter Ducksworth. Every evening, when he was finished with his work at the racetracks, Trevor came to the house to accompany Henrietta back to their home. While she washed the dishes and cleaned up the kitchen, Trevor talked to me about the horses in his charge. I don't think he willingly took me with him to the stables when I asked; he complained that he already had to wake up before the birds and would have to wake up earlier if he had to come to the house to pick me up. My guess is that Henrietta thought I needed some sort of father figure in my life and she persuaded him to bring me along. He had one condition—my father must not know. "The doctor don't like gambling, but is not gambling I do. I get the horses ready for the race."

At the stables I helped Trevor feed the horses and brush them down. We worked in silence though often he would hum a tune I recognized as a hymn I had heard on the radio. Then, after about an hour or so during which he had not said a word to me, he would throw down his brush and towel in the pail of water at his feet and announce: "Enough! We take a break now."

How I waited for that moment! Trevor would unscrew the thermos of hot cocoa Henrietta had made for us, pour some in the cup and hand it to me, and we'd stretch out on the grass, he drinking directly from the thermos. After two or three gulps, he'd begin. He'd tell me about the horses: which came from which breeder, which had the best pedigree, which the strongest legs, which would cut arse on the tracks if the damn jockey knew his business, which was on his last leg and headed for the glue factory. When he spoke of the doomed horses, he'd grind his lips back and forth between his teeth and shake his head, and on many occasions I was sure I saw translucent pearls bloom in the corners of his eyes. They never fell. At the first glimmer of daylight he'd shoo me away. "Go, boy. Your father must be ready for his breakfast."

Those were the days before the races moved to Arima, when I was still a young boy in short pants. Now there were only a few old racehorses left in the stables and Trevor stayed to take care of them. It made sense then that when Peter Ducksworth came looking for advice about potential buyers for his horses, Trevor was the groom he sought out.

Ducksworth had no way of knowing that I was the son of John Baxter, the doctor he claimed had saved his life. He was as surprised as my father when I corrected his mistake, for wanting to keep the times I spent with Trevor a secret, I had given Ducksworth just my first name the day I met him and allowed him to assume that Trevor was my father.

"Émile. Hmm." Ducksworth had made a slight snorting sound, air rushing down his nose. "Well, well," he said, chuckling, "that's a good French name. Émile. Like Émile Zola."

"I was named for a relative," I said, and I explained my mother's ancestry.

He glanced at Trevor, who was talking to another groom. "And so that's why she married your father?" he asked, as if only the great-great-granddaughter of an abolitionist would marry a man as dark-skinned as Trevor.

"They were in love." I don't know why I said that except it suddenly bothered me that he would think my parents—my real mother and father—would have some political motivation for marrying. (He would remember my remark, for that morning at the racetracks when he returned with my father after speaking to a buyer for his horse, he took me aside and observed quietly that my father looked like a man still in mourning.)

Henrietta said Mr. Ducksworth must have been blind to think I was Trevor's son. "You ten times more handsome," she scoffed. "I love my Trevor but the truth is the truth. You tall and slim, not fat and short, and you have that nice long nose, not pug nose like my Trevor, and your lips nothing like his. Your lips thin-thin, like your father's. That's one thing I wouldn't change about my Trevor, though." Her voice softened. "I love his fat lips, like a pillow when he kiss me. But you more handsome. That's a fact." This was Henrietta's opinion, not mine, though I was pleased she thought me handsome.

The first time he met me, however, Peter Ducksworth made it clear he was neither complimenting me on having the name of a distinguished Frenchman, nor was he laughing at me. He was simply making an observation about the disassociation of names from their sources. "Look at me," he said when Trevor joined us. "My name is Peter. *And upon this rock I'll build my church.* Am I Greek? A follower of Jesus?"

Trevor frowned. "You not a follower of Jesus?"

"I am," Peter Ducksworth said, "but He disappointed me. My wife and I prayed for a son. Jesus gave us only daughters."

"You not vex about that?" Trevor's frown deepened. Henrietta said that Trevor was considering joining the evangelical church that had set up a tent close to the Savannah. "Now is only hymns he singing and listening to on the radio," she said. "Not the calypsos we use to dance to."

"Not a bit, old man," Ducksworth said. "I have the nicest daughters. They love their old papa." He pounded his chest near his heart.

When he left, Trevor told me that ever since Peter Ducksworth's wife died, many women tried to get him to marry them, but he didn't want to share his daughters with anybody. Those girls meant everything to Mr. Ducksworth, Trevor said.

"Then why does he seem to regret not having a son?" I asked.

"All man want a son. You'll see when you have children."

"His daughters could marry and then he'd have sons," I said.

"Sons-in-law."

"So?"

"It's not the same," Trevor said, his manner dead serious. "Sons in *law*, not blood, and that man Ducksworth have land. I know if I have a son, I prefer to pass my land to my son who will carry my name, married or not, than to girls who take their husband name and then nobody know it was my land in the first place or the land was in my family for years."

So the day after I went with my father to the racetracks, I told Trevor that Peter Ducksworth was not only selling his racehorses, he was going to sell all his land and move his family to Barbados.

Trevor scratched his head and wriggled his lips. "You know they call Barbados *Little England*." He looked straight at me. "And you know why? Plenty white people live there, that's why."

I laughed. "Mostly black people," I said.

"But more white people than they have in Trinidad. Those English people that drag us here from Africa, they like Barbados too bad. They don't want to leave. That Mr.

Ducksworth know what he doing for sure. He go buy land in Barbados when he sell his land here."

"Yes," I said. "My father told me that Mr. Ducksworth intends to buy a big house by the sea with a lot of land around it."

"And find white husbands for his daughters."

Suddenly I found myself bristling with irritation. I had no interest in Ducksworth's daughters and had thought of Corinne only as a delightful adolescent girl, and yet I found myself defending Ducksworth with more enthusiasm than was warranted by Trevor's remark. "Rubbish!" I replied.

Trevor smacked his lips. "Trini to the bone. Except when it comes to his daughters."

But it was paradise Peter Ducksworth was seeking. So Corinne had told me.

3

And the first time I came to Barbados I thought
Ducksworth was not wrong to think he would find
paradise there, on that island so flat Columbus
had missed it entirely on the voyage that landed him in the
Caribbean, the chain of islands he mistook for India. The
West Indies, he misnamed the archipelago. The slavers too
had missed Barbados the first time they crossed the Atlantic, the bottoms of their ships bulging with human cargo.
For the world being round they needed a high marker to
distinguish where the sea ended and the land began, and,
like Columbus, they had approached the island from the
west where there were no hills. It would take a hundred
and thirty-three years after Columbus first set eyes on the
New World for the British, in 1625, to catch sight in their
telescopes of that ridge of highland to the north and the
east of Barbados that they named the Scotland District.
And then they found on the west and south of the island a landscape so perfectly even, so suitable for planting sugarcane, it seemed a gift from God, His blessing on
their awful enterprise: the Africans they had pillaged and
forced under the lash to plant, harvest, and then turn the
cane into sugar crystals and rum. A gift indeed, for by the
1700s sugar in the Caribbean, mostly from Barbados, was
worth £4 billion and quadrupled in value within the next
sixty years.

But it was paradise, Barbados. Waves of forest-green

edged with wide bands of pristine white sand that slipped into waters so blue, I doubted my eyes when I stood there the first time on that impossibly white sand, refusing to believe what was clearly before me: beds of snow-white coral dazzling in the sun, the water mirroring the blue sky above it. It was as if someone had emptied a bottle of blue ink in the ocean. I had seen the postcards, of course, but they were pictures intended to entice the foreigner, the European from cold lands. I rubbed my eyes, but there it was: blue stretching to the horizon and the sky dipping down to meet it. Paradise. Heaven.

Trinidad, where I was born and raised, was paradise too. At least so Columbus thought when the *Pinta*, the *Niña*, and the *Santa María* had managed to escape the fury of the Dragon and sail without incident into the calm waters of the Gulf of Paria. Four mouths the Dragon had, four *bocas:* Boca de Monos, Boca de Huevos, Boca de Navios, and Boca Grande. Through his telescope Columbus had seen the roiling waters and the cemetery of bones, metal, and wood, the remains of hundreds of sailors and the rotting carcasses of ships the Dragon had vomited onto the ocean floor. *Jesús, María, y José!* All was lost, he must have thought. Then the Dragon rolled over and the channel widened. Boca Grande: the widest of the Dragon's mouths linking Trinidad to Venezuela. Columbus must have dropped to his knees in thanksgiving. *In nomine Patris, et Filii, et Spiritus Sancti.* He looked up and there before him was God's sign that what he had undertaken for his queen in Spain was good and right and he had God's blessing for his mission. For across the plains on the island rose three mountain ranges—one to the north, one in the center, one in the south. "The Holy Trinity!" He praised God who had brought him here, and in gratitude, he named the island

Trinidad for the three persons in the one God: God the father, God the son, and God the Holy Ghost.

But the water in the gulf was muddied and brackish, and that was a disappointment. Soon, though, the men's grumblings turned to delight when plumes of white froth rose in the air, miraculous fountains of water on the backs of blue whales come to spawn in the warmth of the Caribbean Sea. The Spaniards would name the waters Golfo de la Ballena, Gulf of Whales, and so it was until it was renamed the Gulf of Paria for the town in Venezuela. Still, after the clear waters of the Bahamas archipelago, it must not have been pleasant swimming in that brown-stained water. What Columbus and his men may not have known was that they were in the delta of the great Orinoco River, its water heavy with silt scraped from the floor of the Amazon rainforest in its journey to the sea.

Like Peter Ducksworth, I grew up in Port of Spain, on the west coast of Trinidad, facing the gulf. The nearest beach to my home was Carenage. There the sand is brown and pebbly, the water, even on a clear day, murky with the backwash from the Orinoco. So I could understand Ducksworth's desire to spend his last years on that sun-bleached island, where, as the Barbadian poet Esther Phillips riffed, "God borrow colors / From Eden days." Yet when Corinne declared to me with such utter confidence in her father's conviction that they were about to move to paradise, I could have reminded her that even in Eden there was a snake. For I knew of Hurricane Allen that had pummeled that island, flattening its already flattened landscape, ripping apart homes, violently downing power lines. And though Trinidad was not fortunate to be surrounded by dazzling white coral reefs, it was situated in the doldrums, in latitudes below the hurricane belt. We had pouring rain and fierce winds, but nothing like the tropical storms that periodically battered Barbados. I could not know, though, that the threat to Corinne's paradise would be more than churning seas, devastating winds, and pelting rain, that there were snakes slithering in the sand biding their time, waiting for the opportune moment to sink their forked tongues into her flesh.

4

I t would be six years before I would see Corinne again. By then I had learned much more about the Ducksworths through my best friend, Albert Glazal, who was in love with Corinne's sister Glynis, the eldest of Peter Ducksworth's three daughters.

We were all three—Glynis, Albert, and I—students at the University of the West Indies at Mona, Jamaica. I, to the continued chagrin of my father, was studying for a degree in literature. My father wanted me to be a doctor like he was, though the first indication I had of his interest in my career was when I told him that I had been accepted in the English degree program at the university. He had never taken me to his office or to any of the hospitals he supervised. He had never discussed any aspect of his work with me or asked about my studies at boarding school, seemingly satisfied that I had progressed from one form to the next without inconveniencing him in any way with the sort of complaints from the headmaster that disrupted the social and professional lives of many a parent.

"Only girls and feckless men go to university to study literature," my father said when I declared my interest in the subject. "All that nonsense about a make-believe world. Be a man. Live in this world, the real world. Science, my boy. Physics, chemistry, biology. Mathematics. Those are manly subjects. What do you think you can do with a degree in literature?"

"Teach," I said, though I also wanted to add, *write*. I dreamed of being a poet; I had had a few of my poems published in the newsletter of my boarding school, but he would have laughed at me had I revealed my ambition.

My father had no patience with fiction writers. He thought of them as cowards, afraid to face reality without "frilling it up" (his words) with all sorts of stories meant to fool people into thinking that there was some sort of order to the universe, that in the end all will be well; there will be redemption; the good will be rewarded, the bad punished. "But it's all chance," he said to me. "We had no control over how we got here, and we will have no control over our leaving or what happens to us in the in-between." He had similar words for poets. "Weepers and dreamers," he called them. "They are no different from novelists. They believe because they see the sad and the bad in the world they are in control of the things that can happen to us in life; they can show us how we should live, how we can avoid the sad and the bad. But chance rules their lives just the same."

I believe when my father said those things to me he was thinking of my mother. He had loved her and she died. What had happened to her was outside of his control in spite of his years of medicine, in spite of the fact that he was the most important, and perhaps the most knowledgeable, doctor on the island. There was absolutely nothing he could do to save her when she lay writhing in pain on her bed. Someone told me he prayed, though I had never seen him pray or even attend any church. But nothing he did mattered, not his knowledge of medicine, not the prayers he offered to a god he was not certain existed. Nothing changed the course chance—fate—had determined for the woman he adored. She died all the same and he was powerless to bring her back to life. So I did not tell my father that I hoped one day to be a poet, a good poet. I did not tell him that I would be one of those he called weepers and dreamers. I said I wanted to be a teacher.

"To teach what? Where?"

"Literature. In secondary school," I said.

He laughed anyhow. He threw back his head and gargling sounds came from deep within his throat to taunt me. "Secondary school?" he scoffed. "Do you know how much a secondary school teacher makes? How do you think you will support a family with a secondary school teacher's salary? Don't count on me. I'll see you through university, but you're on your own after that."

I met Albert Glazal on the first day of class at the university and we quickly became best friends. I envied him for he had the sort of relationship with his father that I wished I had. My father drove me to the airport, helped me unload my luggage from the trunk of the car, shook my hand, and drove away, leaving me to sit alone in the waiting room until my flight was called. Albert's father flew with him to Jamaica and spent a week there, helping him "settle in," Albert said.

Albert had come to the university to study business. His father, Georges, owned department stores in Trinidad. Albert told me that ever since he was a little boy all he ever wanted to do was to help his father expand the Glazal empire. I should have been more sympathetic with my father when Albert told me this since I could not say that my father's dream was my dream, or that I had given any thought to being a help to him. He had shut me out, though perhaps I use his indifference toward me as a pretext, for I had no stomach for medicine. The sight of blood made me nauseous and, on more occasions than I can count, I had vomited my insides all over Henrietta when she cleaned the wounds on my arms and legs that I got from playing football with my friends in the Savannah. I was a child then, and by the time I became a teenager, blood no longer had this effect on me, yet I continued to have no interest in medicine. Call me selfish. Maybe I should have tried to please my father—he had such little joy in his life. Maybe had I agreed to study medicine or one of the sciences I could have made up for the suffering I had caused him.

I fool myself, of course. Nothing I could have done would have erased my father's pain; my mere presence was the source of the darkness that enveloped him. Albert was a lucky man: he loved what his father loved and his father was pleased with him.

Georges Glazal, Albert's father, belonged to a long line of Syrian Lebanese families who were among the last immigrants to Trinidad during the colonial era. Syrians, we called them, whether they were from Syria or Lebanon, Lebanon having been part of Syria when the first immigrants arrived on the island. Almost all of them were Orthodox Maronite Christians fleeing persecution from the ever-widening spread of Islam across the Middle East. In Trinidad the Maronite Syrian-Lebanese immigrants joined the Catholic Church, which was then, and to a great extent still is, the most influential and financially stable church on the island, Catholicism being the religion of the French planters who, finding no contradiction between their religious faith and their terrible business in human traffic, brought their slaves from the French colonies of Martinique and Guadeloupe to plant sugarcane and cocoa in Trinidad during the years when Trinidad was a mere way station for the Spanish conquistadors, their eyes set on El Dorado in the South American continent.

Albert's great-grandfather arrived in Trinidad in the 1920s. Like many of his compatriots, he began seeking his fortune as a peddler of dry goods, going from house to house in the countryside with a huge brown crocus bag on his back stuffed with all kinds of kitchen utensils and fabrics. Eventually he began selling ready-made clothing his wife sewed, and in a relatively short time he was no longer peddling his goods on his back but had opened the first of many clothing stores that are today owned by the families of the early Syrian-Lebanese immigrants. Albert's father had two of the largest stores. Albert was not yet a teenager when his father put him at the counter of one of them. The boy turned out to be a natural. He loved the business, loved serving customers, loved the pride he saw in his father's face when he tallied up the receipts at the end of the day and noticed the sales were mostly his son's. "You're going to make me a multimillionaire soon," his father said. Albert had bigger dreams: he wanted to be a multibillionaire.

Albert met Glynis in our last year at university, in an accounting class they were both taking. I told him I had met her father briefly, though not long enough to satisfy the questions Albert pestered me with: What sort of man was he? Did he seem strict, set in his ways? I said Ducksworth seemed friendly, a nice man. I didn't tell him what Trevor had said to me; I didn't say Trevor suspected that Ducksworth's motives for moving his family to Barbados were linked to his hopes for husbands for his daughters. *White husbands*. For though it seemed odd to me that Albert would be interested in Glynis's father, I didn't think too much about his attraction to Glynis, certain that it was his intention to return to Trinidad to marry the Syrian girl he was dating who worked in one of his father's stores. I was wrong. Albert seemed enthralled by Glynis and broke more than one plan we had made so he could spend time with her. Then one day he remarked casually that Glynis was the sort of girl who'd make a good wife.

"For you?" I asked, not sensing there was anything more than theoretical rumination in his remark.

"Why *not* for me?" he replied irritably.

"Her father is English," I said.

"I thought he was a Trinidadian."

Trini to the bone. That was what Trevor had said before he added, "Except when it comes to his daughters." I had bristled, but I knew very well what he meant.

Later Trevor apologized. He was not trying to insult my father's friend, he said. Mr. Ducksworth is a nice man. He understands how Mr. Ducksworth feels. He himself would feel the same way if he had a lot of land to leave behind for his children. He'd prefer to leave his land to black sons-in-law rather than to white sons-in-law. Just like Mr. Ducksworth wants for himself.

And the fact of the matter, Ducksworth's position, if indeed Trevor was right, was hardly different from the one the Syrian immigrants in Trinidad had taken and, I imagined, Albert's father also endorsed. They too did not approve of marriage outside of their communities. They wanted their Syrian daughters to marry Syrian men and their sons to marry Syrian women. To be fair, race and culture were not their only concerns; there was property to be considered, the vast commercial holdings these families now owned in Trinidad.

"What would your father say if you were to marry her?" I asked Albert, still fantasizing with the theoretical.

"My father loves me," he said, his words delivered without ornament, without qualification.

I had not anticipated the sharp pain that whizzed through my heart at that instant. It startled me. My chest muscles tightened and for a moment I could not breathe. I thought I had outgrown my longing. I thought I had long since stopped caring. I was not a child waiting for my father to take me in his arms; I was not a teenager wishing that for once, instead of shaking my hand when I returned from boarding school, my father would embrace me. I was a man, and though I had not yet experienced the kind of love my father had for my mother, I could understand how difficult it had to be for him to love me, the cause of his terrible loss. But when Albert so casually responded to my question, leaving no doubt of his conviction, as if there could be nothing in the world more natural than a father's love for his son, *his* father's love for *him*, I felt as if a knife had been plunged into my heart and the world spun before me.

Luckily Albert saw no change in my disposition. I breathed in deeply and the knife withdrew, the wound closed. "Even if he loves you, won't he be disappointed?" I asked slyly.

"You mean that she's not Syrian or Lebanese?" He was challenging me to be direct, to tell him bluntly what I thought.

I yielded to him. "You guys don't intermarry," I said.

"In my father's day, not mine."

Still I pressed him. "There's the business," I said, "your father's stores."

"Yes, the stores." He sighed and clamped his lips together, seeming to ponder my response, but the next moment he was punching my arm and laughing. "Remember where Glynis and I met? It was in an accounting class. An accounting class, Émile! She was beautiful *and* brilliant. I couldn't take my eyes off her. She knew all the answers to the questions the professor asked. And then three weeks ago she asked me to team up with her on an assignment. I couldn't believe my luck. Oh, my father will like her a lot. She's not Lebanese but she has a head for business."

But I did not trust Glynis. There was something about her that had made me uncomfortable the very first day I met her. A feeling, really, nothing I could reasonably base on facts, and yet I could not shake the nagging suspicion that her attraction to Albert was related more to his ambitions than to any genuine affection she had for him.

Albert was olive brown, much darker than his ancestral compatriots who lived on the Mediterranean coastline. His hair was curly. The curls were not wiry knots, to be sure, but they were tighter than the hair of the Syrian Trinidadians I knew, and framed his face like a fitted cap. He was good-looking, though not handsome. His nose was long and fleshy and spoiled what was otherwise an attractive face: dark expressive eyes, a solid chin, a mouth quick to smile. He had a muscular body, wide shoulders, strong arms and legs, narrow waist and hips, but he was of average height for a man, shorter than Glynis, and, as I was to discover, a year younger.

Glynis was, as Albert continually reminded me, beautiful. I saw traces of Corinne in her: the thick mane of hair, though hers was blond, and I assumed dyed, which she wore swept behind her head in a long ponytail that reached just above her waist. No loose strands strayed about her face as swirled around Corinne's. Her hair was plastered to her head and pinned with clips at the sides to keep it in place, nothing there to suggest the girlish carefree innocence I had found so endearing in Corinne. She had Corinne's build, or what I imagined Corinne's build would be at twenty-two. She was tall and slim, her legs long and shapely, encased in tight tapered blue jeans when I met her. I remembered then what I thought that early morning, six years earlier in the Savannah, near the race-tracks. But it was not a young colt that Glynis reminded me of. There was no sprightly playfulness about her, no joyful sparkle in her eyes. She resembled a fashion model, one of those androgynous girls with narrow hips and breasts like pumped-up balloons, the skin stretched taut and shiny, unnatural, spiked heels clicking purposefully down the runway. Beautiful, yes, but unreachable.

And there was something else that made me suspicious of her: the color of her skin. Her family was English; they were white, but they had lived in the Caribbean for generations and the sun had had its effect. Corinne was tanned brown, Peter Ducksworth was tanned brown. Glynis was so pale she could have been one of those English girls who had just arrived on the island. To be so pale, she had to avoid the sun. To be so pale, she had to have made a conscious decision to keep her skin from browning.

I am not unaware of the deleterious effects of the sun. On more than one occasion I'd overheard my father on the phone caution patients about the possibility of melanoma even for dark-skinned people. Perhaps that was Glynis's intent—to protect herself from the disease—though I doubted it was her only motive. She was far too pale, and I had noticed often enough that women who were overly conscious of preserving their white skin from the browning effects of the sun usually did not marry men as dark-skinned as Albert; there were children to consider. But I did not share my doubts with Albert. I held my tongue, and it was good I did, for a week later it became crystal clear to me that Albert's remark that Glynis was the sort of girl who'd make a good wife was anything but casual.

He had invited me to lunch with him and Glynis, claiming he wanted me to get to know her better. "You'll see," he said. "She's a good and kind person. People think that beautiful women only care about themselves, but that's not true. Glynis can't help that she is beautiful."

It was true. Glynis couldn't help being beautiful, and beautiful women often get misjudged for being shallow. The image of a good woman was Mother Teresa—old, wrinkled, sexless. But Glynis seemed to me self-absorbed, as if she were the only audience she cared about and the opinions of others mattered not a whit to her. Yet the evidence I had so far was based on intuition, a poet's intuition my father would have found risible. Her skin was pale, her hair dyed blond, plastered to her head, no stray strands escaping. Did this amount to evidence?

I told Albert I would go with him to lunch with Glynis after we had taken our usual morning laps in the swimming pool on the university grounds. He tried to persuade me to forgo swimming this one time. We wouldn't have time to shower and change, he said, and he didn't want to keep Glynis waiting. But I insisted. There was a chance that a girl I wanted to meet might be at the pool and I was hoping I'd be able to talk to her. I promised Albert we wouldn't stay long; three laps only, I said. He relented eventually and the next day he told me that Glynis had agreed to meet us at the pool.

Alicia was the name of the girl I was anxious to meet. Physically she couldn't be more different from Glynis. Her skin was the color of a ripe cocoa pod, dark-polished brown with red undertones, and her hair, which she wore in a short Afro, set off her dark eyes and grape-colored full lips. The shape of her body was different too. She had the hourglass figure I liked so much in a woman: generous breasts, small waist, and slightly flaring hips.

I had discovered she was a swimmer when I happened to be in the student lounge as she was reading a poem about her love of gliding through still water. I couldn't tell which mesmerized me more: the fluid lines of the verse she read, or the way she read them, her head tilted slightly to one side, her lips rounding off every syllable so that her words were clear and distinct, musical in the way that words in the voice of a true poet can be musical, rising and falling rhythmically, pulling the listener into her dream as inexorably as the evening tide rushes out to the open sea.

I had to find a way to speak to her privately without the crowd that had gathered around her.

She was there at the pool, as I'd hoped, standing at the bottom of the ladder leading up to the diving board, stunning in an orange bathing suit that showed off her curves and complemented her skin tone. I wanted to believe she noticed me. She had looked up in my direction and smiled when Albert and I approached the pool, but someone called out to her and she turned back and mounted the ladder with concentrated determination. I stopped to watch her; Albert did too, though we had both seen Glynis lounging under an umbrella on a deck chair on the far side of the pool, fully clothed in a pink long-sleeved shirt and white linen slacks. But Albert, like me, was caught in the spell of that moment: the vision of an Antillean dancer's body, breasts two plump ripe mangoes, backside high and rounded like twin calabash shells, thigh muscles toned and quivering. She rose on her tiptoes, legs and arms perfectly poised, and bounced, breasts, backside, thighs lifting high in the air on the springs of the diving board. We were transfixed. I heard Albert suck in his breath as she bent, head downward, her body stretched in a perfect line, and dove, a bird swooping through the air, its beak stabbing its prey in the water below.

It was an amazing dive, just a mere ripple on the surface, concentric circles spreading outward from where she disappeared under the pool's blue water. She came up swiftly, the sun setting off a rainbow of bubbles through the tight curls of her short Afro, and when she shook her head, turning it from side to side with the graceful elegance of a long-necked swan, lines of white froth sprayed around her, cascading over her nose and lips. I applauded and she flashed a smile at me but then in an instant was gone, making swift strokes toward the other side of the pool.

"Show-off." Glynis had sneaked upon us, but anyone would have startled us, so absorbed were we following the glistening turn of Alicia's shoulders as her arms sliced through the water and her face disappeared and reappeared each time she lifted her head to breathe.

"Didn't you see me over there, under the umbrella?" Glynis kissed Albert fully on the mouth. "I had to come to get you. Bad boy!" She flicked her fingers across his cheek.

I swiveled my head back to Alicia and Glynis followed my eyes across the water. "She does that so fools like Albert will stop and look at her."

"The only fool I am is a fool for you," Albert replied, and tickled her ear with the tip of his nose. She swatted him away. Gently though. Playfully.

"And what about you, Émile?" She batted her long eyelashes at me. "Did you fall for that trick?"

"She dives like a pro," I said. "She should be in the Olympics."

"But I bet it wasn't her diving that had you staring at her like a fool too."

"Glynis!" Albert took a step away from her.

"Glynis *what*?" she pouted.

"I think she's beautiful," I said.

She looked up at Albert, her eyes demanding he contradict me or at least compliment her on her beauty. She was beautiful too, but the beauty that had transfixed Albert and me was an earthy beauty, a sensual beauty, the kind of beauty that Antillean men crave in their dreams.

When Albert did not respond to her silent plea for attention, Glynis tugged his arm. "I'm hungry. Do you have to go swimming? I've been waiting for you for hours."

Hours was a gross exaggeration. Perhaps she had waited as long as ten minutes, but enough it seemed for Albert to feel guilty. She had caught him ogling Alicia after all. "Can't you wait a little longer?" he asked her, his voice already on the brink of surrender.

"I'm starving," she said petulantly. "If I wait any longer, I'll faint."

Albert turned to me. "Do you mind?" We had already changed into our swimming trunks and it was hot; perspiration was running down both our backs.

"We said we'd go to that Lebanese restaurant we went to last week. Come on, Albert," she insisted. Her mood suddenly changed. She stopped pouting, her eyes brightened, and she clapped her hands excitedly, like a little girl. "Let's go now, Albert. I loved the food there." She threw her arms around him and snuggled against his shoulder, but it was on me she fixed her blue eyes.

I had to twist my head away from her to break the lock of her eyes on mine, and when I did I caught a glimpse of Alicia, water rolling down her shoulders, both arms extended to a man crouched at the edge of the pool, a big grin lighting up his face.

There was no point staying. I had come to speak to Alicia, and I could see now I had competition. Alicia was kissing the man when I turned back to Albert. "No problem, man," I said. "Let's go."

5

Glynis ordered for us. "Hummus, tabbouleh, baba ghanoush, shawarma, kibbe nayyeh." The names of popular Lebanese dishes flowed effortlessly off her tongue. The waiter, a potbellied man in his late fifties with balding hair on the crown of his head which he tried unsuccessfully to camouflage with an embroidered *taqiyah*, was not impressed. Reaching for the *taqiyah*, which kept slipping down the side of his head to expose his shiny pate, he turned his back on Glynis as if she were not there—or if there, inconsequential—and spoke directly to Albert. "So what will you have, sir?"

"What the lady ordered for us," Albert replied with a frown, but he did not chastise him as I would have, for the waiter had been obviously insolent. But Albert was more concerned with drawing my attention to Glynis. "How'd you like that?" he said, smiling broadly at me. "Shawarma, kibbe nayyeh!" He reached for Glynis's hand. "You'd think she was Lebanese."

He was trying too hard. No one would be fooled into mistaking Glynis for Lebanese, especially the waiter who seemed scornful toward her. She may have known the names of Lebanese dishes, but even to my ear her pronunciation was inauthentic, clearly the accent of someone with only a recent acquaintance with the language.

The waiter glared at her and Glynis glared back. "Did you get it all down? What I ordered?"

"Well, did you?" Albert looked up at the waiter.

"We don't have all day," Glynis said.

The waiter curled his lip, grunted something, and pressed his pencil down hard across his notepad.

"Good," Glynis said, fluttering her fingers at him dismissively. The waiter grunted again and he walked back to the kitchen, his hand plastered to his *taqiyah*, which had now slipped to the base of his head.

"I don't know about that waiter," I said, turning around in my seat to take another look at his retreating back. "He was trying to ignore Glynis."

"He thinks I should keep my mouth shut," Glynis said, rolling the cuffs of her pink linen shirt. She glanced up and caught me watching what she was doing. "They use a lot of olive oil," she said. "I don't want it to get on my shirt." She rolled up the other shirt sleeve.

I looked away.

"He's a Muslim. A convert," she explained. "Converts are the most rabid sticklers to the rules, don't you think?"

A Jamaican, I was certain, of African descent. His hair, what remained of it, was coarse, tight curls like coiled wires. His skin was that rich dark brown color typical of the people here, moist, damp, and glowing from the heat of the sun and the humidity rising after the noonday rain. He had on leather sandals, the kind the local artisans made and sold in street bazaars, and wore a long white caftan that was stained with dirt at the hem.

"I wouldn't put it that way," I said. "I wouldn't say *rabid*. I'd say they're careful to obey the rules."

"That women are inferior?" She drew her white polished nails across the folds of her cuffs.

I had no answer for her.

"Well," she said, slipping into the space I had left open, "he disapproves of me."

"Then why do you come to this restaurant?"

"Albert—he likes the food here."

Albert's lips spread in a wide smile. He jerked his head sideways toward me as if to say, *Did you hear her? She loves me.*

I shook my head. "But that was disrespectful, Glynis, the way he ignored you."

"Oh, not to him," she said. "He probably thinks I was the one being disrespectful by not yielding to Albert."

"Glynis is so understanding." Albert leaned over to me. "See what I told you, Émile. My father's going to love her."

"And what did you tell Émile?" Glynis put her hand on his shoulder and pulled him back to her.

"I told him things are no longer the way they were in my father's day."

"You mean in your father's day Syrians only married Syrians, but that's not so today?" She was looking at me when she asked the question, her blue eyes fixed steadily on mine again, and I had the uneasy feeling she was not speaking in general terms, that she wanted me to understand that Albert was the sort of Syrian who would marry a non-Syrian, a Trinidadian Lebanese man who would marry a woman who was not Lebanese. *Her.*

"So when's the happy day?" I asked, feigning indifference.

Albert shifted uneasily in his chair. "I meant to tell you, man," he mumbled.

I held up my hands, my palms wide open. I had asked the question jokingly. I didn't think I would get a serious answer. "No need, no need," I said, desperately hoping my voice had not revealed my shock that my friend, who I knew to be a man careful to calculate the pros and cons of a situation, would make what seemed to me an impetuous decision. But it was the pros and cons of his balance sheet that usually preoccupied him: how much his father should invest, how deep a risk he should take with a new venture. I had never before seen him in a romantic situation, not one that had so thoroughly engrossed him. "I'm happy for you," I added, doing my best to sound upbeat.

"He didn't tell you because he just asked me," Glynis said. "Last night."

"So you've set a date?" *Three weeks ago. That's when Albert told me they had their first date.*

"Albert's going with me to Barbados to tell my father."

"Actually, that was why I invited you to come to lunch with us," Albert said apologetically. "Glynis wanted us to be here—"

"In Albert's favorite restaurant," Glynis interjected.

"Yes, here at Mamoud's when I told you."

"We want you to come with us when we go to Barbados," Glynis chimed in once more. "My father would be delighted to see you again."

I wasn't surprised that Albert had told her I'd met her father, but this was the first time she acknowledged I knew him. "I hardly think he would be delighted," I said. "We barely spoke."

"You are his doctor's son," she responded.

"Your sister was there too, when I saw him on the way to the racetracks," I said. "I remember she fell."

"And of course Daddy helped her up."

Yes, of course. Of course her father would help her little sister when she skated across the mud and tumbled down. But there was a note in Glynis's voice that disturbed me. I detected a sarcastic undertone, a tinge of resentment in the way she expressed the care her father had shown for

Corinne, and I felt compelled to add that her sister's fall had been nasty.

"But she got up. Right?" She lifted her eyes high and wide as if she were daring me to contradict her.

"Yes," I said. "Though she was bruised a little."

"Hardly bruised," she responded, and fingered her napkin. "A tiny scratch that probably healed in a couple of days."

Albert seemed oblivious to this little give-and-take between Glynis and me. "So you see, Émile, you have to come." He reached for the glass of water on the table beside him, and thrusting it toward me, he said, beaming all the while, "My friend is Mr. Ducksworth's doctor's son!" Glynis was quick to raise her glass too, and when hers struck his, I heard the tinkle of wedding bells rippling across the room.

What was I to do but join them? I *was* his friend, and yet as his friend I wanted to tell him that three weeks was not enough time—not enough for either of them to make a decision that would affect the rest of their lives.

I thought perhaps I could distract him, divert his attention back to the waiter, insist that we go to the kitchen and complain to the owner. Anything for a chance to speak to him privately. *Slow down, Albert*, my brain said, but he was watching me closely.

"Glynis is right," he said when I mentioned the waiter. "Three years ago I came here with my father and that waiter was a Baptist. You have to forgive him, Émile." And as if he had guessed the purpose of my detour, he skillfully maneuvered the conversation back to Peter Ducksworth. "As Glynis said, her father would be glad to see you again."

I gargled something about it being a long time since Mr. Ducksworth had seen me. "I was a boy. I look different now."

He put down his glass and placed the middle finger of both his hands in the space between his eyebrows. His eyes focused on me, he trailed the tips his fingers across his brow and down the sides of his temples, and when he spoke, there was a toughness in his voice I had not heard before. "This may seem sudden, Émile, but I didn't see the point in waiting."

I forced myself to smile and said something I didn't believe, or thought I didn't believe: "People fall in love at first sight all the time."

"We did," Glynis said, and slid closer to him. "And we don't want to wait a second more than we have to."

Albert put his arm around her. "So what's your answer, Émile?" His voice had softened, the toughness was gone. "We want you to come. I want you to come. Don't worry about the money. I'll cover the trip."

"We'll only be gone for the weekend. Friday to Sunday. You won't miss any of your classes," Glynis said reasonably. "You must come."

Albert tightened his arm around her. "Glynis found the perfect hotel for us on the beach. For you and me. She'll stay at her father's, of course."

"I'd prefer to be in the hotel with you," Glynis grumbled, grazing his cheek with her lips, "but Daddy won't approve. He's old-fashioned."

"You'll like Barbados, Émile," Albert said. He was offering me an olive branch. He had made up his mind; he was going to marry Glynis. Any attempt on my part to persuade him to reconsider would be futile. "Barbados has the best beaches." And we both laughed when he added, "Not like Trinidad."

Yet I did not miss the anxiety in his voice, nor in hers for that matter. I suspected he was not entirely confident that Glynis's father would approve of him, and in spite of her show of bravado, it seemed neither was she. Was that why they both wanted me to be with them when Albert announced his intentions to Ducksworth? Was I to be a peace offering of sorts? The son of the doctor who had saved his life was the best friend of his daughter's intended. Surely I would be evidence sufficient to erase any doubts Mr. Ducksworth may have.

"Of course I'll come," I said. "But we'll have to share a room. I couldn't put you through the expense of a separate room for me."

"No bother. If it'll make you feel better, I'll book a suite."

"It'll make me feel better," I finally said, then turned to Glynis. "And it'll be good too to see your little sister again."

"She's not little anymore. She's almost nineteen." Glynis adjusted the collar of her shirt and brought it closer to the sides of her neck. "I have another sister, you know."

"Rebecca," I said.

"Yes, Rebecca. She's a year younger than me but she's married."

"Married?" Albert seemed startled by this news. He raised his eyebrows and his jaw fell down comically. "When?"

"Daddy called this morning." Glynis patted his thigh soothingly. "He said Rebecca eloped last week. He didn't find out until last night."

"Eloped?"

"It was a huge surprise. Daddy didn't have a clue."

"Was he angry?"

"Disappointed," she said, and faced me. "I told Albert we were going to have a double wedding," she explained.

"Rebecca promised, but it seems Douglas was in a hurry."

"Douglas is Rebecca's fiancé," Albert said with what I thought was a little too much enthusiasm, as though he wanted me to know he had not been altogether kept in the dark. "Nice fellow." He drained his glass, swallowing the water in big gulps.

Glynis wagged her finger at Albert. "Rebecca's husband now," she said. "And a good-looking fellow too. Wait till you meet him."

Albert passed his hand through the curls on his head. They loosened and then sprang back. "Yes, Rebecca's husband now."

Glynis lowered her eyes and flattened the napkin on her lap. "He's a big catch for Rebecca. Daddy will get over his disappointment. He wanted to give Rebecca away, but he likes Douglas. Douglas's mother and my mother were best friends."

"Well, your father will have a wedding, not a double wedding, but one of the biggest weddings Barbados has ever seen." Albert rubbed Glynis's shoulder affectionately.

She looked up from her lap and rewarded him with a bright smile. "That's why I love you," she crooned.

One of the biggest? Is Albert expected to help finance the wedding?

"I'd order champagne but they don't serve alcohol here. Muslims," Albert said, as if an explanation were necessary. He clapped his hand and waved the waiter over to us.

Glynis leaned across the table and brought her face close to my ear. "Albert's father is not a Muslim, you know," she whispered.

Her warm breath tickled my skin and I felt a spasm of irritation course down my spine. I disapproved of the waiter's manner, but not of his religion. What exactly was she trying to say? What did she wish me to infer?

"Yes, but Albert's family was originally from Lebanon," I countered wickedly.

"So what?" She leaned back in her seat, her eyes challenging me to be more explicit.

Fortunately, before I could conjure an answer, the waiter arrived and was standing before us, facing Albert, his back stubbornly turned against Glynis. "And what you drinking, sir?"

"Albert always orders his special drink," Glynis said to me. Then she raised her voice. "That's what he'll have, waiter." The man jerked his head instinctively around in her direction.

"A specialty of the restaurant," Albert said. "Some kind of a concoction with mango juice, pineapple, papaya, and something else. What? Tell me." He grinned at the waiter. But the man was struggling to recover his composure. Albert was a frequent patron of the restaurant; he did not want to lose his business, but Glynis had barked at him. His lips twitched and he breathed in and out heavily through his wide nostrils.

"So are you going to tell me?" Albert was waiting for his answer.

The waiter cleared his throat. "Secret ingredient," he muttered at last.

"And Albert's favorite drink," Glynis added. There was a triumphant gleam in her eyes as if to let me know she had not relented; the waiter had not cowed her.

When the waiter left, Albert turned back to me. "Then it's all settled. The hotel's not too far from where Glynis's father lives."

"Have you met him?" I asked, certain he had not, but trying one last time to force him to consider the ramifications of his sudden decision. Albert's father may not object, but Peter Ducksworth might. Or so Trevor had led me to believe.

Glynis answered for him: "No, but my father will love him when he does."

I thought I saw Albert wince.

6

We left for Barbados the following weekend. Albert rented a car at the airport, intending to register at the hotel before going on to Peter Ducksworth's house. Glynis said she would take a taxi from the airport; she wanted to make sure her father's house was respectable when we arrived. "Daddy's not the best housekeeper," she said. Albert protested; he didn't want her to go alone in a taxi.

She'd taken a taxi alone many times, Glynis countered. And she was sure the house was in a mess.

"We don't mind," Albert said. "Can't be worse than the rooms at the university halls." He tugged her ponytail playfully and Glynis brushed his arm away, more brusquely than I thought she intended, for when she saw Albert's reaction—a frown creased his forehead though just as quickly disappeared—she stroked his cheek.

"It's just that Daddy would be embarrassed. Truth is, he never did a thing when Mummy was alive. Never lifted a finger in the house, not even to boil water," she scoffed. "Now he can't keep up, even with the maid who comes every day. He tries, but you know what they say about teaching old dogs new tricks."

"What about your sister, the one still at home with him? Surely she helps." Albert said the words that were on my mind as well.

"You mean Corinne?" There was no mistaking the up-

ward curl of Glynis's top lip. I've seen sneers; hers was
more feminine. What I mean is that it was so subtle it
was possible to think she had not sneered at all. But there
was no doubt that what I had seen was a wave of disgust
cross her lips when she uttered her sister's name. "Daddy
thinks Corinne's too pretty to do housework."

Albert put his arm around her. "None of your sisters
can be prettier than you," he cooed.

But Glynis would not to be swayed. We should relax
when we got to the hotel, she said. There's a swimming
pool there and a bar. She'll be safe in a taxi. Barbados is not
like Trinidad. No one is going to kidnap her here.

I chuckled but Albert was not amused. Trinidad was
oil-rich but the money had not filtered down to the poor.
Kidnappings, robberies, drug wars had become a way of
fighting back. But it was in Trinidad he and Glynis would
live when they got married.

Undeterred by Albert's continued protestations, Glynis gave us directions to her father's house and told us to
come in a couple of hours.

"How many?" I asked, my instinctive distrust of her
rising before I could suppress it.

"A couple. Like I said."

"What's a couple?" I insisted.

"Two, you idiot." Albert knocked me with his elbow.

"Well, not to the dot. After lunch would be great."
Glynis swiped her hand over her hair. A habit, a practiced
reflex. Her hair, every time I saw her, was always smooth
and shining, brushed back off her face. She looked at her
watch. "I'd say at about two or three o'clock."

For my friend's sake I tried to make myself believe that
two or three o'clock was reasonable. This would be the first
time Albert would be seeing where she lived. She wanted

to make an impression, to show off the beautiful house her father had bought in Barbados. She was understandably anxious. But the more I thought about her insistence that we arrive after lunch—we arrived at the airport at nine o'clock, and it would be five or six hours from then to the time she said we should come to her father's house—the less I was convinced that she was worried about Albert's reaction to the state of her house. No, more likely it was her father's reaction to Albert that had her stumbling to explain why—when she had claimed her father would love Albert, that he was anxious to meet him—she was stalling.

Albert wanted to unpack immediately. It was hot; I wanted to cool off by the pool with a frosted bottle of beer. But I could tell Albert was nervous, as I suppose I would be if I were meeting my future father-in-law for the first time, so I opened up my suitcase where I had dropped it carelessly on the floor, and pulled out my shaving kit and toothbrush, which were in a transparent plastic food bag stuffed next to my other things that I had packed willy-nilly: T-shirts on top of shorts in no discernible order, bathing trunks, underwear, and socks balled up, a pair of sneakers and sandals on top of them.

Albert had placed his suitcase on the luggage stand, and when he opened it, I was ashamed of the way I had packed. His pants were on hangers attached to a hook at the top of his suitcase, two pairs sharply creased. His polo shirts were neatly folded, the collars pressed down, one placed on top of the other, and though I don't believe this was true, it seemed to me at the time that the polo shirts were layered according to color from light to dark—white, then pale yellow, then deep blue. Next to rolls of underwear and socks were a dark brown leather cosmetic case and two stuffed camel-colored shoe bags.

Albert had told me that his great-grandfather attributed his success to the importance he put on presentation. When I asked him to explain what he meant by presentation, he said that though his Lebanese great-grandfather carried his merchandise in a crocus bag on his back as he hawked his goods from one village to another in the countryside in Trinidad, he always made sure that the fabrics he sold and the clothing his wife and her friends sewed (their first tentative steps to eventual mass production of ready-made clothing they would sell in their stores) were not rumpled. Every morning before he left his house, he was careful to have his wife iron and fold the dresses, the pants, and the underwear, so they looked like new to his customers. "Presentation makes the sale," Albert told me. His father had drummed that advice in his ear. "People will buy most anything from you if you present it well. The same dress they rejected when it was rumpled, they'll buy from you at a handsome price if it's nicely pressed and folded."

Albert stacked his neatly folded shirts in one of the bureau drawers and pointed to the drawer next to his. "You can take that one," he said.

I had not thought of putting my clothes in the drawers. We were here only for the weekend; it was easier to leave my stuff in my suitcase, but I did as Albert instructed me.

He was bending down behind the closet door to place a pair of loafers and white tennis shoes side by side on the bottom rack when I heard him mumble something about Glynis. Not sure I had heard him clearly, I asked him to repeat what he had said. "Glynis," he said. "She's right. We can't just barge in on her father."

We weren't barging in, of course; her father was expecting us. Glynis had told him we were coming.

Albert straightened up and shut the closet door. "I wouldn't like someone to barge in on me either," he grumbled.

"Listen." I put both my hands on his shoulders and shook him slightly. "He's going to like you. He is."

"But—"

"No buts. You're a good guy. You come from a good family."

"Maybe he'll think it's too soon."

The bold confidence he had displayed in the restaurant seemed to be eking out of him. I had thought three weeks was too soon, but I could read in his eyes he wanted me to tell him it was okay. Love is or it isn't. Hadn't I said to him that many people fall in love at first sight? Henrietta told me that within minutes after she first set eyes on Trevor she knew she would spend the rest of her life with him. "That's the way it was for him too," she'd said, "and now it's twenty years. That man love me too bad and I love him just the same." So who was I to say to Albert it was too soon, too soon to propose to Glynis, too soon to plan a wedding?

My father fell in love with my mother at first sight, and if I had not fatally intervened, they would still be together, in love, happy, my father not brooding through the dark rooms of his heavily draped house.

Yet there was a couple I knew, colleagues of my father, who had known each other for years, since they were children. Both came from the same neighborhood, went to the same medical school, shared the same interests in music and art. They got married after they graduated, certain a relationship built on a solid foundation, on years of friendship and love, would last. It didn't. One child later, they divorced.

I told myself I should stop worrying: Marriage is sometimes a crapshoot. Albert's chances were as good as anyone else's. "If Peter Ducksworth wants his daughter's happiness, he won't think it's too soon," I said.

"I'll make her happy."

"I know you will. Any girl would be lucky to get you. A nice guy and handsome too?"

"Liar." But I had forced a smile on his lips.

"Come on," I said. "Let's take a dip in the pool. We have some hours to burn."

Too many hours, it seemed. He was still nervous, worried, restless. We swam some laps in the hotel pool, I ordered beer (he'd only have lemonade; he wanted to have his full wits about him when he met Glynis's father, he said), and we killed more time talking cricket with a group of guys boasting about Sobers. Sir Garfield Sobers, the pride of Barbados, knighted by Queen Elizabeth in 1975 for his prowess on the cricket mound.

"*Still* boasting after all these years?" I couldn't help teasing them. "We're in the twenty-first century, not the old ages."

Albert perked up. He was an avid cricket fan. Never missed a test match, especially when the West Indies team played England. "The last time Sobers played cricket, you guys were in the womb," he said. "Can't beat our Brian Lara from Trinidad. Highest world record. Four hundred not out against England and then a double hundred, a triple hundred."

"A quintuple hundred!" I shouted out, happy to see Albert's gloomy mood broken.

"And a champion runner too," Albert added. "Twenty-eight runs off an over in South Africa."

Beer and rum had made the guys—all Barbadians—

light-headed. They laughed with us too, but they came back with one of their own. Yearwood. "Bowled 153 from 118 balls," a burly chested man said. Barrington Bjorn Beckenbauer Yearwood. Where did his mother drum up a name like that for a black boy? "She was psychic," the man continued. "She knew he was going to play not just nationally, but internationally, and beat out all those white fellas."

We joked some more with the guys. I would have had the rum they offered us, but Albert looked at me sternly and shook his head. He wanted me to make an impression on Glynis's father too. I was his friend. I'd already had a couple of beers; he didn't want me tipsy.

We left for lunch but Albert barely touched his food. At two o'clock he was fully dressed, in a dark blue Ralph Lauren polo shirt, the man on the white horse appliquéd to the top right-hand corner, pressed khakis, polished brown loafers. Was it the briefness of his courtship with Glynis that had him so nervous? Or was it something else? Like being Syrian, Lebanese, his family of Arab descent.

I had intended to wear my knee-length shorts, but I changed my mind, seeing Albert in khakis, and put on my long pants.

"Glynis said two or three. I guess two thirty would be just right." Albert was doing his best to get me out of the hotel, but I didn't think we should arrive too early. I had calculated it would take us only fifteen minutes to get to Ducksworth's house. Albert was not persuaded. "If we leave now," he said, "it'll give us ten minutes or so in case we get lost."

And it was good I had not objected. The directions Glynis gave us took us off the main road to a narrow paved road that ended in two diverging tracks muddied and full of loose stones. Glynis had not told us about the dirt roads, or that the paved one ended. She had just said to keep driving up the narrow road until we came to a big house on the top of the hill. From where we were, we couldn't see a big house. All we saw was a dense cluster of tall trees, and in between, climbing up an incline, were some prettily painted tiny wood houses—some blue, some pink, some orange—all with white wood railings around their tiny verandas.

"We took the wrong turn," Albert said nervously. "Now we're going to be late."

I had offered to drive when I saw Albert fumbling with the keys and he did not resist. I stopped the car to consult the drawing Glynis made for us. Mango Trace. That was the name of the road she had written on the drawing. A man came out of one of the houses holding a toddler on his hip. He was in his underwear: a loose white cotton vest that hung low on his chest, and faded navy plaid boxers, which on closer view I could see were shorts made out of a lightweight material. The toddler was naked, a chubby boy about three years old. He looked a lot like his father: Both had wide brows, dancing eyes, and nostrils that widened at the end. Both had skin that glowed like fresh asphalt after the rain.

"We're looking for Mr. Ducksworth's house," I said to the man.

"No Ducksworth live here," he replied matter-of-factly.

The toddler giggled. "Ducks, ducks, ducky," he chanted. The man tightened his hold and kissed him on the cheek.

"Peter Ducksworth," I said.

Albert slid over me, almost crushing my ribs. "A white man," he called through the open car window. "You know where a white man lives around here?" He handed him Glynis's scribbling.

"Ah!" The man grinned and flung back his head, exposing two gleaming rows of even white teeth. "You make a
mistake." He handed the paper back to Albert. "This here
is Mango Trace, true, but no white people live here. What
you looking for is Mango Road up yonder."

"And does Mr. Ducksworth live there?"

"The white man with the big belly and the yellowish
hair like sand?"

"Yes, that man," Albert said.

"He have three daughters?"

"Yes, yes. Where does he live?" Albert was getting
more agitated.

"One of the daughters done gone and married," he
announced.

The man's wife popped her head out of the window.
She was a pretty woman, with the same glowing dark skin,
her hair cut short in an Afro, smooth round cheeks, black
eyes evenly spaced, a wide mouth, plump lips. She was
holding both ends of the neck of her flowered housedress
close to her chin as if she feared releasing them would expose
her breasts. "Who you talking to, Jimmy?"

The man turned around to answer her. "Some two fellas
asking about the white man who live on Mango Road."

"Ducksworth with the big belly?"

"Yes," Albert said. "We're looking for Mr. Peter
Ducksworth."

"You tell them about how the daughter just ups and
marry, Jimmy? No wedding or anything."

"I was just telling them where—"

"I never hear something like that," his wife interrupted.
"She couldn't wait for her big sister?"

I leaned back in my seat. There would be more back-
and-forth between the man and his wife. We were on a

Caribbean island. Time moved slowly here, inching its way with the sun. In the countryside you woke up before dawn, had breakfast, and began work in the fields when the sun was still behind the horizon. By midday you were home again, beaten down by the sun blazing overhead. Then it was time for a long nap while the sun made its way across the sky. It was a little past two. Jimmy and his family had just woken up.

Albert closed his eyes in frustration. Counting, I thought. He'd have to reach five hundred before he'd get Jimmy's attention again.

"Must have had some row with her big sister," Jimmy's wife was saying.

"You could be right."

"But what row she could have that wouldn't let her wait?"

More back-and-forth. Then the wife said, "Is not right for the younger sister to marry before the old one."

The old one. That got Albert's attention. His eyes flew open. "She's not old!" he shouted. "And if you want to know, there was no row."

"Even so, you have to say it funny how is the plain one get the pretty man," she said, undeterred by Albert's flashing eyes or the veins bulging on his neck.

Good-looking, Glynis had said. Pretty man, Jimmy's wife declared. But if these descriptions of Rebecca's husband bothered Albert, he hid his feelings. "Are you going to tell us?" he asked, speaking directly to Jimmy.

The man glanced back at his wife. "Ernestine, don't go making gossip," he scolded. Then he turned to Albert. "So what was it you wanted again, young man?"

"Directions to Mr. Ducksworth's house," Albert said, doing his best to keep his voice even.

"Back-back your car here and turn around and go back to the main road. Then take the first left turn and go straight-straight up the hill till you see a big house."

And there it was.

It was a huge old colonial-style house, the kind being demolished in certain parts of Trinidad to put up sleek glass-and-metal high-rises, now that money flowed to the island from oil and liquefied gas. (It was reported that over 70 percent of the liquefied gas the US imported came from Trinidad). The house was imposing, standing there on the top of the hill, glistening in the brilliant sunshine. We had driven just about halfway up the narrow road when we saw it. Had we taken the right path we could not have missed it. It rose high above a clearing, a white, two-story rectangular structure with verandas on each floor, white railings wrapped around the front and sides. The charcoal-gray slate roof on top sloped down over it like an enormous hat. Or beach umbrella, Albert said. The house itself was framed on each floor with a long line of tall French windows bordered by olive-green shutters. These were not the sort of shutters one found in the country, meant to be opened to let in the breeze and then shut again to keep out the rain or the sun at noon. Or if they were, they no longer had this function; the sleek windows behind them let in the breeze and kept out the rain, and drapes protected the rooms from the sun. These were decorative shutters, spread open wide like the wings of a giant bird in flight. Tall leafy trees seemed to hug the house on both sides, but in the back there was nothing but blue sky.

As we got closer I could see a white hammock strung between two Julie mango trees on the far right side of the front yard. There was a big-bellied white man stretched out in it.

7

We must have startled him, or he was excited to see us, for when our car pulled up the driveway, he got up so quickly the bottom of the hammock turned upside down and slapped his backside.

Peter Ducksworth: big-bellied, yellowish hair like sand, receding a bit at the hairline, but still full, substantial. He strode toward us, the backs of his sandals striking against his bare heels. "Mr. Glazal," he said, his arm outstretched.

Albert jumped out of the car and practically trotted up the driveway to meet him. "Mr. Ducksworth." He shook his hand vigorously. "Please, not Mr. Glazal. I am Albert."

"And I am Peter," Ducksworth said. "Or Dad, or Pop, or whatever you want, since Glynis has made up her mind."

He was smiling, not a hint of sarcasm in his tone. I wanted to say to Albert: *See, see, there's nothing to worry about.*

"Welcome." Ducksworth grinned, baring gray teeth. Too many years without fluoride in the water in England, a holdover from the days when the royals feared poisoning. Some of them had died that way, from drinking poisoned water. But it had been a long time since any of Ducksworth's ancestors lived in England.

"Glynis has told me all about you." (His teeth were crooked too.) "Prepared the way, so to speak. But I know the Glazals. Not personally. I never met your father socially. We didn't run in the same circles, but I was in his store once or twice. Some years back. Don't know how I missed you. As you know, I moved here, to Barbados. Your father probably kept you in the background, eh?"

Albert flushed, a pinkish stain visible under his olive skin.

"Don't blame him. I kept my daughters in the background too. Wanted you to be a university man, eh?"

"I worked in the store with my father," Albert said. "And when I am done with university, I plan to work with him again."

I cheered Albert silently. *Not meeting your father socially. Not running in the same circles.* We both knew what he meant. Not at the cocktail parties or the dinner parties Trinidad's high society hosted. Definitely not at the Yacht Club.

"In the store. Yes." Ducksworth examined his fingernails. "An entrepreneur. Glynis told me that too. Said that's what you are."

"I wouldn't say that exactly, sir. I mean—"

"And you, young man. What do you do?" Ducksworth cut him off, rudely I thought.

"I'm at university too, sir," I said. "Will graduate in a couple of weeks."

He had aged since I last saw him, more than I would have guessed. He was grayer, paunchier, fleshier, and more sunburned, his face, arms, legs tanned a deep brown. Involuntarily my eyes skated to his rounded belly and he noticed. "Retirement," he said and guffawed, a deep, rumbling sound that was oddly humorless. "That's what it does to you. All that sitting around and eating." He rubbed his belly with his large, brown-spotted hands.

"I'm pleased to see you again, Mr. Ducksworth," I said and stuck out my hand.

He peered at me. Steely blue eyes, eyes like Glynis's. They studied me. "Again? Do I know you?" He took my hand tentatively.

"Émile Baxter, sir. John Baxter's son."

"The doctor's son?"

"My father was your doctor, sir."

His face brightened. The eyes cooled. He tightened his grip on my hand. "Yes, yes. Dr. Baxter. He saved my life."

"I met you at the racetracks in Trinidad, sir."

"Raven." He scratched the back of his head. "I loved that horse," he said sadly. "The man who bought him told me he gave him to his daughter. I didn't want Raven to go to the slaughterhouse. No, no, not to the slaughterhouse. I told your father so. I think he must have persuaded that man to keep Raven. Good man, your father."

Twice now with Ducksworth my father was presented in a light he rarely presented himself to me. *Good man.* I suppose he was, but I wanted a father.

"I'm glad he was helpful to you, sir."

"None of that *sir* business." Ducksworth shook his head and made scissor-like movements with his arms over his chest. "Peter. Call me Peter. You're friends with Mr. Glazal here?"

Albert had hung back behind me; now he came forward. "Émile's my best friend," he said.

"So the best man, I expect." Ducksworth cocked his head to one side. "Come, come. No need to be shy. Glynis told me all about your plans. A big wedding, eh?"

"I came to ask you for her hand," Albert said.

"No need. The other girl just ran away. Nice chap, though. Good family. I didn't mind."

"I wanted to do it right," Albert said. "You being her father."

"Deference to the old man, eh?" He faced his house and cupped his hands around his mouth. "Glynis!" he called out. "Your fiancé is here."

He was wearing an off-white cotton shirt and tan knee-length shorts. The shorts were fastened below the rise of his belly and the shirt, buttoned in one hole, flapped open, exposing a scattering of thin, straight strands of gray hair on the mound that billowed around his navel. Once a handsome man—he had seemed handsome to me six years earlier—the sun, and I suspected rum mostly, had leathered his skin. It was tough and patchy, the lines around his eyes and mouth deepened to shallow gullies.

He had slipped on his sandals but in his haste to greet us (I say "greet" because he had been expansive with his welcome) he had not fastened the buckles. He bent down to fasten them. "Glynis is readying the house," he said. "Seeing about the rum punch." He looked up, winked at me, and then redirected his eyes toward Albert. "You like rum punch, don't you, Mr. Glazal—I mean, Albert? Glynis says there are no prohibitions. You're not Muslim. That's right, isn't it?"

"My family is Catholic," Albert said.

"Converts, I suppose?"

"No. As far back as I know our family's been Catholic."

"In Lebanon?" Ducksworth was standing upright now. The ridges on his brow had gathered together like the folds on a deflated accordion.

"They were Christians. Maronites."

"Maronites?"

"Their founder John Maron was persecuted for his belief that Christ had two natures but one divine will."

"The Holy Trinity," I jumped in, anxious to support Albert. "Catholics also believe in the three persons in the one God."

Ducksworth narrowed his eyes. "So you are saying the Maronites were Catholic?"

"My great-grandfather found a lot of similarities be-tween his branch of Christianity and the Catholic Church," Albert said. "So it was easy for him to simply join the Catholic Church when he came to Trinidad."

"And you are practicing?"

"Occasionally."

"Ah!" Ducksworth exhaled as if he had finally caught Albert in a trap. "Not practicing, eh?" He glanced back at his house. "And here comes Glynis!"

She had changed her clothes. She'd been wearing jeans and a T-shirt when we took the plane from Jamaica. Now she was wearing a sort of gown. Not an evening gown, surely. It was a cotton shift, made of a soft, silky cotton fabric, light blue, the top gathered just below her collar-bone with a thin cord that ran around her neck and was tied in a bow at the back. The rest of the fabric fell elegantly down to her ankles and brushed the tops of the strappy gold sandals that enclosed her feet. (Bright red polish on her toenails, I noticed.) A sudden breeze blew across the front yard and plastered the thin fabric of the gown to her breasts and thighs. I had not thought of Glynis as sexy, but coming toward us, breasts and thighs outlined, the skirt of the gown flapping behind her, I could see what had turned my friend's head. She was still not sexy to me, not in the way I thought of Alicia as sexy as she readied herself to dive into the pool, her hourglass body taut, chiseled. But Glynis would have stopped me in the street had I seen her dressed like that, legs long and slender, the fabric of her dress clinging to her body, her breasts full and rounded like the bottoms of two oversized avocadoes.

When she reached us, she pulled herself up on her toes, stretched out her neck, and kissed Albert on his cheek. He put his arm around her waist, proprietarily, I thought, announcing without words that she belonged to him. "Isn't she beautiful?" he said.

"And isn't my father handsome?" Glynis responded, twisting her body around to face her father.

Albert had complimented her. I would have thought she'd compliment him in return. Ducksworth, though, was pleased. He swung his arm up high in the air, then down past his waist, and bent low in an exaggerated bow before her. A line I'd been forced to memorize in secondary school slipped into my head: *When power to flattery bows.*

"Oh, Daddy," Glynis said, and disentangling herself from Albert's arm, she brought her father's hand to her lips and kissed it.

Albert seemed confused as I was by this display. Of affection? Theater? I could not tell. His lips began to spread into a smile but then pulled back stiffly.

Glynis, to her credit, noticed the distress on Albert's face. She picked up the edge of her gown and twirled around, exposing her bare, pale midcalf. "Albert gave me this," she announced triumphantly to her father.

"Is that what you sell in your store, Albert?" Ducksworth's tone was gruff, the words rolling off his tongue like gravel before he cleared his throat.

"Oh, Daddy, Albert doesn't *sell* in his store," Glynis protested. "Albert *owns* the store. Two stores."

I waited for Albert to correct her, as he always did with me. The stores were his father's, he would remind me. One day he would own many stores, but for now he merely helped his father. But Albert remained silent.

"He said he worked there," Peter Ducksworth grumbled.

"Managing it," Glynis said. "He's the CEO."

"That's my father," Albert murmured at last. "He's the CEO."

"And you are the CEO-to-be." Glynis reached for his hand. "You're always so modest, Albert." She faced her father. "So what do you think, Daddy?"

"About your dress?"

"Daddy!" Glynis stomped her foot in the ground irritably. "Albert! What do you think about Albert?"

"We were talking about his great-grandfather when you joined us. Albert said he was a Christian."

"A Maronite," Glynis said. "And became a Catholic when he came to Trinidad."

"Exactly what we were talking about."

"So you see, Daddy . . ."

She did not say more, but I had the distinct impression that this was not the first time she and her father had talked about Albert's religion. It crossed my mind again that she had left us at the airport not because she was concerned about the condition of her father's house, but, rather, because she was uncertain how her father would react to Albert and needed time to pave the way for our arrival.

I could not blame her. In America—really in the whole Western world, and that included our tiny Caribbean islands—it was too often assumed that all people of Arab descent were Muslims. There were two kinds: the peaceful ones, the kind ones; and then there are those—Islamists we were now calling them—who sneaked up on New York City and Washington, DC. They appeared to be kind, good neighbors, no different from other families on a night out at Pizza Hut. Who was to know one man, the father of the chatty children eating pizza, drinking Coca-Cola, that quintessential American soda pop, would be among the terrorists who would board four planes with razors in their pockets, box cutters, their edges glinting and lethal? Perhaps it could be considered understandable that

Peter Ducksworth would be wary of his daughter's marriage to a man who belonged to a religion that made him
uneasy, but it seemed to me he had already known Albert
was not a Muslim, knew it when he made that sly remark:
You're not Muslim. That's right, isn't it? There was something else
he was intimating. Albert's people came from a country in
that part of the world we had grown to refer to without
distinction of national borders as the Middle East, that
same part of the world where those nineteen men came
from and changed the lives of Americans forever.

Siada, the eldest sister of one of my friends, Indians
from Trinidad, was an honors student at Columbia University, that center of radical liberalism in the sixties and
seventies, students and faculty demanding civil rights for
black Americans and protesting against the war in Vietnam
as immoral and racist. Yet it was there, at Columbia, in the
weeks after 9/11, that Siada was sent running to the bathroom in a panic to escape the hostile stares, even of those
who had claimed to be her friends, and trembling in fear,
where she would take off the hijab that she had worn with
pride for years.

"Well, Daddy?" Glynis was pressuring her father again.
"Isn't Albert a great guy?"

"Too soon to know that. I just met him. But he seems a
decent chap. And his friend's father saved my life."

His response had to be sufficient. He would say no
more; his lips were firmly closed. Glynis slid closer to Albert and did not ask her father to elaborate. But surely Albert's sole qualification could not be that his best friend's
father was the doctor who had saved his life. Surely if her
father could not, or would not, elaborate, Glynis would
sing the praises of Albert, tell her father why she thought
her intended was more than just a decent chap.

For a minute—no, it could not have been a minute; a minute is sixty seconds long, an eternity if there is tension in the air. So though it was probably no more than a few seconds, it felt like a minute before anyone spoke. Then Glynis said gaily, "Why are we standing here? Let's go inside. Corinne has made rum punch for us."

8

Ducksworth led us to the double front doors, and when he opened them, I knew why, as Albert and I had made our way by car up the incline to the driveway, all we saw was the sky behind the house, no trees except at the far sides where the stretch of veranda railings ended.

Elaborate farmhouse doors, Ducksworth's front doors seemed to me. They were made of wide beams of wood attached to each other, each beam running horizontally down to the top step and painted olive green to match the shutters along the windows. Three decorative iron bars, shiny black, with curlicues at their ends, were studded vertically to each door, at the top, the middle, and the bottom. At the center of the middle bars on both doors there were two thick, equally decorative black iron plates, a little more than a foot long, and in one, to the right, a giant keyhole above an enormous door handle.

"We rarely lock the door," Ducksworth said, reaching for the handle. "And as you can see . . ." He pointed to the long line of windows on both floors. "No bars. Safest island in the Caribbean. Has to be. Tourism, you understand. One whiff of crime and the ocean liners don't stop. The police are vigilant here. Very vigilant. No tourists and the money dries up." Ducksworth pushed down the handle and swung open the door.

For a second I was blinded. Blue. All I saw was blue,

shining, dazzling, blinding blue. The sudden blaze of color forced my eyes shut and when I opened them again, I saw it was the sky. Or was it the water? Or was it the sky and that impossibly blue water, like blotting paper, soaking up the blue draining into it?

But I do the blues an injustice to lump them together. There was the gold-stained blue above us, which, though my imagination was telling me otherwise, I knew was sky, for I had seen puffs of cotton-white clouds drift across it. Then my eyes dropped to the line of deep, almost navy blue, but luminous navy blue, at the edge of the horizon. It seeped into azure blue and spread inward to the coast, turning a turquoise that faded to a blue so pale that when it reached the narrow skirt of beach it was almost as white as the sand.

Albert too was stunned, amazed at all that blue, the incredible painter's canvas of blues we saw at the back of Ducksworth's house.

"Daddy's pride and joy," Glynis said.

Ducksworth was grinning from ear to ear. "Do you see why I left your oil-rich island?"

"Yours too, surely," I said.

He turned to me, still smiling. "Mine too, mine too, of course. But I'm settled here. I don't plan to leave. Ever."

"It's incredible. You are most fortunate, Mr. Ducksworth," Albert said. "We have nothing like this in Trinidad. The silt from the Orinoco muddies our waters and—"

The rest of what he was about to say was left hanging in the air for Ducksworth interrupted him. "You'll miss this, Glynis," he growled, pointing to the blues shimmering in front of us.

"There's Tobago. Or have you forgotten, Daddy?" Glynis rolled her eyes. "You used to take us there on holiday when we lived in Trinidad. There are coral reefs in Tobago too, and the water is just as blue."

"Not as blue as here," Ducksworth said curtly.

Was it the thought of Glynis leaving him permanently that had suddenly saddened him? Glynis seemed to think so. She touched his hand, her fingers skimming lightly over his. "Oh, Daddy," she cooed, "Trinidad is a hop, skip, and a jump from Barbados. I could come to see you almost every weekend."

"*Almost* every weekend?"

"Sometimes every," Glynis added quickly, then kissed him.

Ducksworth's lips and nose relaxed, fell into their usual places; he drew in his breath and exhaled. "She's a good daughter, my Glynis," he said.

"And you are the best father." She tightened her hand around his.

I wondered what went through Albert's mind just then. *Sometimes every weekend?* But perhaps Glynis had exaggerated just to put her father at ease. If so, she had succeeded. Ducksworth was grinning again when he invited us to follow him. "Come. I built a deck off the living room. Let's go sit there." He flung out his arms. His shirt flapped open again and I saw that straggly scattering of gray hair. It spread out like wings under his flabby breasts. Barbados has more beautiful beaches than Trinidad, but it had slowed him down, all that lying on the sand, sitting in his deck chair, basking in the blues. *Drinking rum.*

We were standing near the doorway. In front of us was a wide passageway that led directly to enormous glass sliding doors at the back. On one side of the passageway was the living room, on the other the dining room, which apparently was next to the kitchen, for as we walked toward the deck I could hear the faint sounds of ice tinkling against glass and the thud of a refrigerator door. Ducksworth stopped and held up his hand. "Wait," he said. "The rum punch." And then a young woman appeared bearing a tray with four glasses filled with ice cubes and a pitcher of rum punch, the pink stain of Angostura bitters floating on the top.

I would not have recognized her if Ducksworth had not called out her name. "Corinne! Just in time."

How easily I lied to myself and it bothered me that I had. She was not a prepubescent girl anymore, but still, I would have recognized her. She had sprouted up. Legs like the frisky colt I remembered, but there was nothing frisky about this Corinne standing before us. She had a quiet elegance about her, and yet I sensed she had not lost her spunk. Her long thick mane of dark brown hair was no longer parted in two plaits, swinging back and forth past her shoulders; it was pulled back behind her head in a single braid, loosely, not tightly drawn like Glynis's. Wisps of curls still dangled about the sides of her face, curls a young woman would have deliberately arranged to show off her pretty face, except there was no artifice in the way the wisps and curls framed Corinne's. They seemed to have fallen there naturally, almost stubbornly.

She was as deeply tanned as before, coppery brown, her skin glistening like silk. Her eyes were lighter brown than I remembered, but probably so from the bright sunlight streaming through the house. Her teeth had protruded a bit, but now they were even, though her top lip seemed to retain the impression of having been slightly pushed forward over her bottom lip. They were voluptuous lips, sexy lips, and mortified that such a thought would have crossed my mind, I shifted my eyes away from her.

"Daddy, your shirt," I heard her say, and I looked back to see her pointing to Ducksworth's exposed belly.

He laughed out loud but immediately began sliding the buttons through the holes on his shirt. "My daughter Corinne," he said, shaking his head but sounding less as if he were complaining and more as if he were pleased by the attention. "She's taken on my dear dead wife's role," he continued in the same mocking tone between reproach and delight. "She keeps me from being one of those crazy expats who have lived here for years, the ones you see combing the beach day and night."

He was on the third button when Glynis stopped him. "You're in your own house, Daddy." She pulled away his hand. "You can wear your shirt however you want. You're not out in public. Corinne seems to want to keep you on a leash."

I was taken aback by the harshness of her words. *A leash?* I thought Corinne was being solicitous, concerned about how her father could seem to us. He was in his own house but he had not met us before; we were strangers to him.

Ducksworth brushed back his hair that had been tousled by the breeze coming off the sea and frowned. "Where are your manners, Glynis?" he admonished her, retaliating, I thought, for embarrassing his youngest daughter, the apple of his eye. "Introduce your friends to Corinne."

Glynis slipped her arm through the crook of Albert's elbow and drew him to her. "Albert Glazal," she said.

"The fiancé," Ducksworth declared flamboyantly.

Albert's face flushed pink again.

"Not quite yet, but very soon." Glynis looked severely at her father. "There's still the ring to come."

She introduced me next.

"I met him years ago," Corinne said.

I was amazed and delighted that she remembered me.

"Though I must have looked all obzokee," she added. "Mud all over the bottom of my shorts and on my hands and knees."

Years ago I had felt uncomfortable with Ducksworth's use of the Trinidadian vernacular *too-tool-bay* to describe his affection for his daughter. Yet it seemed to me natural that Corinne would use the local expression *obzokee*. Perhaps I was not being fair—again I use the poet's intuition to defend myself—but more than her father, Corinne seemed to me a genuine Trinidadian, a true daughter of our multiethnic society.

"You were a sprightly child," I said.

"Yes, I suppose so. I managed to get up quickly, thanks to you."

Neither a child nor sprightly now, but she had retained the vivacity that was in her girl-child's eyes.

Ducksworth came over to us. "Not for you, Corinne." He took the tray from her hands, though it was clear from the four glasses there that she had not intended to drink with us. "Too young," he said, and frowned at me.

Is he trying to send me a message? I dismissed the thought as unfounded paranoia.

"She's a grown woman," Glynis said, taking a glass from the tray, the tightness in her lips making obvious her displeasure with her father. "Not a child."

"A teenager," Ducksworth declared.

"Who'll be twenty in another year and a half. And in a couple of months she'll be at university on her own."

"Well, she's here now. In my house. And I don't want her drinking," Ducksworth retorted gruffly. "Right, Corinne?"

"Not in your house," Corinne responded. But I did not think Ducksworth caught the subtle defiance in her tone. He stroked her arm affectionately.

"Good girl," he said.

Glynis grunted. She had to go to her room to get a hat, she said. Albert insisted he would wait for her. She flattened her hand on his shoulder and gave him a little push. "Go with them," she said, her voice raised slightly. "I'll be back in a minute."

Ducksworth glanced at her. His lips fluttered as if he were about to say something to her, but he spoke to Albert instead. "Ready?" he asked.

"Ready," Albert answered, and we followed Ducksworth to his deck.

If the view from the living room was spectacular, the view from the deck seemed almost unreal, a fiction, a painter's rendering of an imaginary landscape. The blues were more vivid, as could be expected, for there was nothing in the way to block the direct rays of the sun over the sky and the sea, but now I could see the greens more clearly and they were almost as stunning. At the top of tall trees the leaves were bright lime green and below them a cascade of dark and light greens—emerald green, jade green, olive green, forest green, straw green, moss green—intertwining colors of trees, bushes, and sea grass that rolled down to the shore.

"I'm thinking of putting an infinity pool here," Ducksworth said, filling our glasses to the top with the rum punch. "You know, the kind where the water flows down from the edge of the land and it seems you're right in the sea."

"Daddy's dream," Corinne said.

"And why not?" Ducksworth grumbled.

"Why not indeed? You should do it, Daddy."

"Some day, some day," he said wistfully.

I was about to grasp the white railing on the deck and lean over to get a better view of the trees when Ducksworth called out to me: "Careful. Don't bend over the railing there."

"Yes." Corinne tapped my arm and I stepped back. "Daddy just had it repaired."

"But it's fixed now." Glynis had joined us. "You're always so dramatic, Corinne. There's nothing wrong with the railing."

"Nevertheless, the paint may not be quite dry," Ducksworth said.

Glynis grimaced. *Again taking sides with the apple of his eye.* She was wearing a wide-brimmed straw hat that cast dappled shadows across her pale face through the holes in the weave. She looked glamorous, I must admit, and Albert echoed my sentiments.

"You look like a movie star, Glynis," he said, and her face softened; the grimace disappeared. She touched the brim of her hat and brought it down seductively below her brow. Albert half turned toward me, expecting, I knew, for me to compliment her too, and I did so willingly, nodding and smiling. Pleased that I was as impressed as he was, Albert turned back to Glynis. "Hats suit you, Glynis," he gushed. "You should wear them all the time."

"You should wear a hat too," Glynis said. "The sun can give you skin cancer."

Will she have Albert cover himself too, wear a hat to lighten up his skin?

"Oh, my skin can take the sun," Albert said, pushing up the sleeve of his polo shirt. There was no demarcation between the part of his arm covered by his short sleeve and the part exposed to the sun.

"You spend too much time in the pool." Glynis pulled down his sleeve. "Look how brown you are."

I glanced at Albert, but he did not seem offended. "I'm a Caribbean man," he said simply. He shrugged his shoulders and grinned.

Ducksworth had put the pitcher of rum punch on one of the small round tables that were placed conveniently next to the white wood-slatted deck chairs, each fitted with a plump blue cushion. He picked up the pitcher and refilled his glass. "Here, Émile, come over to this side. The railing is strong here." He beckoned me and I went to the spot he indicated. The drop was steep, but on the far ends, where I had seen the trees at the sides of the house as Albert shifted into another gear on the climb up the hill, the greens sloped down gently until they flattened out to two fat fingers stretching out to the sea and hugging the wide cove below Ducksworth's house.

"Daddy owns that land too," Corinne said, pointing to the fat fingers, two promontories thick with trees on the right and left of the cove.

"Bought all this before land prices skyrocketed." Ducksworth beamed. "It was out of the way, not near the hotels, or the golf courses, or the shopping centers. Off the beaten path, so to speak, far from where tourists usually go. Nobody wanted it."

"He was clever to get it when he did," Corinne said.

"Now squatters live on it," Glynis added dismissively.

"There's only one squatter," Ducksworth responded. The ice in his glass clinked when he shook it in her direction.

"One squatter who brought that woman he lives with and the two children." Glynis flipped up the brim of her hat. Her face was flushed, whether from the sun or from her frustration with her father, I could not tell. "That makes four squatters, Daddy, not one squatter."

"They are harmless." Ducksworth drained his glass. "The man's a fisherman."

"And what about that plot behind their shack? They're growing something there, I know. I've seen plants."

"Vegetables," Ducksworth said.

"More likely ganja. Marijuana."

"Daddy likes having them here," Corinne said.

"They're freeloaders," Glynis countered angrily.

"They give Daddy fish," Corinne insisted quietly.

"Fish for a free place to live? Don't be naive, Corinne. They could bring fish for Daddy all year long and it still wouldn't pay for the use of his land."

"Well, the land is Daddy's and he can do what he wants with it."

Glynis stared at Corinne. I would have blinked under the violence of the light from her eyes, but Corinne held her ground.

"It's Daddy's land," she repeated.

"Now, now, girls." Ducksworth tottered slightly, reaching for the pitcher again. "Let's not quarrel." His words were slurred. He had drunk the rum punch too quickly and it had already gone to his head.

Corinne grasped his arm and steadied him. "Don't you think you've had enough, Daddy?"

He shook her off. "One more," he gurgled.

"You've upset him, Corinne." Glynis put her arm around her father's shoulders. "I'll bring the pitcher for you, Daddy," she said soothingly. "Sit. Sit down." She guided him to a deck chair.

"No more, Daddy," Corinne urged him, but he waved

her away again and she stood there helpless as Glynis filled his glass to the brim. In two gulps, Ducksworth swallowed half the punch in his glass. "To the top," he then said. He stretched out his hand and Glynis refilled his glass.

Albert looked miserable. This was his first time meeting his future father-in-law and he had found himself in the midst of a squabble between the man and his daughters.

Anxious to redirect Glynis's attention, I asked her, "What about your other sister, Rebecca? Will we be seeing her?"

"In the morning," she replied. "We're getting together for brunch at a restaurant near the coast."

Albert wanted to spend more time with Glynis, so he gave me the keys to the rental car and said he would meet me later at the hotel; Glynis would drive him back.

I was just about to pull away when I heard Corinne shout out my name: "Émile! Wait!" She was running toward me down the driveway; a book was in her hand.

I stuck my head out of the car window. "Do you need a ride somewhere?" A foolish question for she had nothing on her feet, neither shoes nor sandals, but my heart had taken a tumble when she called my name and my brain lost reason.

Was it the thought of being alone with her in the car that had set off that boom in my chest? I hardly knew her. I reminded myself she was still in secondary school; I was about to graduate from university.

Perspiration was beading her forehead when she reached me. "I wanted to give you this book," she said. "It's a novel by George Lamming." Her breath came in shallow puffs. "Lamming's the most famous writer in Barbados. He lives in a hotel in Bathsheba. That's close to where we'll be going tomorrow."

She was gone before I could thank her properly, the soles of her feet hitting the hard asphalt on the driveway. A Caribbean girl indeed! Had she lived in the big countries where the temperature dropped, she would have had to wear shoes for most of the year and the soles of her feet would have softened. Here the earth was warm, and a girl like Corinne, accustomed to the scratch and scrape of dried leaves and twigs beneath her feet, and the coarse sand at the beach, could run like that, barefooted on hard asphalt, and she would not flinch.

9

I was exhausted when I arrived at the hotel: too much sun, too many beers at the pool before Albert thought it would be appropriate to leave for Ducksworth's house, and too many rum punches—two glasses on Ducksworth's deck and one more when we returned to the living room.

The sun was setting, spreading a pinkish glow across the horizon and staining the water in the hotel pool purplish blue. I could see a few silvery stars already trying to pop out of the darkening sky and thought I'd swim a few laps to clear my head before the sun was totally gone. By dinnertime, having taken a long, warm shower and washed the chlorinated pool water from my skin and hair, I felt refreshed. When I sat at the dining table I practically gobbled down the sumptuous meal the kitchen chef had prepared: fried flying fish, stewed red beans, white rice, fried plantains, and coconut ice cream for dessert. Then the evening music began—a three-piece steelpan band, which ordinarily I would have welcomed, but I was already beginning to feel queasy from having eaten too much and too quickly, and the glare of the garish colorful lights strung on poles above the dining tables was intensifying a throbbing in my head. By the end of the first rendition of a popular calypso I needed to lie down, so I went to my room to read the book Corinne had given me.

In the Castle of My Skin. It was required reading in secondary school when I sat for the CAPE exam that had replaced the British A-level exam, but I had little memory of it, having studied the book to answer questions on the exam rather than for pleasure. I knew, of course, it was a novel about the early days of independence in Barbados and I flipped through the pages halfheartedly, curious to know why Corinne had been anxious to recommend it to me, not quite convinced that she had given it to me simply because Lamming was an important Barbadian writer and we would be having brunch near the area where he lived.

Some of the pages were dog-eared; nothing remarkable about that. A student would note the passages she would have to remember. Then my eye caught a red line down the side of one of the pages. I opened the book wider and read: *I have always been here on this side and the other person there on that side . . . but they won't know you. They won't know the you that's hidden somewhere in the castle of your skin.*

Was this the reason Corinne had given me the book? Did she hope I'd see this passage red-lined, the flap at the top of the page folded down lower than the other ones?

It fanned my vanity to think so, quelled the discomforting flutter that earlier had stirred in my chest. *Did I really think voluptuous lips, sexy lips?*

I was an elder to Corinne, I reminded myself sternly, a university man. She wanted me to think well of her. That was why she had given me the book, why she hoped I'd notice the lines she had marked. She wanted me to know there were two Corinnes: the one who stood by silently as Glynis plied her father with rum punch, and the one in the castle of her skin who hated the way her father drank, who was concerned about his health. She had not abandoned her father; she had deferred to her sister, the eldest of her father's three daughters.

"Well, Corinne," I said out loud to myself, full of

self-importance, "I did not think less of you." I closed the book and pulled the blanket over my head.

That night I dreamed of Alicia. In the fantasy that blossomed out of the warm cocoon of self-satisfaction I had wrapped myself in as I drifted to sleep, Alicia was beckoning me. She had not kissed that man on his lips; my eyes had deceived me. She had kissed him on his cheek. Now she was smiling at me, a self-conscious smile, a flirtatious smile, as if she had been aware that from the moment I'd seen her at the bottom of the ladder, I had not turned my eyes away from her. That man was not her lover; he was a friend, her swimming coach, she assured me in the dream. I was the one she was interested in.

I woke up the next morning exhilarated. Tomorrow I would fly out to Jamaica. I was expected to give a reading of my poems at a bookstore and I knew Alicia would be reading there too. It would be my chance to speak to her. Today I would have brunch with Corinne and her sisters. There would be no more foolish flutterings of my heart.

The hotel where Albert and I were staying was southwest of the Scotland District where the hilly land in Barbados begins. I say hilly and not mountainous land because the highest peak in the Scotland District is a mere one thousand feet. Our highest peak in Trinidad is two thousand feet, not significant when one considers that Jamaicans can boast of a mountain as high as seven thousand feet, a distinction, though, that tragically made their island easily visible to the British fleet with their terrible cargo from West Africa. In the end, there would be many more enslaved Africans in Jamaica than in Trinidad, which, though having three mountain ranges, was much farther to the south and would require a more lengthy and dangerous voyage for the slave ships. By the time the Emancipation Act was passed, there were a little over eighteen thousand enslaved Africans in Trinidad and over 360,000 in Jamaica.

As usual, Albert was anxious not to keep Glynis waiting, and we arrived on time at Ducksworth's house. Glynis had arranged for Albert to travel with her in her car and for Corinne to go with me. Corinne, it seemed, had to return home early to study for an exam. Did I mind having her trail along? Corinne asked me. She could stay at home and I could go with Albert and Glynis. Glynis objected immediately. "Go with Émile," she said to Corinne. "He will need the company." She and Albert had things to discuss. Corinne snorted. Or was that my imagination? When I looked again, her face was a ripple of smiles.

We were hardly on our way—I was doing my best to keep up with Glynis's car, which seemed to be speeding ahead—when Corinne turned to me and, in a voice somewhat petulant but demanding too, asked what I thought of the novel she had given me.

My eyes still peeled to Glynis's car, I blurted out carelessly, "Oh, many of us live in the castle of our skins."

"Many of us?"

Not sensible enough to keep my thoughts in check, I pushed on, my vanity in full bloom. "There's the you you allow people to see, and the real you you hide from the world. In your castle."

"The real me? You think I'm hiding my true self from the world?"

"I mean the passage you underlined in red." I fumbled through an explanation, though from the scathing tone of her question, I was beginning to guess that I'd probably made a mistake, misunderstood the purpose of the red line she had drawn along the side of that passage.

She slapped her hands on her knees and bellowed. I should have kept my eyes on the road. A truck was barreling toward me on the other side, but she had so disoriented me with her derisive laughter that I turned my head toward her and nearly collided with the truck before the driver swerved to avoid me. Loud shouting, cursing, obscene hand gestures—all on the truck driver's side—before the man finally sped away. In those few moments I lost sight of Glynis's car. I had seen the taillights ahead, but her car rounded a bend and the lights disappeared. At least Corinne had stopped laughing. "Now we're lost." I shook my head and gritted my teeth.

"Don't worry," Corinne said coolly, "I know how to get there."

"Good. I wouldn't want to have to explain to your father that I got you lost in the Scotland District." I looked in my rearview mirror; the truck driver was a good distance behind us. "That was a close call," I said, wiping my brow.

Our narrow escape did not distract Corinne; she interrogated me again. "Did you think that passage was related to me? Or that I had specially marked it for you to see?" She was looking steadily at me.

I felt foolish and mumbled something incomprehensible.

"I thought Lamming would help you understand Barbados," she responded. Then, while I sat there quietly, my eyes fixed forward, our roles reversed. She became the teacher and I the pupil.

Lamming was writing about the colonial experience, she said. He was writing about the pull and tug of the child of the colonies, his affection for the mother country, and at the same time his anger for the subservient role he was forced to play in a country that was his own.

The car windows were open and when I turned toward

her, loose curls from the front of her hair were blowing around her face. She swiped them away from her eyes as she continued to lecture me. Suddenly, though, as I shifted the gears, climbing higher toward the Scotland District, she shifted her tone and announced, her voice weighted with sadness: "Lamming's not my favorite novelist."

"But you gave me—"

"As a novelist, I find him too didactic," she said quietly.

"Didactic?" I was not surprised by her choice of word. I had heard that criticism hurled against Lamming many times before. In America, critics use the term *protest litera-ture* and in that literary bag some lump the greats—James Baldwin, Richard Wright, Ralph Ellison.

"Surely you know what didactic means." Her plait was unraveling at the ends. If it were not held at the nape of her neck with some sort of elastic band it would have unrav-eled completely. "Lamming should trust his readers more," she said. "He's writing a novel, not a political tract." She grabbed her loosened hair, pulled it to one side, and faced me. "Don't you agree?"

I felt compelled to defend Lamming. "You have to re-member he was among the first," I said. "He had to do more than tell a story; he had to give people a sense of who they were. Are."

She grunted.

I said more. I said it was important to understand what Lamming and writers like him meant to the Caribbean in the early days of independence. "The islands were just coming out of decades of slavery and colonialism. Years of saying yes to massa, years of being taught that massa was superior to us."

She slumped down in her seat. *Good*, I thought. *I am re-storing the balance you tried to reverse. I am the teacher now; you are the student.* I went on and on. I said we needed writers to give us a mirror of our true selves. I said the mirror massa gave us was distorted. Massa told us we had no history, no culture, no language. The only history we had was the one he gave us; the only culture and language we had were what he taught us.

She twisted her body away from me and stared out of the window.

That is that. No more speeches. I'd had enough of accusations like hers against the poets and novelists of the early postcolonial days. I switched on the radio. A calypso was playing, a tune I knew, about the new political party in power in Trinidad. I began humming along and my mind drifted, my body relaxing under the warmth of the sun pouring through the windshield on my face and arms and the cool wind blowing through the window, fanning away the heat. I rounded the bend at the top of the pear that was the shape of Barbados, and now the sea side of the road began to look familiar to me. The Atlantic. It beat against the eastern shores of Trinidad, huge waves dashing against the coast and fierce trade winds bowing down the coconut trees so low the fronds almost touched the ground. It was the same here, the wind and the sea smashing against the land with such ferocity that only solid black rocks pocketed with deep crevices survived like lost strays in the water, the remaining land ground to coarse dark sand. But here there were no coconut trees and above the sand the hills rose, brown and gray, spotted with green, but mostly with dried ocher-colored bushes, hardy weeds. Heather, I thought. The moors of England. I had not been to England, but I was well schooled on my island that was once a colony. *Wuthering Heights.* Heathcliff galloping on his horse through the moors. And that stretch along the eastern coast of Barbados, on the other side of the road, away from the sea, looked to me like the moors.

"So were you talking about me?"

The suddenness of Corinne's voice breaking into my musings startled me. I whirled around in her direction. "What? What did you say?"

Her voice was calm when she answered me, the sort of calm that should have forewarned me, as her tone was in stark contrast to the question she asked: "Did you mean me? My family?"

"Your family?" I asked, confounded by her question.

"When you said *massa.*"

I had totally forgotten our previous conversation. *Argument?*

"Our family were the ones bringing those slave ships to the West Indies," she said.

"Long ago," I murmured.

"We stayed. We had slaves."

"Not you."

"My great-great-grandfather."

"Your great-great-great-grandfather," I said, regretting I had spoken so harshly. My talk of massa had apparently wormed its way into her conscience. "You're a Caribbean girl," I reassured her.

"Yes, a Caribbean girl," she repeated softly. And she was. First Trinidad, and now Barbados was her home. Not even her grandfather would recognize those dastardly Englishmen, cracking their whips across the bloodied backs of Africans chained by their necks and legs, all that stunning beauty around them, paradise—the tall leafy trees, the bright green grass, the golden sun, the pristine white sand, the glistening turquoise waters—made a mockery by the obscenity of their cruelty.

She stuck her head through the window and threw

out her hands, her hair blowing in the wind. "Whew!" she shouted. "Like a bird."

"Don't do that," I said sternly. "You could get hurt if a car comes by."

She ignored me and pushed her head out farther. So I drove on with her like that, her hair tangled about her face, her hands outstretched in the wind. Another twenty minutes and a building appeared high on top of a bluff. "Is that where we're going?" I pointed to it.

She pulled her head back inside the car. "No," she said, and began to braid her hair, her face losing all the gaiety that seconds before had illuminated her pretty eyes and tanned cheekbones. "We're not going there. That's the hotel where Lamming lives."

"But you wanted to see him, no?" I asked, puzzled.

"He's in America," she said, and paused. Then in a voice so low I barely heard her, she murmured, "It's ironic, isn't it?'

"What is?"

"What you said to me earlier about Lamming devoting his novels to helping Caribbean people restore their identity and see the islands as nations. Now he spends half the year teaching at a university in America." She tightened the locks on her braid and sighed. "But I suppose he must."

I suppose he must. I repeated her words silently to myself. We control our own government, our own economies, but we are yet to see the value of our artists. Lamming must go to America to make a living. His people claim to adore him; they are proud of him; he is their national hero, but they don't understand or *want* to understand that artists cannot live on air, the sun, and the sea.

My father was harsh with me when I said I was going to study literature at university. *I want to be a teacher*, I told him. He scoffed. *You'll never make a living,* he declared. How much more would he have derided me if he knew my plans to be one of those weepers and dreamers he called poets?

"So," Corinne was insisting, "don't you think it's ironic?" I conceded it was and she settled back in her seat and closed her eyes, but not before saying, "He loves Barbados, you know. His home is here."

I took my eyes off the road and glanced at her. Gold rays from the sun skimmed across her face, setting the ends of her hair aglow, her skin gleaming. Drenched in the brilliant sunlight pouring over her, her head lying sideways, quiet and still on the back of the seat, she looked almost angelic, and in spite of my resolve, I felt that flutter again in my heart.

A few miles later a silvery roof glinted in the sun. "Is that it?"

She opened her eyes and sat up. "Yes. That's where we're going. Pull in where you see Glynis's car."

10

He was a handsome young man. Golden. I do not mean so metaphorically. His hair was blond with streaks of dark and light gold; his eyebrows, which were a bit bushy, were also blond, his skin tanned, but golden brown. He was wearing knee-length shorts, pale-colored khaki, but they could have been gold too for they had a yellowish tint and were just a shade lighter than his skin. His blue short-sleeved shirt was the color of the sky and buttoned in only two places, so when the ends of the shirt flapped open with the breeze blowing from the ocean, I could see a flat stomach and a scattering of light golden strands of hair.

He was the first to rise from the table where he and Rebecca sat, joined already by Albert and Glynis. "Douglas." He stretched out his hand. "Douglas Fairbanks."

I thought he was joking and I played along. Fairbanks was dark-haired, but this Douglas Fairbanks before me was just as tall and broad-shouldered, with a narrow waist, sculpted arms and legs, movie-star looks. "The swashbuckling star. I've seen your movies," I said, and shook his hand.

"No." Rebecca stood up and came behind him, dark brown hair bobbed close to her ears and freckles sprinkled across her tanned face. "His name really is Douglas Fairbanks. But he's not a movie star." She wrapped her arms around his waist and sank her chin in the well of his shoulder.

"She's right," Douglas said. "No relation to the Hollywood Fairbanks, I'm afraid."

"But more handsome," Glynis said. I swung my head around at the sound of her voice. She was shaking her finger at Rebecca. "You should appreciate your man, Rebecca. He is more handsome than a movie star."

Rebecca giggled and Douglas blushed, his golden skin shining brighter.

"Husband," Rebecca said, correcting Glynis. "He's not my man anymore, remember? He's my husband."

Glynis was golden (though dyed blond, I had guessed) and Douglas was golden, and I couldn't help thinking that physically she was a perfect match for him. As if she knew what Douglas was going to wear (but how could she?), she was dressed in similar colors: a light-blue-and-white tie-dyed halter top and pale cream slacks. I felt a twinge of pity for Rebecca with her dark coloring shadowed by all that gold gleaming off Douglas and Glynis. She was wearing a chocolate-brown print dress that hung inelegantly down past her knees and did little to reveal her figure, which, however, seemed attractive enough. She was slim, not thin, and all the curves were in the right places as far as I could tell: firm breasts, a waistline when she moved, strong legs, shapely calves. But if Douglas were a movie star, she was certainly no Mary Pickford, and yet as she tightened her arms around his waist and looked up lovingly into his eyes, I could see why he had married her. Not many a man would have been able to resist those liquid-brown eyes peering up at him with such pure adoration, as if he were a god and she his grateful, obedient servant.

"You eloped," Glynis said dryly.

Rebecca unwound her arms from Douglas's waist and

ran to her sister. "Will you forgive me?" She threw her arms around Glynis's neck.

Glynis freed herself from her sister's embrace and patted her hand. "There's nothing to forgive," she said. There was neither warmth in her voice nor sincerity in her faint show of affection.

Rebecca, though, was elated. "See, see!" she said to Douglas, laughter bubbling up her throat, her eyes shining. Bright eyes, but they struck me as less than intelligent. It might have been wrong of me to make this assessment on a first meeting, but she seemed the sort who would do anything to avoid causing the slightest whiff of unpleasantness to her sister. "I keep telling you, Douglas," she whined, "Glynis forgives me. Forgives you." She tickled him under his chin. He squirmed, twisting his broad shoulders, his body contorting with pleasure, but then (instinctively, it seemed to me) he glanced across to Glynis, and when he looked back at Rebecca, all traces of the frivolity that a second ago had widened his lips vanished.

Glynis snorted, her lips drawn back tightly. "So, were you able to find your way up here all right, Émile?" She faced me. "I told Albert he shouldn't drive so fast."

Albert's head was lowered over a pink drink that he was swirling in his glass with a greenish swizzle stick. I couldn't tell whether he was embarrassed or not, but I didn't believe it was his decision to leave me behind, for when Glynis gave him the keys to her car, he told me emphatically that he'd slow down if he didn't see me.

"You didn't have a problem, did you?"

Albert was still concentrating on his drink as if he wanted to avoid my eyes, so I didn't mention my near brush with the side of a lumbering truck. "We made it here in one piece," I said.

Glynis turned to her sister. "I was certain you knew your way to Bathsheba, Corinne. And I thought you'd see my car not far from there, on top of the hill. You've been here before, haven't you?"

Here was an outdoor dining area, covered with a gray-and-white-striped awning, in front of a small restaurant. I had seen the glinting roof but not Glynis's car, and would have kept going had Corinne not pointed out the car to me, shadowed under the galvanized roof of a shed next to the restaurant.

There was no paved road to get to here, only a rutted dirt track, though it was wide enough for a car. The architect— and I do not use this word simply to flatter him—had an artist's eye. He had set the restaurant into the hill, and the outdoor space where we were sitting was built on a ledge that had either formed there naturally or been carved out of the rocky terrain. Most of the furniture and fittings in the indoor restaurant and outdoor space were made from natural objects. The walls of the restaurant were covered in brown burlap attached to beams of wood that fell horizontally from the ceiling to the floor which, like the floor of the patio, was made of roughly cut gray slate. The tables and chairs were almost the same gray-brown color as the vegetation around us, and black miners' lamps, powered, I guessed, by kerosene—for there was no electricity in the area—were hung on hooks on lampposts. Color beyond gray and brown and black was in the utensils, in the cups, saucers, and plates, and in the cotton table coverings. Some were bright red and glowing orange, others sunlit yellow, sea blue, or grass green, and in the center of each table was a tiny pot of purple African lilies.

Corinne pulled out a chair opposite to Glynis's and sat down. "Daddy brought me here a couple of times," she said.

"When?" Glynis locked eyes with her.

"When you were at university."

"See, see what I told you, Albert?" Glynis turned to him and waited for his corroboration, but Albert had a blank expression on his face and didn't seem to know what he was expected to say.

"And what was that?" Corinne asked.

"That Daddy indulges you. Gives you whatever you want."

Rebecca laughed. A cackle, really. It filled the space around the table with an unsettling echo. "They are always at it," she said to Albert. "You'd better get used to it. *Who does Daddy love best?* It's a stupid game. Daddy says he loves all three of us. That's the answer, Glynis."

Glynis had said nothing about love, though perhaps that was what she meant: her father acquiesces to Corinne's wishes because he loves her best.

Rebecca stuck out her tongue and wiggled her shoulders. "Ta-tee-dah." A childish expression; it nevertheless failed to camouflage the anxiety in her eyes.

"So, Émile, what do you make of our little family?" Glynis asked, deliberately disregarding Rebecca. She narrowed her eyes and reached across the table for Douglas's hand. "He's a wicked boy. Rebecca and I planned to have a double wedding since we were little girls. I promised I'd wait for her, and she promised to wait for me, and you, Douglas, spoiled it all."

"It wasn't all Douglas's fault," Rebecca said, then planted a kiss on his lips. Douglas immediately withdrew his hand from under Glynis's. "I was the one who couldn't wait. Anyhow," Rebecca added, turning back to Glynis, "your wedding is going to be in Trinidad." Glynis looked sharply at her and Rebecca pressed her hands over her nose and mouth. "Sorry," she whispered. "Sorry."

Albert glanced at me. I shrugged, puzzled as he was. On our way to the house, we had talked about the wedding. Albert had told me he assumed the reception would be held at Ducksworth's house. All brides want their family to host their weddings, he had said. Wasn't that the custom? Now he cocked his head toward Glynis questioningly.

"I was going to tell you later tonight," she said. "You aren't angry, are you?"

It was difficult to tell if Albert was angry or not. He was smiling, but with his lips only; the smile never reached his eyes. "I'm just surprised," he said.

"But not angry?"

"If it's what you want . . ."

"It won't be a problem, will it? I mean the money? If it is, Daddy—"

"No, no," Albert said quickly. "My father would be delighted. Honored to host our wedding." The furrows that had gathered on his brow smoothened out. He had recovered. He put his arm around Glynis's shoulder and she slid close to him.

The waiter arrived, bringing greetings from the owner of the restaurant, André Lambert. "Mr. Lambert's sorry he couldn't be here to welcome Mr. Ducksworth's daughters personally," he said. "If he had only known . . ."

Corinne leaned over to me. Her father was good friends with Keith Goddard, the previous owner of the restaurant, she whispered in my ear.

The waiter coughed. He was prepared to take our orders if we were ready, he said. And for a while there was happy chatter around the table: who wanted what, what was the specialty of the house, what was really appetizing today, what would the waiter recommend? The cook had just finished making a batch of corn fritters and fried fish, the waiter informed us proudly. We placed our orders, and when the man left, Glynis lowered her head, and shifting her eyes from the dining room where he had disappeared and back to us, she said sotto voce: "There was something strange about that arrangement between André Lambert and Keith Goddard. Odd, if you ask me."

"Odd how?" Corinne raised her eyebrows.

"Odd. And you know how."

"Daddy liked Keith and he likes André," Corinne said simply.

"And that makes it right?"

"It makes it what it is. Keith's dead. And that's that."

Glynis shook her head. "You always say such silly things, Corinne."

Corinne sat back in her chair, seeming to think the better of beginning another quarrel with Glynis.

"Tell them about the engagement party," Rebecca said brightly.

Perhaps Glynis also wanted to avoid a confrontation. Albert had accepted her decision to change the venue for the wedding without argument. His father would be honored, he said, and yet she must have noticed, as I did, that he seemed distracted. When the waiter asked for our order, she had to ask him twice if he wanted corn fritters, which I knew were his favorite. So now she grabbed onto the line Rebecca had thrown out to her. "Daddy wants to give us a party," she announced happily, and caressed Albert's cheek.

"An engagement party?" Albert looked decidedly relieved, his smile this time genuine. "When?"

"Soon after our graduation. Engagement in Barbados, wedding in Trinidad. Won't that be fun?"

"That would be terrific."

"It'll be a small party, of course. Not too many people."

"I think it *should* be a small party," Albert said, matching her enthusiasm. She was his fiancée. He loved her. "I like small parties. It's generous of your father to throw us one."

"Daddy's generous," she said.

No one contested her remark, but I remembered the look on Ducksworth's face when he teased Albert. *No need to be shy. Glynis told me all about your plans. A big wedding, eh?* He seemed to be gloating, I had thought then. And I couldn't help wondering now if indeed, in spite of her protestations, Glynis's decision to have the wedding in Trinidad *was* about the money. Ducksworth was rich, but Georges Glazal was richer; he owned land and two stores. I had expected that Mr. Glazal would contribute to the expenses for the wedding, but now it seemed he was to finance it entirely.

We chatted some more, mostly exchanging superficial information about music—who liked what and who didn't. Douglas declared that he liked Jamaican reggae. Rebecca chirped up predictably that she liked it too. Glynis said she thought reggae was too loud and strident. Douglas, in a swift change from his previous position, said she had a point. You couldn't hear what someone was saying to you when the band started playing, he said. Rebecca said they were both right: reggae is great but it's too loud. No one asked Albert for his opinion; he kept stirring his drink and sipping it slowly.

Talk turned to sports. Douglas said Americans had usurped our sports. They took our cricket and made it baseball. Now they want us to lump our football and rugby together and call it soccer, he said. One of my schoolmates in secondary school had been the captain of the Trinidad football team. I mentioned his name and turned to Albert who also knew him, but before he could utter a word, Douglas cut across me with an anecdote of his own, and Albert slouched lower in his chair.

More and more I began to notice that there was little conversation between Douglas and Albert. Albert would begin to say something to us and Douglas would interrupt. Finally I brought up the subject of our future careers. Douglas said he wanted to be a businessman, an entrepreneur. Albert perked up. "That's what I plan to do," he said.

And for the first time Douglas addressed a question directly to him: "With your father?"

"We have plans," Glynis said before Albert could answer.

"I expect in Trinidad," Douglas pressed Albert. "But I hope in Barbados too."

"As I said, Douglas, we have plans." Glynis frowned at him. Douglas grinned; his lips spread apart, revealing his polished white teeth.

"Okay, okay," he said, and threw up his hands in mock surrender.

On the surface, it appeared that Glynis's intent was to keep Douglas in the dark about whatever plans she had with Albert, but I felt her chastisement of Douglas was a ruse, a pretense, that it was more likely she thought that this was not the place, not the time, not in front of Corinne and me, to discuss her plans. Douglas seemed to have got her message, and I began to wonder if the real reason Glynis wanted to go ahead of Corinne and me, and why she probably encouraged Albert to drive fast, was to get a chance to speak in private with Douglas about those plans. I was suddenly tired of them and their games. "Well," I said, and stretched out my arms, making a false show of a wide yawn as if I were exhausted, "all this sun makes a man sleepy. You guys are more ambitious than I am."

"How so?" Glynis peered at me.

"All your talk about business and being an entrepreneur. I plan to be a teacher after I graduate."

"Oh, I think being a teacher is pretty ambitious," Corinne said energetically. "It's a huge responsibility, helping to guide young minds."

I could have kissed her right then. A brotherly kiss, of course. Then, brushing the curls off her forehead, she declared, "I want to be a poet."

She shamed me. I had withheld my true ambitions, but she had the courage to name hers.

Glynis laughed and Rebecca joined in. "Corinne is such a dreamer," Rebecca said.

"Well, the truth is," I said, facing Corinne, "I want to teach, but I also want to write poetry."

Again, there was a lull in our conversation. Uncharacteristically, Albert ordered a rum punch. "Make that more punch than rum," he said to the waiter.

"And make mine more rum than punch," said Douglas, ordering his third drink.

"Not to worry," Rebecca said when she saw me glance skeptically at Douglas. "We plan to stay until evening. But make this your last one. Okay, Douglas?"

"Okey dokey," he replied, winking at her. Then, out of the blue, he turned to Albert again and asked: "Were you born in the Caribbean or in Lebanon?"

"Here, of course. Like you. You in Barbados and me in Trinidad."

"But your father?"

"My father and my father's father," Albert said.

"Your father's father?"

"Yes." Albert crossed his legs and then added nonchalantly, "As I suppose were your father and your father's father."

Good for you, Albert, I applauded him silently.

Rebecca spoke up. "Except in Douglas's case, his family goes back way further than that," she said cheerfully. "Further than his father's father."

"As far back as the slave ships," Corinne murmured.

"What's that?" Douglas's face turned from pink to red and tiny hard knots rose in wavelets from his jaw up the sides of his face.

Corinne was right, of course, to sense the underlying malice in Douglas's tone. He was unfairly grilling Albert, attempting to intimate that he was a foreigner to our islands, an interloper. But both Albert's family and Douglas's family could be said to be interlopers; both had come to the Caribbean to make a better life for themselves. There was a difference, though, a deep chasm separating them. Albert's family had started at the bottom, as mere hagglers, their goods strapped to their backs, sweat draining into their mouths as they forged their way in the broiling sun from village to village. Douglas's family had made their fortune on the backs of African men, women, and children they had enslaved, chained, and brutalized, forcing them to work from sunup to sundown planting sugarcane and cocoa for them.

But couldn't one say the same for Corinne's people? Her family was English. Didn't her people come to the Caribbean for the same purpose: to rape the land, to exploit the people, to bring Africans on slave ships to do their bidding? If I could distance Corinne from the cruel past of her relatives, why not be as generous to Douglas?

"It's not the past itself that counts," I said. "It's what we make of the future from the past."

Douglas looked at me, his eyes glistening with gratitude. "Well said, Émile. I like your friend, Glynis. He's an intelligent man, forward-looking. The past is the past. Why bring it up? Good man, Émile."

It was not exactly the praise I wanted. The past to me was also the present. It affected our thoughts, our actions. I had been to Ducksworth's house, saw where he lived—in a mansion on top of a hill with a spectacular view of the sea. He owned the land where his house stood, the two fat fingers extending out to the sea too. To get to Ducksworth's house, we had to pass tiny shacks. Black people lived in those shacks, the children of the enslaved Africans Ducksworth's people had brought in chains to the Caribbean. How much had changed in their lives? They were poor; Ducksworth was rich, still as rich if not richer than his people who had made their fortunes from the suffering of others. Ducksworth lived on Mango Road. The man who showed us the way lived on Mango Trace, minutes away, but miles from the world of the Ducksworths.

"The past informs the present and the future," Corinne said, still not ready to concede her point to Douglas. "The lives we live today are the result of the lives our families lived in the past."

"So serious, so early!" Rebecca sat up and waved her hand in the air. "Dessert! Let's have dessert. Waiter!"

And so, thanks to Rebecca, the late morning ended on a somewhat conciliatory note, if not a happy one, the dark cloud of history swept away with coconut custard pie, sapodilla ice cream, tea, coffee, lemonade, and another pitcher of rum punch, while all around us the brilliant sunshine illuminated the hilly windswept landscape and the frothy cotton-white caps of powerful waves unfurling against the craggy black rocks stranded in the roiling waters of the

Middle Passage, the spotless dazzling blue sky a silent witness of a past few wished to remember.

Corinne needed to leave. She had to prepare for an exam the next day, she reminded us. Glynis said she would stay a little longer with Rebecca and Douglas. She still had not completely forgiven Rebecca, she said, pouting her thin lips. "Eloping without telling me! Wicked Douglas. Naughty you, Rebecca." She squeezed her sister's arm affectionately, though I detected a hint of violence in the way her fingers dug deep into Rebecca's flesh, leaving a pink impression. Rebecca squirmed and rubbed her arm, but she didn't complain. In the next second she and Glynis were laughing uproariously, calling their sweethearts to join them.

Corinne stood up. "Well, I guess we'll leave the lovebirds alone," she said.

Her sisters were still laughing and teasing each other when we said our goodbyes. Douglas shook my hand and I slapped Albert on the back. I said I'd see him later, though it was on the tip of my tongue to wish him good luck. I was glad I didn't. He might have thought I meant to say so ironically when I would have wished it in all sincerity.

As we were trundling down the dirt road back to the paved road, I looked in my rearview mirror. The lovebirds were huddled together: Douglas and Rebecca, Glynis and my poor friend Albert.

"Poor Albert." We had reached the sea side of the paved road when Corinne echoed my unspoken sentiments.

I had just warned her again of the dangers of putting her arm outside the car. "You can get struck by a passing car," I'd said. "Like that truck that almost ran into us."

She was catching the wind, she told me, her hand cupped as if she could indeed scoop up the salt-laden wind blowing from across the glistening ocean. She looked so happy I did not have the heart to stop her when she refused to heed my warning. "Poor, poor Albert," she said again.

"Why poor Albert?" I asked cautiously.

"Didn't you notice?"

"That he hardly spoke?"

"That Douglas cut him off every time he tried. He was downright impolite to Albert."

"Maybe Albert preferred to listen rather than speak," I said, lying, of course, though hoping it was the truth. Douglas would soon be Albert's brother-in-law; it would not be good for there to be enmity between them.

"Maybe they have something up their sleeves," she said.

"Something like what?"

"Glynis is cunning. Sly like a fox. Didn't you notice how she tricked poor Albert into bankrolling the wedding?" She clicked her tongue. "Plans? Hah! Whatever it is she has in mind, when poor Albert finds out, it will be too late."

I didn't like how she was talking about Albert and I quickly stopped her. "He's not poor Albert," I said. "And you're wrong. Albert was just surprised Glynis would want to have the wedding in Trinidad. I think he was pleased. Very pleased."

"And I hope he'll be very pleased when he learns about her plans," she said.

"Glynis didn't say I *have plans*," I responded irritably. "She said, We *have plans*, so whatever plans she has Albert must know."

"Did he tell you? You're his best friend. Did he mention any plans to you?"

She was making me uneasy. "No, it's really none of our business, I mean *my* business, whatever plans Albert and his fiancée have," I said perhaps a little too brusquely.

She said nothing for a while and began humming, a tune that strangely imitated the whistling of the wind. She had pulled in her hand but the car window was open and her hair was blowing in all directions. "All right," she said at last, pushing away strands of hair that were stuck to her bottom lip. "You can't tell me Douglas's question was innocent."

"Are we on the same topic?" I asked her. "Are you still talking about their plans?"

"You know what I mean. His question to Albert. *Were you born in the Caribbean or in Lebanon?* He darn well knows Albert is Trinidadian."

"You got him, though, with your comment about his family coming with the slave ships. I was proud of you."

She seemed pleased by my compliment and began to whistle again. Then abruptly she stopped. "Did you think she was angry?"

"Who?" I glanced over at her.

"Glynis, of course. Rebecca was giddy with happiness— she caught the handsome big fish."

"Big fish?"

"Douglas," she said.

"And why would Glynis be angry?"

"If you didn't notice anything when we were leaving, then I won't tell you."

But I *had* noticed. Maybe Glynis was simply teasing Rebecca—*Naughty you, Rebecca,* she'd said—but it seemed like Glynis actually meant to hurt her when she plunged her fingers into her sister's arm.

Corinne tapped her chin. "Rebecca better be careful," she said.

"About what?"

"About nothing. If you choose to be blind . . ." Once

again she stuck her head out the window. In seconds, she was back again. "Douglas doesn't like Albert," she announced.

"That's a ridiculous thing to say." I made no attempt to mask my anger. "He just met him."

"You don't understand."

"What is it I don't understand?"

"WMDs."

"WMDs?"

"That whole Iraq War."

I slowed down the car and turned toward her. "Now you have me completely in the dark."

"Douglas doesn't like Arabs," she said flatly. "That's why he eloped. He didn't want to have his wedding with Glynis and Albert. None of his family did. It was personal with them."

II

Before I dropped her off at her father's house, Corinne told me the whole story. She said Rebecca had been showing off when she claimed she was the one who wanted to elope. Rebecca didn't have that kind of influence over Douglas, Corinne said. Douglas wanted to elope because he didn't want to get married in the same ceremony with the man whose people were responsible for his brother's death. Albert's people were from Lebanon, and Hezbollah, one of the most fearsome terrorist enemies of Israel and America, was conceived in Lebanon, he told Rebecca. Hezbollah was responsible for the terrorist attacks on New York, the Pentagon, and the fiery crash in Pennsylvania. Hezbollah was responsible for the Iraq War that followed, in which his brother had been killed.

Corinne said that when she corrected Douglas, pointing out that it was al-Qaeda that attacked the US, he dismissed her. Hezbollah and Iran were silent accomplices, he argued; they gave money and military support to the operation. If not for Hezbollah and Iran, that terrible plan would have failed. So to Douglas, it was Albert's people, Hezbollah, who were responsible for the devastation in America, the deaths of thousands of innocent civilians, the deaths of thousands more good Americans who fought to avenge the murders. The death of his brother, Ralph. He would elope, marry in a civil ceremony in the courthouse, before he would stand at the altar in a church next to a man who had his brother's blood on his hands.

Ralph, Douglas's brother, had been a doctor. He had graduated from an American medical school and completed his residency at a hospital in a Midwestern American state. Though there were no guarantees, he fully expected to get an H-1B visa that would allow him to practice medicine in America. That visa would pave the way for him to a green card, then to American citizenship. He had a fiancée in Barbados. He planned to marry her when he got the H-1B visa. His expectation that a teaching hospital in America would sponsor him for the visa was not unfounded; he had friends who had succeeded in achieving this path to citizenship. America needed doctors; doctors from foreign countries were cheaper than American doctors. They made less demands, accepted smaller salaries, were willing to work in poor urban areas or in isolated rural communities where even newly minted doctors, with little or no experience, were loath to practice. American doctors had huge loans to pay back for years of medical training; they could not afford, or were not willing, to work in some backwater hospital and delay the years before they could make real money.

Then 9/11 happened and changed the way America viewed immigrants. More restrictions were placed on H-1B visas and hospitals were no longer as willing to sponsor the foreign-born doctors. Immigrants were aliens, a term generally applied to creatures from outer space. Extraterrestrials. Aliens were suspect; they could make themselves resemble real Americans. See what those men did? They looked harmless, didn't they? Eating at McDonald's, Wendy's, Pizza Hut. Buying groceries and furniture at Costco, BJ's. *Signing up for flying lessons.* Yet no one wondered why they were more interested in getting the plane up in the air than in landing it. No one wondered because they seemed like regular Americans. Now, after 9/11, teaching hospitals were put on notice. Aliens could not be trusted. They might pretend they are one of us, they might swear they are here to help the underserved, the poor, but you have to watch them; you can never take your eyes off them. One day they might blow up your hospital.

But America did not count on how lucrative the medical profession could be, how in a few years a young doctor, well placed in a well-to-do neighborhood, could become a millionaire; how foolhardy it could seem to a young doctor that he or she should sacrifice years of study, sixty-hour workweeks, sleepless nights, not to mention their parents' savings, on missionary work.

Douglas's brother Ralph, however, was more than ready to be a missionary if being a missionary would open the golden gates to American citizenship. He moonlighted in places where they asked no questions, went undercover, became an illegal alien, subject to arrest, detention, and deportation. Those were scary days for him. He prayed a lot; his fiancée prayed a lot; his family prayed a lot. And then, in 2008, Washington granted some aliens the MAVNI visa, Military Accessions Vital to the National Interest.

The MAVNI was not an act of charity, of generosity, on the part of the American government. The Iraq War had not turned out to be the triumph the American president had promised: a couple of weeks, maybe a few months at the most, and the Iraqi people will fall on their knees, throw roses on the tanks that rolled through their streets, willingly surrender their rich oil fields to repay the American taxpayer for the cost of their salvation, for rescuing them from the hands of a brutal dictator, who just might (some evidence was there, though not confirmed) have been the one to have masterminded the second worst attack on American soil, but who, in any case (once more the evidence was squishy, but there was the president's father who had to be avenged) had WMDs, weapons of mass destruction, that could turn the air we breathe toxic, fatal for every man, woman, and child in America.

What a fairy tale! Young rosy-cheeked men and women, young black men and women hopeful for a more just tomorrow in the country of their birth that had not always been fair to them, were now bleeding on Iraqi soil, brains blown to bits, arms, legs, torsos flung in all directions in a guerrilla war that seemed to have caught the generals by surprise. The American military services were desperate, especially the army.

The MAVNI program that was passed by the US Congress and signed by the president was offered on a one-year trail basis. It promised doctors like Ralph an accelerated route to citizenship, the green card almost immediately if the doctor was willing to serve three years of active duty or six years in the Selected Reserve. Ralph chose the shorter route. He jumped at the chance to come out of the shadows, to practice medicine without the fear of deportation hounding his waking hours.

It was an IED, one of those insidious homemade bombs cooked up in kitchens and back alleyways, that almost killed him, though ultimately he wished it had. He woke up in a military hospital, the sheets that covered him flat below his knees. He had been trying to staunch the blood flowing from the wounds of a young man, still in his teens, when the IED detonated beside their makeshift clinic. His legs were blown apart.

Corinne told me that Ralph went into a deep depression that even the promises of his fiancée—that she loved him just the same and would never leave him—could not relieve. One day—he was home by then, in Barbados—he persuaded a fisherman to take him fishing and when they were far out in the ocean, Ralph disappeared. The fisherman said the sky had suddenly darkened but in the center there was a ring of light. Like a saint's halo, he said. He turned to show it to Ralph, but Ralph was not there; he had disappeared. There was not a ripple in the water, but the fisherman believed that Ralph had thrown himself in the sea and drowned. Not so, said Mrs. Fairbanks. Her son would never commit suicide. "God sent that light to take my Ralph home to heaven."

Douglas was not consoled; he was not as forgiving as his mother. He grieved for his only brother, his best friend, his companion, the one who had taught him all he knew. And he blamed the Iraqi people for his death. He blamed all Arabs. He blamed all Muslims. He blamed Albert, though Albert was not a Muslim, though Albert was a Christian and a Trinidadian, and had never been to Iraq. But Albert was ethnically an Arab; his people had come from Lebanon; Lebanon was the breeding ground for Hezbollah.

A	lbert and I left the next morning, I to return to Jamaica, Albert to Trinidad to buy an engagement ring for Glynis but mostly to ask his father if he would host his wedding reception. Georges Glazal loved his son, so I could not imagine he would object, though certainly he would think it strange that a young girl would cede that privilege to the man's family. I doubted, though, that he'd share my cynical view of Glynis's motivation. For Albert was right: his father would consider it an honor to host his son's wedding.

Our flights were thirty minutes apart so Albert and I went to the airport together. Glynis and Rebecca came to see us off. Neither Douglas nor Corinne was with them.

I felt an unsettling rush of disappointment when I saw that Corinne was not in the car. Before I could rein in my tongue, I blurted out half-mockingly: "Corinne didn't want to say goodbye to me, huh?"

Glynis was not fooled by my tone. She eyed me suspiciously. "You didn't expect her to come, did you? It's Monday. She has school. Have you forgotten?"

I felt exposed and embarrassed, and angry at myself for being disappointed. Corinne was a girl, still in school. *Alicia.* Alicia was the woman I was anxious to see.

Rebecca was profuse with her apologies. Douglas had to help his father with some repairs he was doing in the house, she said. "Douglas is his father's only son. Well,

I mean, now that Ralph is not with us. Ralph was Douglas's brother. He . . .” Pause. Deep breath. She started again. “Well, Dad—that is, Douglas's father—is getting up in age. He can't lift heavy things as he used to. We're living with them. That is, I've been living with them since Douglas and I got married. We have to contribute. Not that Douglas's father is poor—they are doing fine. That is, they have money, not a lot, but enough for them. Still, we have to do what we can. We . . . Ralph's medical bills . . .”

“No need to apologize,” Albert said, and stopped her torrent of false starts and stammers.

Did he already know what Corinne had told me? Had he suspected that it was not passion, impatience to make Rebecca his wife, to have her in his bed every night without the curfews Ducksworth was said to have imposed on her, that caused Douglas to persuade Rebecca to renege on her promise to Glynis for a double wedding? Did he know about Ralph?

“I understand.” Albert put his arm around her. Nothing in his expression gave me a clue as to what he understood. His face at that moment was inscrutable. But Albert was the sort of guy who bore no grudges; he was easygoing, quick to forgive a slight.

Clearly relieved, Rebecca giggled, bobbing her head up and down. “You're such a nice man. Such a nice man, Albert. I really think—”

Glynis tugged her skirt. “Enough, Rebecca,” she said sternly.

But Rebecca had more to say. Douglas was really very sorry, she said. He had planned to see Albert off. “He likes you, Albert,” she said.

Albert removed his arm from around her shoulder.

"He's the brother-in-law of my soon-to-be wife," he said. Again that inscrutable expression.

"But he really does like you."

Glynis tugged Rebecca's skirt once more and pulled her firmly by the waist to her side.

A devious thought snaked into my head. Maybe Albert had paid the entire bill for the brunch we had at that restaurant on the hill. Maybe that was why Douglas supposedly liked him. I had left my share on the table, but at the hotel I discovered that Albert had slipped the money back in my pocket.

It felt good to be back at the university, to have something definite to do, no guessing games between my professor and me. If I didn't submit the final research paper for my degree on time there would be consequences. What consequences there would be for Albert in his marriage to Glynis was a question that could only be answered in the future. Albert was an intelligent man. Surely it must have occurred to him that those questions Douglas had lobbed at him about his family's background were not well intentioned.

Peter Ducksworth was no less intrusive, though one might say he had a right to ask questions; his daughter, after all, would be marrying Albert. Still, I thought the way he probed Albert about his religion was unkind, bordering on malicious. But Albert said he loved Glynis, and I was learning how far a man would go in pursuit of his heart. I could not say I was in love with Alicia, but I had fantasized about the possibilities of an attachment with her, convincing myself on the slim evidence of a dream that the man in the pool meant nothing to her romantically. It was on the basis of that fantasy alone that I had turned down Albert's invitation to accompany him to Trinidad, giving up the chance to see my father, as well as Henrietta, whose kindness I sorely missed.

That evening I looked for Alicia in the bookstore where we were both scheduled to read, she after me, but I was soon swept away by a group of friends and, when the room filled up, I could not find her.

My turn came and I read a poem about my mother whom I had never seen, or if I had, it was behind that murky film that distorts the vision of newborns. Of course, I had seen photographs of her, and imagining she was alive when I was a child, I had composed a poem about her beauty and her boundless love for her only son. The applause was satisfying, not thunderous. I hadn't expected thunderous applause, but I could tell the audience was pleased, that they liked my poem.

"Cold." Alicia caught me by surprise. A visiting poet, one who was the second Caribbean poet to win the Nobel Prize in Literature, had just congratulated me. He had slipped into the room just as I was beginning to read and slipped out again as a murmur went through the bookstore from a group of people who recognized him. Still in a daze, my head lingering in the direction where he had disappeared through the back door, I had not seen Alicia as she walked up to me. The poet, of course, was Derek Walcott from the island of St. Lucia. Before Walcott, the Nobel laureate was the poet Saint-John Perse from Guadeloupe. Nine years after Walcott, V.S. Naipaul, a novelist this time, would be our third Nobel laureate for literature, though Naipaul would claim a debt to England and India first, and only days later acknowledge that his formative years, until age seventeen, were shaped in Trinidad.

"Your hand." My hand was hanging by my side and Alicia had taken it into hers. "It's freezing."

She was more beautiful than I had recreated in my fantasy. She was wearing white—a long skirt that flowed softly down to her ankles and a tight-fitting sleeveless top with a wide scoop neckline that revealed the crest of her full breasts rising gloriously like a glistening wave on a sunlit sea. Against all that white, her skin shone, cocoa brown, gleaming under the bright lights in the room. She released my hand and like an idiot I murmured, "Sorry," and rubbed my hands together.

"No," she said, "that was very moving. Powerful! I saw Walcott congratulating you. Your poem really touched him. Too bad he had to leave. Men usually sanctify their mothers, but the woman you wrote about was real. You must have had a great mother."

I wanted to say something other than "sorry," something about not knowing my mother and yet being pleased that she liked my poem, that Walcott liked it too, but at that moment the moderator announced her name.

"Wish me luck," she said, fluttering her fingers in a little wave to me as she mounted the podium. Her legs—the long, taut legs that arrested me when she rose on her toes at the tip of the diving board—were covered, and yet with every step she took up to the podium they seemed more seductive to me, the shape and color tantalizingly visible beneath the gauzy material of her skirt. I wished her luck. Secretly I wished myself more luck.

Her poem was surprisingly political, though I should not have been surprised. I had found out that she was a law student but my fantasies had got the better of me and I had fashioned her into a student of a subject that was not so prosaic and unromantic. Yet, though I did not know it then, that poem would trigger a pivotal point in my life, one that would bring me closer to Corinne than I had foreseen.

It was a poem about Christopher "Dudus" Coke, the notorious gangster from Jamaica who was found guilty in 2011 of exporting marijuana and cocaine to the US. For weeks US authorities had searched for him in Jamaica's Tivoli Gardens where he was a god, the savior of that impoverished village. It was Dudus Coke, the people believed, who protected their children from the violence that erupted daily on the island, reputed to have one of the highest murder rates in the world. It was Dudus Coke who fed and sheltered them when government officials turned their backs. It was Dudus Coke who gave them jobs.

Over seventy people were killed in the raids to smoke out Dudus Coke, seventy people who hid him in backrooms and in dugouts in their backyards, who willingly offered their bodies as human shields to protect him. Even when the prime minister caved in (the word was that he too was involved in hiding Dudus from the US), the people still refused to give him up. Eventually he was captured, though it was said he was on his way to the US Embassy to surrender to the American government. He didn't want any more killings in his name, he reportedly claimed. He loved his people too much to have them suffer for him. The mourning lasted weeks; drums beat for him, echoing through the warrens and cramped spaces in Tivoli Gardens. The women wailed, the men pumped their fists and swore there'd be retribution.

Alicia did not attempt to exonerate Dudus Coke for his crimes; she cataloged the vicious murders he was accused of committing. She told of an instance when he had dismembered his victim with a chainsaw, but her poem was mostly targeted to the Jamaican government, to the prime minister in particular. The prime minister and his deputies had betrayed the people, thrown them to the mercy of drug lords like Dudus Coke. *The children are suffering / The children are starving / The children have no place to sleep and the prime minister don't do nothing.* Words to that effect were a constant refrain in the stanzas she read.

Alicia got the loudest and longest applause of the evening. My hands were cold after I read my poem. They had betrayed me. They had remembered my longing for my mother when I was too young to have learned the futility of resisting fate. Her hands were beaded with sweat, with her passion, her anger at the injustices rained down on the children of Tivoli Gardens. Trails of perspiration rolled down the sides of her face. Her bodice was damp and clung to her skin, exposing the outlines of her white lace bra, and I am ashamed to say that my eyes lingered on the two perfectly shaped mounds spilling over that white lace.

A crowd gathered around her—students, faculty, local poets, people from the neighborhood. I stood outside of the crowd. She caught my eye and mouthed, *Wait!* When the crowd dispersed, she walked over to me. "Doing anything later?" she asked.

"No," I said. "Do you have anything in mind?"

"A group of us are meeting at the Irie Café. Why don't you join us?"

The man was there, her swimming coach, as I had imagined him to be. He walked over to where we were standing and swung his arm possessively around her neck. She smiled and rested her head on his shoulder. What more proof did I need that I was a dreamer?

"Michael. Émile." She introduced us, and with one arm still around her neck, Michael shot out his other hand to me.

"I saw you at the pool," I said, shaking his hand.

He grinned. "Saw me or my girl?" He had found me

out, but he was not about to humiliate me. "You can't see anybody when Alicia is on the diving board. True?"

"True," I said, and my heart sank.

He was a handsome man, tall, lanky limbed, with a broad strong nose, thick eyebrows, eyes that crinkled when he smiled. His hair was styled in dreadlocks, caught in a black band at the nape of his neck. They made a stunning couple, Alicia in white, he in a navy dashiki and light-beige linen pants; Alicia brown as a cocoa pod, he dark as a ripe governor plum, both of them fit, in the flower of their youth.

I chastised myself for that unimaginative phrase I had used in more than one poem when I was a teenager. *In the flower of their youth*. It was how I had described the girls I saw at the botanic garden in Trinidad, but Alicia and Michael, standing next to each other, did remind me of that stage in a flower's life when the bud opens and the flower that blooms is the most beautiful it will ever be.

"She's a first-rate swimmer," I said, determined to be magnanimous. "And a talented poet."

"I tell her so all the time." He kissed her on her forehead. "See what I tell you, Alicia? From the mouth of one poet to another. Can't say I understand too much about poetry, though."

"Michael is a civil engineer," Alicia explained. "He's going to build highways for us, map out better roads for Jamaica."

"The girl loves me." Michael laughed, showing his perfectly straight teeth.

"No, really." She gave him a playful shove with her elbow. "Michael's going to be doing important work for Jamaica. Needed work."

"Engineering is important," I agreed, not wanting to

spoil the happiness so clearly lighting up her face.

Michael tapped his chest with his free hand. "But I have to give you poets respect. You reach into our souls. Here." He pressed his closed fist over his heart and held it still. "I loved my mother too. But she's dead now, long gone."

In spite of my jealousy, I found myself liking him. He had a warm, inviting smile, not a shadow of guile or pretentiousness about him. He seemed an honest man, the genuine article. "Mine too," I said. "She died giving birth to me."

He loosened his arm around Alicia's neck and placed his wide palm on my shoulder sympathetically. "Alicia," he said, "tell Mr. Émile Poet to come with us to Irie Café."

I had assumed he was a Rasta—the dashiki, the dreadlocks—and with a name like Irie Café, I prepared myself for an evening breathing in the mind-numbing smoke from ganja spliffs, ubiquitous in such places, and having to endure the ear-splitting beat of reggae. Irie Café was nothing like I imagined. It was a middle-class Rasta restaurant, those words *middle class* and *Rasta* seemingly contradictory until you saw the clientele. There were families with children there, young people my age laughing and joking with each other, businessmen in suits, and staid professionals engaged in lively conversation. Not a person was bleary-eyed, not a person was slouching listlessly in his seat. Not a whiff of ganja anywhere, the reggae music soft, subdued.

Some, both the men as well as the women, wore the tam—a knitted cap in red, gold, and green—that I'd seen on many Rastas. It covered their heads entirely, ballooning out in the back where it was weighted down with thick long coils of dreadlocks. Others, though, had their dreadlocks uncovered. These were well-cared-for dreadlocks, no frizzy ends poking out between the loops, the locks swept attractively from the face and tied in the back, the women letting a lock or two drop seductively over their foreheads.

I do not mean to imply that everyone had dreadlocks. Like two of the men at the table where Alicia and Michael were ushering me, several men in the restaurant had close-cropped hair like mine, and more than a few women had either straightened their hair or were wearing it natural, styled in an Afro like Alicia's. But I was definitely in a Rasta restaurant, the walls lined with framed pictures of the chubby-faced Marcus Garvey in military garb, a plume of long, thin, whitish cords gathered together like the fly whisk some African chiefs favored flowing out of the top of the helmet on his head. It was Garvey who had urged American and West Indian blacks to look to Africa for their freedom, promising that one day a black king would be crowned to rule over the continent. That king was Haile Selassie of Ethiopia. His followers were Rastafaris: *Ras*, meaning head, prince, chief; *Tafari*, Selassie's birth name.

Photographs of Selassie at varying stages of his life were hung next to pictures of Garvey: Selassie with a short beard, a long beard, a black beard, a gray beard; Selassie as a boy in simple dress, a gold cross dangling on a cord around his neck; Selassie the bejeweled emperor, a gold crown like a large upturned tumbler on his head, jewels draped over his robe; Selassie the military man, clutching a gold sword at his side, standing erect in a dark jacket, a green sash and thick gold ropes looped across the front, ribbons and medals pinned to his chest, rows of gold buttons attached to wide epaulettes on his shoulders.

There were also photographs and paintings of Bob Marley on the wall: Marley the reggae king, a marijuana joint, fat and round as a Cuban cigar, clamped between his lips; Marley the Rastafari ambassador, who had brought the social classes in Jamaica together—rich, poor, and in between—with his reggae music, his lyrics appealing for freedom and social justice across the world. He had made reggae popular in the Western world, dreadlocks fashionable even among whites. The Irie Café a safe place for Jamaican families who loved reggae and jerk chicken.

Alicia's friends gathered at the Irie Café would not have condoned the corruption widely believed to have been rampant during the time of Selassie's imperialistic control over his country. It was Bob Marley's entreaty to the world for peace and harmony that appealed to them. And it was One Love, Brotherly Love, that was the topic of a heated discussion later at the table, after we had dined on a sumptuous meal of peppery jerk chicken, rice, steamed vegetables, banana fritters, and mounds of green salad topped with chunks of ripe mango and avocado, and had cooled our tongues with ginger beer and mauby.

While we ate, the conversation was light: the usual queries about mutual friends and family. Someone, a woman who had been to the reading, asked about my mother. "That was a lovely tribute to your mum," she gushed. I thanked her but I did not repeat my history. Michael clapped his hand on my shoulder and nodded approvingly.

It didn't take long, though, for talk to turn to politics, Alicia's poem making a convenient entrance point. "You're right, Alicia, not to water down the crimes Dudus Coke committed," one of the men with the close-cropped hair said. "Dudus was a vicious criminal. It's no lie that he tortured the men who didn't do what he ordered them to do. He was the biggest drug lord in Jamaica, but you have to give it to him for what he did for the people in Tivoli

Gardens. If not for him, a whole lot of them would have starved."

Others joined in, going back and forth about Dudus Coke: whether he deserved the punishment he got, whether the prime minister and his government ministers should go to jail too since they profited from Dudus's crimes. The man with the longest dreadlocks, a lawyer, said that a lot of government officials took kickbacks from Dudus and yet it was he, not the health minister, who paid for the vaccines the children needed. One woman said that mothers lived in constant fear for their children, but Dudus sent guards to protect them. They talked on and on, no one justifying Dudus's terrible crimes, but no one absolutely condemning him either. "What we need is to form a coalition with some of the community members of Tivoli Gardens to put pressure on the government to improve the living conditions there," someone said. And they began to talk about how and when they would form such a coalition. I was quiet for so long listening to them I thought they had forgotten me until one of them asked: "So what are you going to do after you get your degree, Émile?"

Awed by their selflessness, their commitment to One Love, to Brotherly Love, and emboldened by their courage, I blurted out, "I want to be a poet."

"But how do you plan to make a living?" Alicia asked, not unkindly. She was a poet; she understood more than most the near impossibility for a poet to make a living with words.

"Teach," I conceded.

"Yes," the man who asked about my future plans said encouragingly. "We need teachers. That's a good thing to do. Maybe you can work with us. Be part of our coalition."

"He's from Trinidad. He's going back home." I thought

Alicia said this a little too quickly and zealously. It was as if she wanted to send me a clear message: there is absolutely no hope of a romantic relationship between the two of us.

"He's going back home, we know that, Alicia," Michael said softly, and then he turned to me. "But spend a little time with us, Émile. You only know the Jamaica of the university. That's a world of its own there. Get to know the real Jamaica before you leave." He reached over to me with his glass. "Come, tell me you'll stay for a couple of weeks after you graduate."

I clinked my glass against his. "Not a bad idea," I replied. "But as Alicia said, I have to make a living."

"A couple of weeks, then?"

"A couple of weeks if I can find work that will pay me. Then I have to go back."

And, as it turned out, I didn't return to Trinidad. I didn't become a teacher either, at least not for many months, both decisions linked to my father. They were decisions that would deepen my relationship with Corinne so much so that it would not be long before she would take full possession of my heart. Alicia, too, would become more important to me than either she or I could have guessed that evening when she seemed indifferent as to whether I left or stayed in Jamaica. And because of her, because of the political positions she so passionately defended, I would find myself involved in the messy affairs of the Ducksworths.

13

That June, Albert and I got our degrees. I had turned twenty-two three months earlier.

My father did not come to the graduation ceremony. I had not expected him to and I was surprised when he called to congratulate me. As usual, our conversation was strained, though somehow I felt (I had no rational explanation for this feeling) he wanted to let me know he loved me.

"So it's all done?" he inquired.

"Yes," I assured him, "I have my degree."

"Any of that nonsense about being a teacher?"

"I have to find a job," I said.

There was a long silence on the phone. I could hear him clearing his throat and then sipping some liquid. Water, I assumed, for he was an avowed teetotaler.

"I suppose you can come back here." An invitation? Not quite, but his voice had lost its usual gruffness.

"I've sent my resumé to the Ministry of Education in Trinidad," I said. "I'll stay here while I wait to hear from them."

Again the silence and the clearing of his throat. "I'll give you something that should tide you over until then," he finally said.

I couldn't believe he was offering to support me some more. I needed the money. He had paid my tuition, my boarding and lodging, as he had promised, and had given me a monthly allowance. I had expected all that to end when I graduated. "Don't count on me," he had warned me. So I had saved quite a bit of my allowance, though not enough to last beyond a month.

"Just for a few more weeks," he said.

"Father . . ." Suddenly I found myself choking up.

"No need," he said quickly before I could continue. "I've already deposited some money in your account."

"Father . . . I . . . Thank you so much."

"Look, Henrietta wants to speak to you." And he was off the phone.

Henrietta was whispering when she got on the line. "He changing, Émile. I think he see now you all he has."

"Maybe I should come home then."

"No," she said. "He want you to be with your friends. Come later when you ready."

She knew me well, Henrietta. *When you ready*. I was not ready, not ready to go to the dark, dreary rooms of my father's house where I knew I would have to stay until I made enough money to find a place of my own. I wanted to be with my friends. Albert had insisted that I come to his engagement party in Barbados and had booked a room for me in the hotel where we had stayed. In Barbados I would be in the light, in the brilliant sunshine, surrounded by all that turquoise water. The sun shone in Trinidad too, but wherever I would go I would carry the darkness of my father's house with me.

And I was looking forward to seeing Corinne again. Oh, I told myself that I wanted to find out more about Douglas's brother. I needed to warn Albert to be careful, to let him know that Douglas was carrying a knife with a sharp edge pointed at him, that Douglas blamed him for his brother's suicide. The truth, though, if I allowed myself to admit it, was that it still bothered me that Corinne had not come to the airport to see me off. When I dropped her at her father's house, she had promised. "See you tomorrow," she had said.

I had new reasons for wanting to spend more time in Jamaica. I was intrigued by Alicia's friends, by their idealism. I had not known anyone—certainly none of my father's doctor colleagues—willing to sacrifice their careers to help the less fortunate. I wanted to find out if they would succeed in persuading the government to do more for the poor in Tivoli Gardens.

One month more in Jamaica, I told myself. It would take that long for the ministry back home to place me in a school—that is, if there was a vacancy.

My father did not come to Jamaica for my graduation but Georges Glazal was there for his son's. I hadn't had a chance to meet him when he came three years before to "settle" his son in Jamaica, but now that I finally did, I took to him right away, predisposed to find him likable because of the things Albert had said about him, things I envied: he was a father who loved his son unconditionally. I had had reservations about his acceptance of a daughter-in-law who was not Lebanese, but Albert was confident his father wouldn't object. "My father loves me," he said without forethought, without reservation.

I would guess he was well over sixty. There were wrinkles running horizontally across his forehead and vertically along his cheeks but they were shallow wrinkles, soft and moist. He had not yet grayed though his hair had receded past his crown, but at the sides of his head, down to his ears, there were tufts of dark brown curly hair. His nose was thick, long, and curved at the end, a substantial nose, the formidable nose his son had inherited. He was much shorter than Albert and stout, yet I could not say that Georges Glazal was not an attractive man. It was his genial demeanor that drew people to him, a ready smile that rose to his eyes, crinkling them upward until they seemed mere slits behind his large black-framed glasses. I suspected, however, that his easygoing manner was the learned expression of a man who had made his fortune by getting people to like him, by convincing them that nothing would make them happier than owning the goods he sold to them. I did not find this aspect of the man hypocritical. On the contrary, I found it admirable. Georges Glazal's ancestors had made their fortunes by their charm, rising from mere peddlers of dry goods on the dusty roads of country villages. Now a son was the owner of two profitable stores in the city. When Mr. Glazal wasn't smiling, I could see the fierce intelligence in his eyes behind those thick-framed glasses. He was a man who understood the give-and-take of trade, a smart man who would not be easily fooled.

Corinne was worried that Glynis could lead Albert into a quagmire. Glynis was cunning, she said. Like a fox. Glynis could make Albert go along with her plans—whatever those plans were—and it would be too late afterward for Albert to change his mind. But I also knew Albert. He had not only inherited the texture of his father's hair, his formidable nose, and the coloring of his complexion, but also an affable manner that I knew from experience camouflaged a keen intelligence. Albert was no fool. If Glynis's plans were in any way connected to his father's fortunes, he would share those plans with his father, and his father would not be swayed to do anything that would damage his business or his son's inheritance.

We traveled together to Barbados—Albert, his father,

and I—for the engagement party. It was, as Glynis had said, a small affair at her father's house. Besides Glynis, Albert, Rebecca, Douglas, Corinne, Albert's father, and me, there were three of Glynis's friends and an older married couple, who, I correctly guessed, were Douglas's parents, the mother as blond as Douglas, with the same greenish-blue eyes, her skin as golden, the father as fit and handsome. There was another person there too, whom I almost missed: a stately Indian man with a thick bush of white hair, sitting in the corner apart from everyone else, nursing a glass of pink lemonade with an air of seeming indifference except I noticed that his eyes scanned the room as if he were making mental notes of everyone there. He was an odd presence in a charcoal-gray suit, dressed as if he were at a business meeting and not at an informal family gathering. I introduced myself. "Émile. Émile Baxter," I said. He simply shook my hand but did not give me his name. I tried to engage him in conversation and his one-word responses made it clear he did not wish to be disturbed. Nevertheless, when Ducksworth called us to toast the happy couple on his deck, the man rose immediately to his feet and joined us.

It was late afternoon and the sky blazed bright with the fiery colors of the dying day: the sun a big glittering round ball fanning out a palette of oranges and reds that dissolved into shades of amber and turmeric, and casting a tunnel of golden light across the darkening sea. Peter Ducksworth stood with his back to the railing, framed by all those sunset colors and the black silhouettes of the two lush green promontories that stood as sentinels guarding the cove at the bottom of the steep drop that fell from the edge of his house to the sea below. He had dressed for the occasion, shoes rather than sandals, and a white linen

suit and pale-blue shirt that matched his eyes, but I suspected he'd had a drink or two before he filled his glass with
champagne for his eyes were glazed. When he spoke, however, there was no hint of the slurring I had heard the last
time I saw him down several glasses of rum punch in quick
succession. After he was sure we were all gathered on the
deck, he fished out a silver spoon from his pocket, brushed
back his slightly rumpled hair, and tapped the side of the
tall champagne flute he was holding. Conversation around
him died down.

"To my daughter Glynis on this happy occasion." He
raised his glass toward Glynis. She beamed. The diamond
on her finger glinted in the light of the descending sun.
Albert (or his father) had spared no expense.

"And to my soon-to-be son-in-law." Ducksworth bowed
to Albert. "May you have a long and happy life together."

There was a ricocheting chorus of "Here, here." More
well wishes from Peter Ducksworth for his daughter's happiness, more praise for Albert, a man, he said, who had a
solid head on his shoulders.

Georges Glazal lifted his glass (he had asked the housekeeper for sparkling water when she offered him champagne) and smiled appreciatively, and I could only surmise
that there would not have been such genuine delight in
his eyes had he thought the marriage of his son to Ducksworth's daughter was not in his son's best interest. "To my
son and my soon-to-be daughter-in-law," he declared loudly.

"Here, here" resounded again across the deck. Instinctively I glanced at Douglas. His lips were sealed. Corinne
was standing next to me and her eyes flashed triumphantly
from Douglas to me as if to say, See, I told you so.

"More champagne," Ducksworth called out to his
housekeeper. "I have something to say."

Corinne grasped my hand and held it tightly. I could not tell if she was nervous about what her father might say, or if she was worried he would drink too much. I decided on the latter. "It's only champagne," I whispered to her. "He'll be okay."

Ducksworth waited until his housekeeper refilled our glasses, and then facing Glynis and Albert, who had their arms around each other's waists, he began: "If you, Albert, and my daughter Glynis could have a smidgen of the happiness I had with my darling wife . . ." His eyes turned misty and he tipped the glass to his mouth, gulping down most of the champagne. Corinne made a half-step toward him and I put my hand on her wrist and brought her gently back to my side.

"If you could have . . ." And again Ducksworth stopped, this time to brush away a tear that had settled in his right eye. Glynis rushed over to him and wrapped her arms around his waist, pressing her face into his chest.

"No, no." Ducksworth disentangled himself from his eldest daughter's tight embrace. "This is not a time for tears. It's a time for joy. Go back, Glynis."

Glynis stumbled backward. Albert stuck out his hand to help her, but she stepped forward again.

"No!" It was a command this time, yet before we felt the shock of it, Ducksworth's voice softened. "Let her go, Albert. Go next to your sister, Glynis. Stand next to Rebecca."

By now everyone's eyes were glued to Ducksworth; no one moved. The only sounds were the rhythmic crashing of the waves onto the beach and the eerie screeching of seabirds wheeling across the sky, the setting sun lighting fire on their pale gray wings, and then the nosedive, their heads pointed downward, beaks stabbing the unwitting fish in the blackening water. Strange, I thought. Hungry so late in the darkening evening.

Satisfied he had our attention, Ducksworth's eyes fell first on Glynis and then on Rebecca. "I have an announcement, a gift to make to my daughters." He looked over at Corinne. I could tell she was as curious as I was, but apprehensive too. Her eyes were open wide, her head strained forward. "Not to you, Corinne." Ducksworth shook his finger at her. "Not right now. There'll be time for you. I want to make a gift to my newly married daughter and to—"

Rebecca would not let him finish. "Oh, Daddy." Her eyes sparkled, and she clapped her hands to her mouth. "Oh, Daddy!"

"You couldn't wait, Rebecca, but I can see why not." Ducksworth made a wide gesture with his hands toward Douglas's parents. "You have a fine son," he said. "A fine young man."

Mrs. Fairbanks mouthed, *Thank you*, and sniffled into her handkerchief.

"And I mean to give you a gift too." Ducksworth was now looking back at Glynis. "On the occasion of your engagement to Albert."

Glynis bit down on her lip. Her eyes glistened.

"A fine young man, your intended."

"You're too kind, Daddy. Too kind." Glynis blew a kiss to her father.

Ducksworth seemed not to have noticed the kiss. His head was tilted upward and he was squinting, peering across the room as if he were searching for something or someone. I followed his line of vision and saw he was looking directly at the white-haired Indian man in the charcoal-gray suit who was leaning against the wall at the entrance of the deck. "Well, I'm not like some besotted fathers we know, eh, Gopaul?" Ducksworth called out to him.

Gopaul straightened up, raised his glass, and gave a brief nod to Ducksworth.

"So I won't ask my daughters to swear how much they love me, eh, Gopaul?"

Gopaul laughed, a guffaw really, the sort of guarded acknowledgment an employee might give to his employer in case he had misinterpreted his meaning.

Rebecca, though, wasted no time in reassuring her father: "But we do, we do love you, Daddy. You are the best father a daughter could have." Her face shone like the moonlight.

"Better than the best," said Glynis, glancing briefly at her sister, her brows contracting before she turned back to smile brightly at her father. "I don't know what we would have done without you. After Mummy died, you were like mother and father all in one. So I love you twice as much. I love you with all the love I had for Mummy and all the love I've always had for you. Two times more."

"And I more than two times," Rebecca piped up.

"I three times. No, four, five times."

Rebecca grinned, a childish chortle rising from the back of her throat, yet there was something else I saw, something in her eyes, a cold determination that surprised me, for she had seemed to me ever willing to yield to her big sister. "I a hundred times more!" she declared.

But Glynis exceeded her. "And I more than life itself."

"More than life itself." Ducksworth smiled and puffed out his chest. "See?" he said to us who were witnesses to this extravagant display of filial love. "See how my daughters fight over me?"

What could any of us say or do but applaud? Glynis

and Rebecca ran to their father's side, each one embracing him, throwing her arms around his neck.

"See! They will strangle me with their love. Enough, enough," he said. But he was beaming, clearly thrilled with their public display of affection for him.

Corinne had not applauded. Her arms were crossed tightly over her chest. She seemed frightened.

"And you?" Ducksworth unwound his daughters' arms from his neck. "What say you, my youngest daughter, my joy?"

Corinne slid behind my back.

"Come forward," Ducksworth beckoned her. "Let me see your lovely face. Hiding from your father, are you? But you see . . ." He turned around to us. "She's hurt. I didn't mean to leave you out, Corinne." He stepped toward her, cooing: "You'll get your turn. I'll have something for you too."

"You don't have to, Daddy," Corinne said softly, coming out in the open. "You don't have to give me anything." She was standing in front of him now.

"But I do. You are the sweetest daughter a father can have."

"And I love you."

"How much?"

I think when Ducksworth asked that question he was halfway jesting. He already knew, had much reason to assume, Corinne loved him deeply, but she hesitated. For a split second she said nothing, and he became impatient, agitated. He had made a show of his certainty of his daughters' love for him and now one, his youngest, the one he called his joy, the apple of his eye, was hesitating, making him wait for her answer. *Embarrassing him.* "How much?" he repeated. "Your sisters say they love me too. More than life itself, Glynis said. Do you love me more than life itself?"

"I would do anything for you, Daddy." Corinne's bottom lip was trembling.

"Then tell me. Tell everyone here." Ducksworth's voice grew gruffer, almost menacing. "Tell them how much you love me."

I had not thought Ducksworth was drunk yet, but I was beginning to think he was losing control of mind. His eyes shifted from one end of the deck to the other, settling on no one. There was a man who lived not far from my father's house who had eyes like that. Every afternoon he sat on the same park bench digging his nails into the palms of his hand as if the pain (I saw blood on his palm once) would stop him from doing something bad, something cruel. Henrietta said his wife had left him. Whenever I passed by him I would hear him mumbling, "I thought she loved me."

Ducksworth came closer to Corinne. He was shorter than she and had to raise himself on the tips of his toes to bring his face next to hers. "How much?" he asked her again, his breath upon hers.

A deathly silence hung over the room. We were all uncomfortable, hoping for something or someone to break the tension building in front of us. And Glynis did. "Just tell him, Corinne!" she cried out. "Tell him what he wants to hear. It's my engagement party. You're spoiling it. Or is it that you don't love Daddy as much as Rebecca and I do?"

Corinne looked into her father's eyes. "I love you as much as a daughter can love her father," she murmured.

"Speak up. Speak up. I didn't hear you clearly," Ducksworth grumbled.

"My sisters have husbands. Rebecca does, and Glynis will have a husband soon. They must love their husbands, and when I have a husband, I will love him too. I cannot give you all my love. I will have to share my love with my husband."

Her response was reasonable; more than that: she had the authority of the Bible on her side. Genesis 2:24: *A man shall leave his father and mother and shall cleave unto his wife*. Even after her husband died, Ruth remained faithful to his people, walking away from her own.

Ducksworth blinked and his face paled. "And how much will I have?" he asked, chastened, but so consumed by hubris he could not back down.

"An equal share," she said. "Half."

Ducksworth grunted, twisted his head to one side, and clamped his lips together as though to force his tongue to stay still in his mouth. *Half!* That was all she would give him. But he seemed to know Corinne well enough not to demand more. She might not lie like her sisters. She might embarrass him again, tell him the truth, and perhaps the truth wasn't what he wanted.

Douglas's mother came to his rescue. "Peter!" she called out to him. He spun around, startled out of the fog that had enveloped him. "How long are you going to keep us waiting for your announcement?"

"A-a-announcement?" he stammered.

"Yes, the gift."

"For Glynis and Rebecca." Douglas's father had joined her.

Ducksworth passed his hand across his brow as if to wipe off perspiration that was not there, but that slight physical act seemed to restore his emotional equilibrium. He glanced at Corinne. I half expected her to recant, to apologize to him, but her lips remained closed. I wanted to hug her right then and there, totally impressed by her courage, her integrity. She would not compromise the truth

for the sake of flattering him. Faced with her continued silence, Ducksworth turned away from her toward the sea.
He closed his eyes and sniffed the salt-filled air.

"So? Are you going to tell us?" Douglas's father asked.

Ducksworth swiveled around and opened his eyes. "I
left Trinidad for this." He paused, sniffed the air again.
"Marian would have loved this," he murmured. "A house
on a hill facing the sea."

"My mother." Corinne's voice shook when she whispered
in my ear.

"You see there." Ducksworth's voice was strong again.
He pointed to the two fat fingers extending out to the sea.
"There are two pieces of land, one to the right and one to
the left of the house. This land we are standing on makes
it three, three for three daughters, as I know Marian would
have wanted. And so to you, Glynis and Rebecca, I give the
land to the right and left as my wedding gifts."

"Now? You mean now?" Rebecca sang out excitedly.

"The land is yours. I'll have the deeds drawn up. You
can choose which side you each want."

Overwhelmed with gratitude, Rebecca thanked her father over and over. Glynis thanked him too, but with none
of the squeals and squeaks gushing from Rebecca's mouth.
She was waiting for more. *What about the house and the land it's
on?* I could practically hear the question rumbling through
her head. She didn't have to wait long for the answer.

Ducksworth drew in his breath and when he exhaled,
his nostrils flared. *"As much as a daughter can love her father,"* he
mumbled. I was not sure everyone had heard him clearly,
but I did, and I could see from the way Corinne reddened
and lowered her head that she had heard him too. "Not to
matter, not to matter." He breathed in again, a shallower
intake of air this time that softened the muscles that had

grown taut around his mouth. "You are sisters, all three of you." He looked at each one in turn, his eyes fixed steadily on them. Rebecca flinched and turned away. Glynis and Corinne held his eyes but, I thought, for different reasons. Glynis's eyes shone with her determination to prove to her father that she was the strong one, the one who really loved him. Corinne was pleading silently for him to forgive her. She had not meant to hurt him.

Ducksworth signaled his housekeeper and she refilled his champagne flute. He drank long and deep. "We have a saying in Trinidad," he began again. "*Blood is thicker than water*. You know what that means?" We knew, but no one responded. "It means that blood binds us, blood binds us forever. Your mother's blood and my blood." He was speaking directly to his three daughters now. "Our blood binds you three sisters forever, binds your children and your children's children. I will not be the one to break those bonds. So to you, Corinne, who I have loved, who I thought loved me—"

Corinne leapt forward and grasped his hand. "No! You are wrong. I loved you. Love you now."

Ducksworth shook her off. "You've had your say." He drew back his lips, a snarl exposing pinkish gums and gray teeth. "Now I'll have mine," he growled. "Duty compels me, duty and loyalty to my father and to his father's father. *Love.*"

Corinne winced as if he had struck her. I reached for her arm and held her still.

"It was with the money from my father's land that I bought this house and land. And I will pass what was given to me, and what I earned in my lifetime, to my progeny. I will not be the cause of discord among my daughters after I die." Ducksworth paused. "So to you, Corinne," he continued (he had not taken his eyes off of her), "I leave my house and the land it stands on."

Glynis sucked in her breath, the sound audible enough that Albert turned to her, alarmed. He put his finger to his lips and shook his head. *Glynis*, he mouthed, urging her to be silent.

"But I still have my wits about me." A vein popped out from Ducksworth's hairline, blue and swollen, and ran down his forehead to the space between his eyebrows. "I am not some doddering old man." He pulled off his jacket and tossed it on the railing. "I am virile!" he shouted out. He unbuttoned the right cuff of his shirt, pushed up the sleeve, and flexed his arm. There was muscle there, but like the arm of an aging boxer, below it the flesh hung soft and flabby.

We were all taken aback. I saw Douglas's mother tighten her hold on her husband's arm. Mr. Glazal had a glass of water in his hand; he tilted it to his lips and in the abruptness of that action, a thin trail of water ran down his chin. Albert and I exchanged nervous glances. Rebecca and Glynis drew closer to each other, their bodies forming a tight knot as though shielding themselves from what could come next.

Only Corinne seemed to know what to do. She stretched out her hand again toward her father. "Daddy." Her eyes were welled with tears. "Daddy." The sound of her voice, pleading, full of love and concern for him, seemed to calm him. His lips softened and shaped themselves into a smile. For a brief moment his eyes lingered on Corinne, with affection I thought, but then he turned to the Indian man with the thick white hair. "Mark this, Gopaul." His voice was strained, but he was no longer shouting. "The house and land are hers, but after I die. After I am gone from this

earth. I will not be put out of my house. *By any of my daughters.*
I will have a place to live. See to it, Gopaul."

I was certain now: Gopaul was his lawyer, not just a
guest who'd come to celebrate the engagement of Glynis to
Albert. Ducksworth had distributed his property among his
daughters, but while he was alive he wanted the protection
of the law.

Gopaul reached into a pocket inside his jacket and took
out a pen and a small notebook. I could not see what he
was writing, but I could tell from the expression on Ducksworth's face that he was pleased Gopaul was doing as he
had commanded. As he had planned all along, it occurred
to me.

Satisfied, Ducksworth clapped his hands. "Come, everybody! There's food inside. Music!" He motioned to Douglas. "Turn up the stereo!" And in minutes the somber mood
that had blanketed us on the deck was lifted with the raucous rhythms of a calypso.

When Albert had a chance to speak to me in private, he
cornered me in the living room. "Put out of his house? Why
would Mr. Ducksworth say a thing like that?"

I told him what my father had told me. Ducksworth
thought he was dying, sailing to Byzantium, and when my
father pulled him out of his delirium, he was determined
to have his paradise on earth. This house above the sea is
paradise for Mr. Ducksworth, I said. It means everything
to him.

"But why say he was not a doddering old man? And
why would he think his daughters . . . ?" Albert stopped
himself short.

The wheeling birds so late in the evening, wings on fire. I shivered
involuntarily.

"I don't know," I replied, but I told him the story. My

degree was in English literature, Albert's was in business. Ducksworth might not have read the play either, but there was ancestral pride. Stories by the great English playwright would have been recited around his family dinner table. "Perhaps he was thinking of the aging king who made the mistake of giving away his property to his daughters while he was alive. He gave them his land and his castle and they put him out."

"Put him out? All of them?"

"Not the youngest. She was kind to him. But he had disinherited her."

"The others then?"

"Yes," I said. "The other two."

Albert tossed his head as though mulling over what I had said. "They must have been mad," he said at last.

"They made *him* mad. Insane. But, as you can see, Peter Ducksworth isn't taking any chances."

"I hope you're not suggesting that Glynis . . ."

His face had darkened and I quickly reassured him. "Never," I said. "She loves her father too much."

But Ducksworth had ensured that neither Glynis nor Rebecca could ever put him out of his house. He had divided his property among his three daughters. Glynis and Rebecca would own their share now but the house would remain his until he died. Then it would go to Corinne. Corinne had disappointed him; he was unhappy with her, but he did not want discord among the sisters after he was gone.

That was Lear's intention too. *That future strife / May be prevented now,* the king said in his moment of greatest clarity before he made the fatal mistake of confusing flattery with love.

14

I was worried about Corinne and early the next morning I called her.

"Daddy and I have made up," she said, dismissing my anxiety as an overreaction to what she claimed was merely a family squabble. "He had too much to drink last night. I explained it all to him in the morning and he understands. He knows I love him."

For her own sake I wanted to believe her, but I had seen when her father pushed her away from him. Surely it would take more than one night's sleep to cool the anger that had swelled within him. Yet there must have been some truth in what she claimed. He had not denied her an inheritance, the biggest part of his estate in fact.

She sensed my disbelief and hurried to assuage my doubts. "I promised Daddy he'll live out his days in his own house. I'll make sure of that. I told him no one will ever take his place in my heart. He was the first man I loved. He gave me life. Without him, I wouldn't be here on this earth. I'll love him forever."

My head had not caught up with my heart. I didn't fully know then how much she would mean to me. Still, ego—call it manly pride—made it impossible for me to resist asking: "And what about your husband? Will you love him forever too?"

"Oh, Émile," she chided me. "Of course I'll love my husband. Why else would I marry him?"

It was a satisfactory answer, a good answer, yet right then I empathized with Ducksworth: she'll love her father forever, but she'll love her husband too.

When I was a boy on the brink of adolescence, my friends and I, our hormones beginning to rage, would try to puzzle out the existential questions of life, most having to do with our relationships with our future wives. "Suppose you were in a boat with your wife and your mother far out in the sea and the boat capsized but neither your mother nor your wife could swim—who would you save?"

I did not have a mother, so of course for me it was a no-brainer. "My wife!" I belted out eagerly.

A boy much older than my friends and I, already a cynic or posing as one, happened to be passing by. He laughed at me. "Poor innocent," he said scornfully. "Don't you know you can get another wife but you can never get another mother?"

So this must have been Ducksworth's thinking too. Corinne should love him with her whole heart, not half her heart. She could not get another father.

We had breakfast at the same restaurant on the hill in the Scotland District. Mr. Glazal was leaving before lunch and Albert wanted him to see more of the island than the flat landscape edged by white sand and turquoise waters that seemed to stretch for an eternity in front of his hotel. "There's a rocky side too, the Atlantic side," Albert informed Mr. Glazal proudly, as if laying claim to Barbados, which I supposed he could since it was the home of his wife-to-be. "It'll remind you of the sea in Trinidad going up to Toco," he said.

Ducksworth did not come with us. He wanted to see to his business right away, he said. By *business* we all understood he meant going to the lawyer (Gopaul, I presumed) to draw up the deeds for the land he had promised Rebecca and Glynis. Glynis beamed and pecked him on his cheek. "You're the best father in the world," she said, the words tinkling like wind chimes as they left her lips.

Corinne tried to persuade Ducksworth to join us. He'd had a full day entertaining his family and friends, she said. He needed to relax now and have his daughters pamper him. "The sun is out, but it isn't too hot. Just the right weather for a trip down the coast. And you like André Lambert, Daddy," she reminded him. "It would be good to spend some time with him. Catch up. You can do your business tomorrow."

She had made him a cup of tea, the way he liked it— strong, piping hot, with evaporated milk. He took the cup from her hands and she kissed him on his forehead. "Yes," he said, and looked up at her with unmistakable affection, causing me to reconsider my fears. Perhaps she was right: he had forgiven her. "I like André Lambert," he said. "And I miss his friend Keith Goddard. It would be good to catch up."

Glynis clamped her hand on Corinne's arm and cast her blue eyes lovingly on her father. "Didn't you say your lawyer was going out of town, Daddy?"

"Yes, next week," he said.

She shook her head disapprovingly. "Never leave for tomorrow what you can do today, Daddy."

So we left without Ducksworth, and as we drove down the slope from his house, Albert at the steering wheel, Glynis next to him, and Corinne, Mr. Glazal, and I in the backseat (Douglas and Rebecca would meet us at the restaurant), I turned and saw him through the rearview window, hat on his head and papers stuck under his arm, walking briskly toward his car.

We took the same route I had traveled with Corinne, up that strip of land the locals called the Gold Coast. On that day with Corinne my attention had been pulled in all directions: the near accident with the truck, keeping up with Glynis's car, parrying points with Corinne about writers like Lamming, and still trying to catch glimpses of that astonishing sea. But now I found myself drawn to the sprawling hotels, one after the other, Barbados's Gold Coast, protected from the prying eyes of the public by high walls that rose from the edge of the road. Tiger Woods had married his Swedish girlfriend in the most luxurious of these places. It was rumored he had spent millions, shutting down the entire hotel for days with the lavish parties he hosted.

"Keith Goddard owned a restaurant here too before he moved to the place where we're going," Glynis said.

Mr. Glazal perked up. He had said little since we left the party the night before, though I had overheard him praise Ducksworth as I walked behind them down the driveway to the car. "That was a generous gift you gave to Glynis and Rebecca," he had said.

Ducksworth shrugged. "They are my daughters." His voice had been flat, curiously emotionless.

"I'll make it worth your while," Mr. Glazal replied cryptically.

Now Mr. Glazal was asking about the restaurant business. "Why did Keith Goddard move? Seems he could have made a lot of money here."

"His chef liked the hills in the Scotland District," Glynis said.

"His chef?"

"André Lambert. Keith died and now André owns the restaurant. Keith left it to him."

"Gave it to him?"

Glynis kept her eyes on the road before her. "He loved him," she said matter-of-factly.

Albert explained: "This was a gold coast for rich gay men too . . . still is."

"And poor men. Pretty men," Glynis added.

"Then AIDS came . . ." Albert said.

"And some of the poor pretty men got infected," Corinne said.

Glynis swiveled around, her eyes glittering. "What are you trying to say, Corinne?"

"Keith Goddard died of AIDS. André was not infected," Corinne replied tersely. She was sitting between Mr. Glazal and me, Mr. Glazal behind Albert, who was driving, and I at the other end. I could feel her body stiffen when she sent that volley back to Glynis. Mr. Glazal looked expectantly at Corinne. "It's the price of the tourist trade, Mr. Glazal," Corinne said, answering his unspoken question.

"What Corinne is trying to imply," Glynis said, dragging out the words with exaggerated emphasis, "is that Mr. Goddard was the one with the virus. He was a white Canadian man. André, as you will see when you meet him, is a black man."

"Oh?" Mr. Glazal took a deep breath.

"They were lovers," Glynis explained, her voice choked with disapproval.

"Lovers?"

I could not discern from Mr. Glazal's tone whether he was merely curious or whether behind his question lurked judgment of the relationship between Keith Goddard and André Lambert, for as that one word left his lips, he turned his head toward the window and I could not see his face.

"André was more than a lover to Keith Goddard,"

Corinne said, the effort it was taking her to control her irritation at Glynis making her sound peevish. "André was Mr. Goddard's chef, bookkeeper, bartender. He brought in the customers."

"And Keith was good to him," Glynis said. "He left his restaurant to André."

Albert reached back across his seat and touched his father's shoulder. "He wasn't married, Dad," he said gently. "And he had no children to give his fortune to."

"Except André. Keith was married to André," Corinne said. "Not legally, but in every other way."

"Strange," Mr. Glazal said, and leaned back on his seat.

He was not young, but pretty, yes, though pretty is not the right descriptor. He had a model's beauty; a natural, I thought, for the cover of *GQ* magazine on an issue about men over forty. He was around that age—that was my guess—closer to fifty than forty, though. He had the attractive salt-and-pepper hair some men are fortunate to have, the salt sprinkled lightly on the crown and sides of his head, suggestive more of a man of experience, a man who had lived the good life, than one hurtling toward the void. And he was tall, slim shoulders, slim waist, slim hips. But what struck me the most about André Lambert, what I first saw as he came to greet us at the driveway, was his radiant skin. I suppose what gave the impression of his radiance was the sun blazing behind him, bright and golden, and he coming out from that darkened sheltered dining room in a white chef's smock, long white pants, his skin by contrast so black it was almost blue, glistening with the thinnest layer of sweat. He shone, he glowed.

"Glynis! Corinne!" He kissed them on both cheeks. "And you must be the lucky man." He extended his hand to Albert. Profuse apologies to Albert for not being at the restaurant when we came previously, warm greetings to me and Mr. Glazal.

"I detect an accent," Mr. Glazal said, shaking his hand. "French?"

"*Oui*," Lambert replied.

"Guadeloupe?" Mr. Glazal asked.

"Martinique."

"They speak perfect French in Martinique, you know." Mr. Glazal inclined his head to his son and lowered his voice as if imparting confidential information to him. "Your great-grandfather had thought of going there from Lebanon before his friends persuaded him to come to Trinidad."

Lambert heard him. "Yes, like Martinique, you were a colony of France too," he said.

"Except Lebanon fought for its independence."

Lambert threw up his hands and said good-naturedly, "*C'est la vie.*"

I thought he would have been offended by Mr. Glazal's remark. It was a source of pride for the Lebanese people that in 1943, years before Algeria was finally victorious, they had booted out France from their country. *Booted* was Mr. Glazal's word to me when he gave me this brief history. It took Algeria almost twenty more years, following a brutal guerrilla war, the Algerian women as formidable as their men, hiding bombs and guns in their baskets at the market, for that country to gain its independence from France in 1962. I have never forgotten the scenes of the stoic defiance of the Algerians and the indescribable torture they suffered, indelibly captured in the 1966 movie *The Battle of Algiers*, which was banned in France and her colonial territories, including Martinique and Guadeloupe. Of all the people to have given me a copy of the film was my father. He gave it to me when I was leaving for university. "Take a look," he said, "and know the price people are willing to pay for freedom."

I did not know what made my father give me that film or say those words to me—I knew little of his past life—but I would have reason to recall his words years later and to be inspired by them.

If Lambert was insulted by Mr. Glazal's veiled criticism of Martinique, that to all appearances the people there seemed comfortable with their country's status as an outpost of France, he gave little indication. "Martinique is France," he simply said.

And so it is. If a Frenchman wants to live and work in Martinique where the sun shines almost every day, where the sand is white, the sea blue, he can do so with almost the same ease as would an American moving from one US state to another. If he wants to set up a business there, where labor is less expensive, he can. He can choose to holiday in Martinique, build his vacation house there, or, if he prefers, live there permanently.

When I first went to Martinique, curious to see the island where my French ancestors had enslaved Africans, I was shocked to see white Frenchmen cleaning the streets, selling fruits and goods at the roadside, serving in restaurants, washing dishes, even one or two begging for alms. My first instinct was to view this reversal of labor as just retribution, but soon I began to wonder about the local people. "Are there jobs for them?" I asked a Martinican. "Oh, France takes care of them," was the answer.

André Lambert may not have intended for us to take his remark literally, but it seemed to me then that Martinique *was* indeed France, the ties binding the island not only economic, but cultural too. French writers and philosophers are adored in Martinique as they are in France, the cuisine and style of dress on the island very Parisian, the French spoken casually in the streets Parisian too. Yet two of the loudest voices decrying French colonialism were Martinicans: the philosopher Frantz Fanon and the poet Aimé Césaire. And there was the incident I had witnessed one night at the end of a Bastille Day celebration: a huge fire on the beach and around it scantily dressed young people dancing to the ferocious beat of conga drums. I could have been somewhere in Africa way back before the Europeans came. Then too there was the statue of Josephine, the Martinican wife of Napoleon. I had seen it bloodied with red paint, the head chopped off. It was said that Josephine had encouraged Napoleon to reinstate slavery as proof of her loyalty to France and the purity of her European blood.

"I had relatives in Martinique," I admitted to André Lambert, feeling compelled to stand in solidarity with him against Mr. Glazal's insinuations, which, with a cooler head, I later realized were spoken without malice. Lebanon was indeed politically independent; Martinique was still tied to France.

Lambert studied my face. "What were their names, your relatives?"

"Fornier," I said.

"Ah!" He scratched his chin. "There was an Émile Fornier. He was an abolitionist. He freed his slaves and took them with him to Trinidad."

"My mother's family," I said.

"You have a good name, Émile."

My mother's gift to me. I beamed.

"I didn't know we were in the presence of a member of a distinguished French family," Glynis said.

I knew her intentions were ill-willed. Still, I did not retreat. "My mother was," I said.

"They went back to France," Lambert explained. "There was a backlash from the slave owners. Émile threatened their livelihood and they chased the family back to France."

"So you are no longer a member of a distinguished family?"

"I'm afraid not, Glynis. I am just my father's son."

"Daddy's doctor's son," Corinne said triumphantly.

Glynis eyed her scathingly before turning back to Lambert. "So what are you giving us for breakfast, André?"

"The best breakfast you've ever had."

"Can't wait," said Albert, and rubbed his stomach, seemingly relieved that Glynis had stopped sparring with me.

"Well, to the kitchen."

When he left, Corinne told us that André Lambert was not always a chef. He had a degree from the Sorbonne, had taught high school in Paris for a few years, but was unhappy with teaching, and decided, when he was well into his thirties, to enroll in a culinary school. "It took him years, but he finally did what he always wanted to do," Corinne said.

Glynis chuckled. "You mean it took him so long to know he was gay?"

Corinne ignored her and continued talking about André Lambert. "He met Mr. Goddard in France. André was working as a sous-chef in a big restaurant, and the chef, who knew Mr. Goddard, introduced them."

"And that, as they say, was that." Glynis clapped her hands.

We were so engrossed in Corinne's tale that we hadn't noticed Douglas and Rebecca arriving.

"At last, relief from Corinne's interminable stories!" Glynis belted out.

Douglas sprinted toward us, leaving Rebecca behind, and, without a word of greeting to any of us, he scooted across the bench where Glynis was sitting next to Albert, practically pushing Albert to the edge.

The situation was awkward. There was Albert hanging on to the side of the bench, Rebecca, her eyes lowered, fussing with the hem of her dress, and the rest of us looking on in amazement as Douglas put his arm around Glynis's shoulder and gave her a wet kiss so close to her mouth that had she turned her head just a smidgen, their lips would have met. I was stunned; Mr. Glazal's eyebrows shot up but his son played it off and pointed at Douglas. Smiling, he said, "Nice T-shirt."

Douglas tightened his arm around Glynis's shoulder. "Do you like it?" he asked her. He and Rebecca were wearing khaki shorts and sea-blue T-shirts with the word *Barbados* scrawled across the front in white.

"You look like tourists," Glynis said, pushing him away, but obviously pleased by his unabashed affection for her.

"Proud to be Bajan," Douglas said, and tossed his head with a preening swagger.

Albert readjusted himself on the bench. "We saved the two seats in front of us for you and Rebecca," he said.

In fact, Albert was the one who had insisted that Corinne, Mr. Glazal, and I sit on the chairs at the sides of the table. "So Douglas and Rebecca can sit next to each other," he'd said.

"Yes, go away, Douglas." Glynis waved him off, laughing. "Go sit next to your wife."

As if taking his orders from her alone, Douglas sprung

up, trotted to the other side of the table, and pulled out a chair for his wife.

Rebecca looked flustered, not knowing whether to be angry with her husband or grateful to her sister for reject- ing his advances, as innocent as they might have seemed. I remembered Corinne's odd question after we left the restaurant the day I met Douglas. Did I think Glynis was angry? Corinne had asked me. When I didn't respond, she had declared enigmatically: "Rebecca better be careful."

And I remembered too my first reaction when I saw Douglas. It seemed to me then that Glynis was more suited to him than Rebecca.

Douglas plunked down on the chair next to his wife, leaned over to her, and making no attempt to lower his voice—indeed, he seemed to want us to hear him, or at least Glynis to hear him—he said, "You should wear dresses more often, Rebecca. Doesn't your sister look beautiful?"

Glynis was wearing a white linen sleeveless dress that fashionably complemented her pale skin and blond hair, and though we were under a wide umbrella that completely shaded our table, she had not taken off her dark glasses or the wide-brimmed straw hat I had seen on her once before when she had joined us on her father's deck.

Albert was magnanimous. "Well, you look beautiful too," he said to Rebecca.

Rebecca flashed him a grateful smile, but I could tell she was smarting. She reached for her glass and gulped down her water.

Douglas seemed not to have noticed or cared he had offended her. He turned to Mr. Glazal. "So you're leaving today? Sorry you didn't get to see more of the island. The Harrison Caves, for example."

"Oh, I heard about them. Stalactites and stalagmites.

And there's a place down there that apparently looks like a cathedral—"

"It's impressive," Douglas cut him off, then turned back to Glynis. "Did you order for us?"

Glynis bent her head sideways and batted her eyes. "What do you think?"

Perhaps it was an overactive imagination that led me to conclude there was a hint of flirtatiousness here. In any case, Albert didn't seem to share my observation or give the slightest indication he was bothered by Douglas's casual dismissal of his father. "Glynis ordered mimosas for you," he said, answering for his fiancée.

Douglas arched himself toward Rebecca. It looked almost as if he were about to embrace her, but their bodies did not touch. "Of course, not for Rebecca," he said merrily. "Rebecca doesn't drink." He winked at her.

"What nonsense!" Rebecca pulled herself roughly away from him. "I just don't drink alcohol this early in the day. Do you, Mr. Glazal?"

"I don't have alcohol at all," Mr. Glazal said.

"It's cultural," Douglas murmured.

"It's for my health," Mr. Glazal said dryly. "I drank too much when I was young. I want to keep my brains sharp. "

Douglas clasped his hands over his head and seemed at a loss for words. Had Mr. Glazal just insulted him, implied his brain was dull because he drank alcohol? He rolled his eyes upward to the ceiling and knitted his brow as if pondering the possibility.

Our drinks arrived. Albert, like his father, had orange juice, as did the rest of us, while Douglas and Glynis sipped their mimosas.

"Well, we just have a few hours before Mr. Glazal leaves," Glynis said, filling the silence that had fallen on the table. "I think we should talk about our plans."

I glanced across to Corinne, whose eyes shot up. She had warned me: *Glynis is cunning. Sly like a fox.* "Plans?" Corinne asked sharply. "What plans?"

"Douglas's father has offered to help us get rid of the squatter," Rebecca said brightly.

"The squatter?" Corinne frowned. "Daddy has no problem with the squatter."

"Yes," Glynis said, "but now the squatter is on our land. My land, actually."

Glynis did not have the deed in her hands, but we all knew that her father was on his way to have the deed drawn up. Right now, as we were sitting sipping our drinks, he was probably in Mr. Gopaul's office finalizing the details. He had probably already signed on the dotted line.

"So you have determined which side will be your sister's and which yours and Albert's?" Mr. Glazal asked, sounding more like the businessman he was than a father who was merely inquiring about his son's interests.

"Albert's?" Douglas murmured into his mimosa.

"Yes, Albert's." Glynis frowned at him. "Don't forget that Albert and I will be married soon." She turned back to Corinne. "Mr. Glazal has agreed . . ."

"Mr. Glazal has agreed to what?" Corinne's face reddened.

"Let me explain," Albert began. "My father has agreed to—"

"No!" Glynis reached for his arm and pulled him back. "I'll explain." She lowered her voice. "Rebecca and I have been talking. Daddy has never done anything about those two pieces of land. Remember what he said about Mummy? That Mummy would have wanted him to buy it?" She was speaking to Corinne now as if she were an adolescent who needed to be schooled.

"He said Mummy wanted to live on a hill that faced the sea," Corinne responded harshly, not at all placated by her sister's change in tone.

"Yes, but Daddy said if Mummy were alive she would have wanted him to buy all of it, the hill and the two pieces on either side."

"And so?"

"Don't you see?" Rebecca whined.

"Not now, Rebecca," Glynis snapped, silencing her.

"What am I to see?" Corinne asked with exaggerated patience.

"Mummy would have seen the potential." Glynis was no longer speaking in a soothing tone. It was obvious Corinne was determined to oppose her.

Mr. Glazal cleared his throat. "Is there a problem?" he asked.

"No, not at all," Glynis said quickly. "Corinne will understand when she has all the facts."

Corinne sat forward. "I'm listening."

"Rebecca and I have been talking," Glynis repeated. "Douglas agrees and so does Albert."

"They agree about what?"

"The baby boomers. They are old now, most of them close to their seventies, and they are living longer. True, Mr. Glazal?"

"I don't know about baby boomers. I'm seventy-four. I hope I live as long as my father did. He died at ninety-eight."

"See what I mean, Corinne? Look at Mr. Glazal. He's full of life. Still running his business."

"But not everyone wants to be working when they are that old," Rebecca interjected again.

Glynis shot her a withering glance. "Let me finish, Rebecca. Corinne will understand. She's a smart girl."

She took a sip of her mimosa, her eyes fixed steadily on Corinne.

"Understand what?"

Glynis put down her glass. "We want to build retirement flats," she said. A statement of fact, not to be questioned. Except Corinne did.

"Retirement flats? Where? On the land Daddy gave you?"

"They'll be pretty flats. They'll slope down to the beach below."

"The only decent beach below is in front of Daddy's land," Corinne said emphatically.

"And he hardly ever uses it."

"That's because he didn't go ahead with his original plans to build steps down from the house."

"You know he couldn't afford to do that. Not after the storm."

Corinne had told me that shortly after they came to Barbados, the island was struck by a devastating storm and to protect his land, her father had a construction company stack huge boulders around the two fingers that stretched out to the sea. They protected the beach at the cove, but there was no money left to build the steps he had envisioned. To get to the beach he had to depend on friends to take him there by boat.

"When we build the flats, we'll make the steps and a pathway from the flats to the steps. It'll be easy for Daddy to get to the beach then," Glynis said.

Glynis was boxing her in. Her father would have the access to the beach he had long wanted and the people in the retirement flats would have a path to the steps that would get them to the beach. Corinne glanced helplessly at me as if hoping I could give her a counterargument. I looked away. I didn't want to take sides against my friend; Glynis was his fiancée.

Then something dawned on Corinne. "The beach doesn't belong to Daddy or to either of you," she said defiantly.

It was the law in Barbados. All the beaches were public lands; they belonged to the people. Of course the hoteliers knew how to get around the law. They were permitted to erect their massive structures within a short walking distance beyond the shoreline. There, close to the beach, they put swimming pools and recreation lounges. On the beach itself they set up cabanas and rows of white deck chairs with sea-blue cushions and sea-blue umbrellas, all very pretty but signaling to the local people that this was theirs and anyone not connected to the hotel would be trespassing. But the law demanded access for the local people, so between the tall walls which rose from the edge of the street at the backs of each of the hotels, the hoteliers cut out alleyways. The difficulty for the local people was that the alleyways were so narrow and the vines that grew around their borders so thick, you could drive down that Gold Coast and miss the alleyways entirely.

"I didn't say it was Daddy's beach," Glynis replied, undeterred by Corinne's accusation. "But you can't disagree that Daddy's going to like getting to the beach without having to depend on friends to take him on their boats."

"And I suppose you discussed this with him?"

"No. Not yet."

"And the squatter? What will happen to him when you build your flats? He lives there with his wife and children."

"He's not married."

"She's his wife."

Glynis sniffed. "Common-law wife, not legitimate wife."

"They have two children. Toddlers."

"He's on Daddy's land. My land now."

My land now took the wind out of Corinne. "That man built his home there," she said, her voice more subdued.

"Home?" Glynis sneered. "Is that what you call some planks of wood covered with burlap bags?"

"You have no heart," Corinne spat out.

"My heart has nothing to do with this. It's the law. You can't just decide to live on someone else's land."

I wanted to put my arm around Corinne, to comfort her. She had fairness on her side, but not the law. Once the land was legally Glynis's, she had the right to evict the squatter.

Douglas broke the impasse: "Why don't we wait until André joins us?"

"André? What does André have to do with this?"

I was as surprised as Corinne to hear Douglas ask this question. Glynis had already expressed her disdain for people who were gay and I assumed Douglas shared her view.

"There'll be a restaurant," Albert announced cheerfully.

Corinne spun around. "Where?"

"So the people in the retirement flats won't have to leave the area for their meals," Glynis explained.

"On which side?" Corinne was facing her again. "Your side or Rebecca's?"

"That's the problem," Glynis said, wrinkling her brow as if confronted with a moral conflict.

"In the middle," Douglas said.

"In the middle of what?" Corinne went pale.

"Between the two strips of land, silly," Rebecca chimed in. "Between Glynis's land and mine."

"On Daddy's land? In Daddy's house?"

"We'll give him one of the flats, of course," Glynis said.

"So you'll put him out of his house?"

"It'll be the centerpiece of the retirement condos. A five-star restaurant. André is famous. We'll hire him to be the chef. People will come from all over the island to eat there."

"You mean you're going to turn Daddy's house into a restaurant? Put him out?"

"Oh, don't be so melodramatic, Corinne."

"He won't go," Corinne said softly.

"He'll like the restaurant," Glynis said. "We'll name it after him. Something like . . ." She threw her hands in the air flamboyantly. "Peter! Peter's Place on the Hill! That's what we'll call it. Daddy'll love it. He could welcome the guests."

"No," Corinne stammered, but her voice had dipped down low. "Daddy wants to stay in his house. He told you so. At your engagement party he told you so. He said he won't be put out of his house."

"Nobody's talking about putting him out of his house," Glynis said soothingly.

"You want him to give up his house."

"And move into a beautiful apartment where everything is new, new kitchen, new furnishings. And he'll be with other people his age. *And* he'll be able to go to his beach."

"You heard him, Glynis. He won't be put out."

"Rebecca is gone, and I'll be gone soon. You'll be going to university in September," Glynis said reasonably. "Daddy won't need all the room he has now."

"It's not about need. He wants all the room he has now. He worked all his life for this house." Corinne's eyes were beginning to spring water. *Don't let the tears fall,* I begged silently. I could see she was fighting to hold them back.

"Don't be romantic, Corinne." Glynis's voice now vibrated with sarcasm. "Daddy inherited the money for his house. He didn't work for it."

"For most of it," Corinne said adamantly.

"And now the house is practically yours, Corinne," Rebecca joined in again.

"The house is Daddy's. That's where he wants to live." Corinne's lips formed a hard straight line, her jaw stiff.

"You can talk to him. You can convince him he'll be happy in one of the flats. He'll listen to you," Rebecca said plaintively. She lowered her eyes and drew her fingers across the water condensed at the bottom of her glass. "Daddy likes you best."

"Daddy loves all of us," Corinne responded vehemently.

"But you best. Right, Glynis?" Rebecca lifted her eyes and waited for her sister's corroboration.

"He gave you the biggest part of his property, his house and the land," Glynis said flatly, speaking directly to Corinne. "What more proof do you want?"

"Yes, what more?" Rebecca echoed, her lips, like Glynis's, upturned in a sneer.

So there it was: the source of the animosity between Corinne and her sisters. How long had Glynis and Rebecca felt this way? For how many years had they seethed with resentment? Their father loved their youngest sister more than he loved them.

I had no siblings, no experience to compare with theirs, but I imagined I would be jealous too if my father bequeathed more to them than to me. It would be undeniable proof that he preferred them, loved them more.

Was it guilt that silenced Corinne at that moment? When her father died she would indeed receive the largest share of his property. I think she was hoping to ease the sting of that guilt when she turned to Albert's father. "Is this what you agreed to, Mr. Glazal?" she asked.

Mr. Glazal had been quiet, sipping his drink and studiously examining the decor in the open patio where we sat and in the dining room behind us, as if he were considering André's choice of colors for one of his stores.

"Mr. Glazal," Corinne addressed him again, "is this what you want?"

He put down his glass and faced her. "It seems like a good plan. A nice place for people to live when they are older," he said simply.

"And Daddy?"

"I won't do anything without your father's permission."

"The land is ours now," Glynis declared.

"I promised Albert as a wedding gift from me to invest in your project, the retirement flats on the land your father gave you and Rebecca," Mr. Glazal said. "But I'll have nothing to do with your father's land, Glynis, unless I have his permission."

André was approaching us with loaded trays. He put them on a folding table and signaled to his waiters to begin serving us. "Everything okay here?" He rested his hand lightly on Corinne's shoulder.

"Family business," Glynis said, and then, just as he was about to leave, she added, "I think you might be interested in our plan to build retirement condos. We'll need a restaurant."

"Condos? A restaurant? Where?"

"We'll fill you in with the details later. Can you come back?"

"Yes, yes, of course." André smiled, and before he left, he tapped his finger on his temples and said to Albert,

"You are going to marry a very smart woman."

"I know," Albert said. "And beautiful too."

The waiter placed a carnival of mouthwatering colors on the table: a large bowl of buljol glistening with olive oil, the shredded saltfish shimmering with slivers of gold and silver mixed with chunks of tomato, red sweet peppers and translucent pieces of onion, and next to the buljol a platter of avocado and hard-boiled eggs sliced to show their centers—yellow, white, and green nestled on a bed of crisp watercress. The aroma was irresistible and I was hungry. I had passed up the hotel's breakfast of omelets, sausages, and ham for this Caribbean feast, so I welcomed Mr. Glazal's intervention when he declared, "Business later. Let's eat now." No one objected, and for about thirty minutes or so there was no more talk about retirement condos, or about a restaurant in Ducksworth's house.

When the busboys came to clear our plates I braced myself for a resumption of the quarrel between Corinne and her sisters, but Mr. Glazal stood up and announced that he needed to leave right away. "I don't want to miss my flight," he said.

Glynis seemed relieved. She rose immediately. "Émile will take you to the airport. Won't you, Émile? Douglas will drive us back. And take Corinne home too," she added quickly. "Daddy would be worried if we're not back in time for tea. Corinne, you can let him know we're going to spend the day here." So they both went with me, Mr. Glazal insisting on taking the backseat and Corinne sitting next to me on the passenger side.

All the way to the airport Mr. Glazal seemed distracted, giving only one-word answers to the questions I asked him about his stay in Barbados, which, given the intensity of the discussion earlier, I had the good sense to limit to his opinion about the beach and the blue water and the people he had chanced to meet. Soon he was not answering me at all and when I looked in the rearview mirror, I saw he had his eyes closed though I was certain he was not asleep. At the airport, he kissed Corinne. "Take care of your father," he whispered in her ear. (I was close enough to hear him.) "He wants what's best for his children."

I hardly had the chance to open the car door for Corinne after we returned from saying goodbye to Mr. Glazal at the ticket counter, when, her voice trembling with indignation, she practically shouted to me: "But my sisters do not want what's best for him!"

I tried to calm her down. "Your sisters love your father. They said so. You heard them at Glynis's engagement party."

She flounced down on the front seat. "Hypocrites! They flattered him because they wanted his land. I told you Glynis was up to no good. I bet you didn't believe me."

"Believe what?"

"They planned this all along. Did you see how Douglas cringed when Glynis said he'd drive them home?"

I had noticed, seen Douglas's shoulders cave forward, his nostrils flare, his eyebrows shoot up, but he didn't protest.

"Douglas can't stand Albert, but he kept his mouth shut. And Glynis made sure I left with you. They don't want me around. Or you either."

"Come on, Corinne," I said. "Be sensible. Only yesterday your father announced he was giving them the land."

"She'll use André. She can't stand gays; she has nothing but scorn for them, yet she'll use André because she knows he's the best chef around. *It's business not personal.* That's what she'd say.

"And maybe to André it'll be business not personal too. He's no fool, I can tell. I don't think he'll go into business with Glynis with blinders on."

"Glynis was just biding her time. She knew one day Daddy would give her the land."

"She could not have known it would be so soon," I said reasonably.

"Daddy drinks too much. Glynis must have put the thought in his head. She must have caught him when he was weak, when he was drinking."

I made a stuttering attempt to stop her from conjectures she could not support, saying something foolish like all daughters love their fathers; all daughters want what is best for their fathers. Her sisters would never do anything to hurt him. It was just an idea they were exploring. They will definitely make sure to get their father's approval before they do anything rash.

She would not let me finish my litany of platitudes. For platitudes they were. History is replete with stories of mercenary daughters hastening the demise of fathers whose earthly goods they are impatient to possess.

"I told you she was cunning," Corinne said. "Albert put a ring on her finger, but she has attached a string to it and will lead him around like a sheep."

This was not the friend I knew. "You're wrong. Albert has a good head on his shoulders."

"We'll see," she said. "But you can be sure I won't talk to my father for them. If they think I will join their little scheme to move Daddy from the home he loves, they are crazy. Daddy left Trinidad for this place. It was his dream to have a house on the top of a hill looking down on the sea. They want to put him in an apartment at the bottom of a hill with people milling around him on all sides. He loves his space in his house. He loves being king of his castle, doing what he wants. He loves roaming around in his rooms, knowing they are *his* rooms. He loves sitting on his deck watching the sun come up at dawn and go down again in the evening. He loves the changing colors of the sea, how it looks as if a robe of golden threads is spread over it in the mornings, how it turns silvery in the evenings, how it's pink and red at sunrise and sunset. I won't be part of Glynis and Rebecca's scheme to displace him. I won't."

15

The next day, before I left for Jamaica, I dropped by the Ducksworths' to say goodbye. Only Corinne was at home; her sisters had taken their father for afternoon tea to his favorite café in town. "They're going to try to butter him up," Corinne said. She didn't think they'd succeed; her father loved his house too much. They wouldn't be able to persuade him to give it up for some fancy flat just so he could walk to the beach, she said. But she was worried. She'd be leaving for university soon and her father would be alone to fight their slings and arrows.

"Alone?" I asked, puzzled. "Even if you stay in one of the university's halls of residence, you'd be less than an hour away from your father."

"Oh, no," she informed me. "I'm not going to stay in Barbados. I'm going to Jamaica."

I was surprised by her response. When she told me she was accepted at the University of the West Indies, I had assumed she meant the campus in Barbados.

"It was always Jamaica," she said. "Daddy still thinks of me as his little girl, but I need my independence. Glynis and Rebecca are wrong to think he loves me best. I was a child when my mother died and Daddy felt protective of me. I guess he thought they didn't need him as much as I did."

Is that all it is? A father protecting his youngest child who lost her mother, not that he preferred her to them? That seemed to be what she believed, or what she comforted herself by believing.

"But I'm grown up," she said. "I'm not a little girl. I'm a woman."

"Not so fast," I said jokingly. "You're still a schoolgirl."

She swiped my arm and pouted. "It's good you're leaving now."

Why is it good I'm leaving now? A young girl's playful blabbering, I told myself, and swatted the comment away. I couldn't let my mind play tricks on me; I had things to do. I had to focus on my future. I had to find somewhere to live and secure a job while I waited to hear from the Ministry of Education in Trinidad if there was a teaching position for me.

Albert stayed a few days longer in Barbados. There was the matter of getting the business started up, he said. We had lunch before I boarded the plane for Jamaica and, still unable to shake off the uneasiness I felt when Corinne questioned Albert's loyalty to me, I took the chance to ask my best friend why he hadn't told me about his plans to build retirement condos on Ducksworth's land. "For that very reason," he said. "It was Ducksworth's land. Glynis thought her father would give it to her one day, but she had no idea it would be so soon."

He told me they were in the speculation phase. He had mentioned the plan to his father and got his tentative agreement to invest. "I'll still be working with him in his stores," he said, "but we thought it would be a good idea to start a business here. We may want to open a store in Barbados one day."

"What about André Lambert?" I asked. "Seems he's going to be very involved."

"That was Glynis's idea," he said. "Lambert is supposedly one of the best chefs on the island. Glynis may have objections to his lifestyle, but she can't deny he's a great cook and knows how to make a place look spectacular. You know gay people have a better sense of style than we straight men do. It's in their genes."

"Their genes? You can't be serious." I laughed and he joined me.

"Look at how he decorated his restaurant. We never would have had the instincts to put all those bright colors against those dark walls—bright blue, green, red, yellow. *Purple?* And yet it all works—the place looks fantastic."

Our laughter eased what could have been a tense moment between us, made more difficult had I mentioned Corinne's vigorous objection to a restaurant in her father's house. But Albert's father had made his position clear: he wouldn't invest in a restaurant in Ducksworth's house unless Ducksworth gave his permission.

Still, I wondered about Douglas's involvement. What was he going to contribute? He and Rebecca were living with his parents, and though Rebecca seemed to imply they were needed—Douglas was helping his father repair the house, she said—I thought it was a ruse to cover up the sad reality that the man was unemployed and depended on his parents for his livelihood.

Albert seemed too happy looking forward to his marriage for me to inject my suspicions into the fairy-tale romance he had spun for himself. He wanted to make Glynis happy, and this venture she had planned with her sister and brother-in-law was what seemed to make her happy. So I didn't mention my fears that Douglas's sole motivation was to put money in his own coffers; that if Corinne was correct, Douglas had nothing but resentment and dislike for Albert, possibly bordering on hatred; that as ridiculous as it sounded, he blamed Albert for his brother's death. I kept my own counsel and hoped Corinne was wrong.

The dean of students at the university had agreed to allow me to stay in my room for another week, two more weeks if there weren't new students needing the place. When I arrived there was a note stuck under my door; it was from the dean. I was nervous to open it, certain it was going to say I had only a week, or maybe days, before I had to vacate the room. I put down my suitcase, opened the bottle of water I had brought with me, drank it halfway, and then sat down to read my sentence. It was as I had feared. The dean wanted to see me. *Immediately*, he wrote.

It was early afternoon and I knew the dean would be on campus, so I went right away to his office. He welcomed me warmly and my apprehensions grew. He had the reputation of delivering bad news with an icebreaker, something pleasant to ease the blow to come.

"So, Mr. Baxter," he began. (He was a formal sort of guy who wore a jacket and bow tie at all times on campus in spite of the Jamaican heat, and addressed all the students by their title.) "I didn't know you knew such important people in high places here."

I looked at him, perplexed. "Who do you mean?"

"Oh, don't play games with me, Mr. Baxter. Hugh Cumberbatch QC. He is one of the biggest donors to the university. He said he was a patient of your father's."

QC: Queen's Counsel, counsel to the British Crown, an honorific given to a barrister of exceptional achievements. Jamaica was politically independent, but it was part of the British Commonwealth; the reigning monarch of Britain was still its titular head of state. To be a QC, a silk, Hugh Cumberbatch had to be a brilliant man.

"I've never met Hugh Cumberbatch QC," I said.

"Well, your father saved his life. The doctors here

weren't able to do anything for him, so he went to Trinidad and your father operated on him, made him a new man. Some father you have, Mr. Baxter. His reputation follows him here to Jamaica. I knew your father was a doctor, but why hadn't you mentioned that he is *the* Dr. Baxter?"

I couldn't say because my father was ashamed of me, that my father disapproved of my course of study. That he thought only girls and feckless men go to university to study literature. I simply shrugged my shoulders.

"You should have told us. Told me. We could have invited Dr. Baxter here."

For what reason? But I didn't ask the question. Instead, I waited for him to inform me.

"I know Dr. Baxter is a busy man but he may have been willing to give a lecture," he said. "The premed students would have been inspired by him."

Dr. Baxter was my father; I was his son, not his student, and there was little he wanted to do to inspire me.

"Maybe next year." He picked up an envelope from his desk and handed it to me. "Here. This is for you." The envelope was addressed to me. On the top left-hand corner was the name *Hon. Hugh Cumberbatch QC.* "Mr. Cumberbatch has found a job for you and a place to stay," he said, opening his desk drawer. "Would you like to see what he looks like?" He pulled out a photograph and passed it to me.

The man in the photograph was smiling into the camera, dark, intense intelligent eyes, a shock of white hair styled in a short Afro, polished dark skin with a reddish undertone. "Always in the sun," the dean said, "and fit as a fiddle. Still plays tennis though he's close to eighty-five. Went to school with Naipaul in Trinidad. You've read Naipaul, I suppose."

I nodded vigorously. "Yes, indeed, sir."

"Well, you'll want to read your letter." And placing his hand firmly on my arm, he ushered me to the door.

Once outside his office I tore open the envelope. A key fell out. I picked it up and read the letter.

Dear Émile, the letter began, *First let me congratulate you on completing your studies. Your father is quite proud of you. Very proud, I must say. He told me so.*

I felt a rush of blood to my head when I read those lines, but I composed myself and continued:

Unfortunately, I will be out of the island for the next couple of months so I will not have the privilege of meeting you in person. Your father, however, has asked me to assist you in finding an apartment and a job. I am happy to do so, for your father gave me more than a man can give another man. He gave me back my life. I suppose he told you about my surgery.

He had not. He never told me anything about his work. Hugh Cumberbatch QC was the second person to say to me that my father had saved his life. Finally, after all these years, did my father want to save mine too?

I read on. There was an address. Mr. Cumberbatch was apologetic. The apartment he found for me was at the back of his house. It was his housekeeper's place. She had died recently but he and his wife would not need to hire another housekeeper anytime soon since they would be away for about ten months in all. The place was tiny, he wrote, but had all the necessities: bed, bathroom with all the linens, dining table and chairs, and a small kitchen, fully equipped. I was to use the key in the envelope to open the door. I shouldn't worry about break-ins; his house was alarmed and he had hired a security service to patrol the place at night. The letter continued:

I've arranged an interview for you with Tony Lee at the Jamaica Examiner. Mr. Lee needs men who can read and write, men who can write a decent sentence, if you know what I mean. You are to call his secretary at your convenience for an appointment with Mr. Lee. Here is her phone number: 555-1111. Mr. Lee will be expecting you.

Sincerely,
Hugh Cumberbatch QC

The *Jamaica Examiner* was an important daily newspaper on the island. What job could that paper have for me? As far as I knew the *Jamaica Examiner* was not connected to any high school. I had told my father I was going to be a high school teacher.

It bothered me that my father would assume he could control my future, could determine my career path, and yet this was the first time he had so directly and pointedly reached out to help me. It was difficult for me to suppress my gratitude, my feelings of pure relief. I decided to call him.

Yes, he said, he knew I had my heart set on being a teacher, but Mr. Cumberbatch QC had told him that Mr. Lee needed help with his newspaper. "Isn't that why you went to university? To learn to write pretty words? I told Mr. Cumberbatch you know how to write pretty words."

Pretty words. He didn't mean to insult me. He simply had no practice commending me and this was the closest he could come to apologizing, to saying I hadn't wasted my time at university.

"It'll be a couple of months before the schools open again for another year," he said. "I didn't think you'd mind helping out and getting paid for the work."

I didn't mind.

His voice was unsteady; at times he coughed. I asked if he was ill.

"Not at all, young man. Not at all," he said, and coughed again.

He was lying, but there were rigid boundaries between us and I knew I could not press him further. Still, I said, "That cough. I suppose you're taking something for it."

"I'm a doctor. Or have you forgotten?"

The gruffness I was accustomed to hearing in his voice had returned. There was no point in prolonging our conversation. He would only get sterner with me. "I'll follow through with Mr. Cumberbatch's recommendation," I said, and thanked him.

"Glad to be of help," he gurgled, and another wave of coughing rattled up his chest.

I wanted to say he should take care of himself, get treatment for his cough, but he would only answer as he had before: *I'm a doctor.* We ended the call with the usual pleasantries.

In the sweltering heat of the midmorning, I made my way through the narrow, crowded Kingston streets looking for the building that housed the *Jamaica Examiner.* A cacophony of noises blasted my ears as I crossed from one street to another: horns blaring, cars screeching as they braked suddenly to avoid colliding into each other in the congested traffic; heart-pounding music pumping out of speakers on the shoulders of muscular men; women in tight pants, bottoms high and wide, exuberantly greeting each other; shoppers—young, old, male, female—bargaining with store owners for the colorful clothing hanging on long metal poles that extended out to the pavement from the dark interiors of densely packed stores; indigents pleading for money and food, and at every corner vendors hawking their goods.

Sweat was pouring down my face and back, the humidity so thick I was sucking the air like a donkey. I stopped to buy a bottle of water at a small café and when I came out, there, to my great relief, was the sign for the *Jamaica Examiner* on the other side of the street. An enormous van that had blocked my view moved along and I could see it clearly now, a one-story decrepit old colonial building, the plaster peeling from the façade, Demerara windows, the wooden louvers faded and cracked in places, tilting outward on fat poles. My hopes rose when I noticed the glass windowpanes behind the wooden louvers; they were closed and frosted. A century-old building but someone had the foresight to install air-conditioning.

In his letter, Mr. Cumberbatch had instructed me to make the appointment with Mr. Lee's secretary. She was the consummate professional when I called, consulting her appointment book—I could hear the pages turning in what I imagined was one of those thick, wide, leather-bound books—and then asking me for dates and times that would be convenient for me. She was checking her book again, mumbling apologies that Mr. Lee's calendar was quite full at this time of the month, when I heard a male voice shout out: "Who's on the phone, Susan?" She must have covered the mouth of the phone, for her voice was muffled when I heard her mention my name.

"Tell him to come right away."

"When?"

"Today. What do you think *right away* means, Susan? Tell him to come now."

So there I was at high noon when the sun was blisteringly hot, my face and back dripping with perspiration, ringing the doorbell on the solid wood front door of the *Jamaica Examiner*.

"Crime. Bandits. Thieves. Murderers. Drug lords, what have you." Mr. Lee came out of his office to greet me. "We're wired up. Alarmed." He pointed to the solid door and the closed windows which I could now see had wires running up their sides and at the top and bottom. "Jamaica has become the Wild West of America's past. We don't have cowboys, but we have drug lords. Just the same. The killing and lawlessness just the same. No law but their law." He scratched his head and smiled grimly.

He was probably thirty, thirty-five at the most. I had already assumed from his surname he was Chinese, but he was biracial. His skin was brown, his nose flat and wide, his eyes narrow and slanted, his hair curly and yet spiked in places as though the straight hair from his Chinese ancestors was in a battle with his African roots. Unlike the Chinese in Trinidad, the Jamaican Chinese had come to the Caribbean islands almost by accident. Their original destination was Panama, where their plan was to work on the railroad that was to stretch from Panama City to Colón, but yellow fever began to decimate them, and by some kind of strange political arrangement, the Panama investors agreed to send them to Jamaica in exchange for black Jamaican laborers. The Chinese arrived in Jamaica without their women, and for years, until the Chinese women arrived, they cohabitated with, and sometimes married, the Jamaican women. I imagined that Mr. Lee was the progeny of such an alliance.

"You're a godsend," he said, shaking my hand. "I just lost a man. Come, come in my office and we'll talk."

Apart from the doors to the restrooms, there was only one other door, which I assumed led to his office at the back of a large open space crammed with five desks—four for the reporters and another, closer to the door, where Susan sat. She had spoken so formally to me when I called that I was surprised to see she was so young—probably still in her twenties. Her appearance matched her voice, though. She was a reasonably attractive, fairly slim brown-skinned woman, but her hair was fashioned in a severe bun behind her head, and she was wearing a suit: a navy jacket buttoned to the top (which I was certain remained buttoned when she left the building and was outside in the sticky heat), and a matching pencil-thin skirt that clung to her hips. She came around her desk to shake my hand and I noticed right away that though she was slim, she was well endowed back there. I caught Mr. Lee glancing down at her bottom just as I looked up, and it occurred to me, not unreasonably, that he was romantically involved with her, and that her style of dress and formal demeanor were just a smoke screen to fool his customers.

"They're in the field," she said, somewhat apologetically, pointing to the empty desks.

There were stacks of newspapers and loose sheets of paper everywhere: on the floor, on the desks, and between the desks. Cable wires, knotted and tangled, ran across the room from computers and phones. In one corner was a line of metal file cabinets with silver handles, most of them partially open, wads of paper spilling out. There was a water cooler in another corner next to a small table with an electric metal teapot and a basket full of tea bags, sugar, and powdered cream packets. Only Susan's desk was un-cluttered. She shrugged and opened the palms of her hands in resignation when she followed my eyes. "You should see the place when the reporters come back. I've cleaned it up a bit," she said.

Mr. Lee laughed and ushered me into his office.

It was not much larger than a closet, books piled everywhere and in every direction: on the shelves lining the walls and at the feet of his mahogany desk. Sprawled haphazardly on the desk itself were stacks of newspapers, magazines, and sheets of paper, some with typing on them, others covered with handwriting. He sat down behind the desk and pushed away a pile of newspapers to the side with the sweep of his hand, clearing a space for me in the front.

"At least it's cool in here. The bandits forced us to lock up, lock the doors and windows, but we got air-conditioning in exchange. Cooler now?" he asked.

My skin was rapidly getting dry, and I was breathing more easily. "It feels great," I said.

"Sit." He indicated an antique walnut office chair with a wide seat, generous armrests, and a rack of evenly spaced narrow wood slats on the back. It was fixed to a metal swivel that immediately lurched from side to side when I sat down, and then unexpectedly rocked backward when I leaned into it. My legs flew into the air and just as I thought I was about to fall, the chair settled forward again.

"They don't make chairs like that anymore." Mr. Lee grinned mischievously. "Stole it from the original owners of the building. Englishmen. Comfortable, no? Even without a cushion?"

Comfortable, but I would have to adjust my posture. I sat up straight to avoid being rocked backward again.

"Knew what they were doing, those Englishmen," he added. "Got their workers to pay attention when they came to the boss's office."

I sat up straighter.

"So, you have a degree in literature?" He pressed his

elbows on the desk and studied me. "Mr. Cumberbatch told me you got first-class honors."

Did my father tell Mr. Cumberbatch QC I made first-class honors? He seemed unimpressed when I told him. "I've always loved reading," I said.

"Excellent. Excellent." He rubbed his hands together. "And writing too?"

I said I had written a few poems.

"Poems?"

"Short stories too, but I'm better at poetry."

He banged his fist on his desk. "You are just the man I'm looking for! Put some poetry in that prose, I always say to my reporters. Let your words sing, let them have rhythm. Throw in some imagery, simile, metaphor, symbol, that sort of thing." He lowered his voice. "You use simile and metaphor in your poetry, Émile?"

"Well, in some of my poems—"

"Onomatopoeia? Alliteration?" His eyebrows gathered expectantly.

"Sometimes . . ." I began cautiously.

He clapped his hands. "That's what I mean. That's what the poetic eye can do for prose. Dress it up, throw in some magic. You agree?" The voice lowered again conspiratorially.

I would not have used those words; I would not have said that the purpose of poetry is to dress up prose. But I concurred with the magic. "About the job, Mr. Lee?" I asked, anxious to know where this unorthodox defense of the effect of poetry on prose was leading.

He lifted his hands, palms up. "Tony, please. They'll laugh at you out there if you call me Mr. Lee. Call me Tony." He flipped through the stacks of paper on his desk and pulled out a sheet of typed paper. "Here. Read this. Tell me what you think."

It was a poem by Alicia, the poem I had heard her read at the bookstore, no less. I read it quickly. "It's a remarkable poem," I said. "She has talent."

"Just as I thought. I'll send out one of my reporters to contact her."

"No need," I said. "I know her."

"Well, well. This is really my lucky day." He clasped his hands behind his head and rocked back and forth on his chair. "You've come just in time." Then, resting his hands down and sitting forward, he told me he had an idea he'd been hoping to put into action a few weeks earlier but the man he had hired for the job left unexpectedly. "More money," he said. "My competitor offered him more than I can afford. I hope you're not going to ask for a lot." He regarded me sternly. "We pay a decent wage here, but you can't get rich on this job."

I told him I needed just enough to support myself. I didn't mention I might not stay long on the job. In the first place, I didn't know how soon I would get a teaching position, and I also didn't want to frighten him away. The man he had hired had left without giving notice. I needed to convince him that I would not abandon the job. Whatever it was, I would see it through. I was also intrigued. He had handed me a poem that Alicia had written. I was curious to know the connection between her poem and the project he had in mind.

"A literary arts magazine," he said. "I want to put it as an insert in the Sunday papers. You know . . . something people can pull out and read at their leisure. There's lots of talent in Jamaica and it's going to waste."

"Indeed," I said, thinking of the readings I had attended at the university. Most of the students whose poetry I admired would stop writing once they had their

degrees. Writing—fiction, poetry—is for dreamers, my father would say. It did not put food on the table. Better for
them to focus on their professional careers: law, engineering, business, medicine. That's where the money is for the
comforts they believe will make life worth living.

"People need outlets for their creativity," Tony grumbled. "It can't be all music and dance. I have no objection
to the music. I love reggae. Bob Marley and the Wailers. I
cut my teeth on that music with Marley. And dancehall!
Love it too, but people need inspiration, they need something to make them think, to make them understand their
lives, to give them hope that things can be better. I think
literature does that, don't you?"

This man spoke my language. I was beginning to like
him a lot.

"I mean, take this poem. You read it and you want to be
a better person. You see how complex human beings are,
how we are tempted by money and fame. I mean, look at
the way this woman talks about Dudus. She condemns him
for sure, but she leaves us thinking that if conditions were
better, if we didn't live in such a materialistic world,
a dog-eat-dog world, maybe Dudus would have done
something better with his life."

I sensed he didn't need confirmation from me on the
views he expressed, so I remained silent as he talked on
and on about the bad things Dudus did and the good, the
same opinions I had heard among Alicia's friends at the
Irie Café. Finally he stopped and passed his hand through
his hair. The spikes stood up like stubborn blades of grass
on a manicured lawn. "Just spinning my wheels," he said,
suddenly bashful. "More than you want to hear, I suppose."

"Oh, no," I hurried to assure him, "I agree with everything you said." I wasn't sure if that was the right re-

sponse. He did not seem the sort of man to be influenced by flattery, though it was not my intention to flatter him. I was already convinced of the power of poetry.

"So you'll do the job?" he asked, dismissing my comment.

The job was to edit a small insert of four pages that he planned to publish once a month in the newspaper. "Just a beginning," he said, "until we can see the interest." I was to put out a call for submissions of poetry, fiction, and essays, and select which ones would be printed in the insert. "You'll be in charge of editing. I don't want any badly written work to appear in my newspaper. We have standards to maintain, you understand? Think you could do this?"

Do I think I can do it? I couldn't dream of a better job. I couldn't have hoped for work more meaningful to my aspirations to become a better poet. I couldn't get back to my hall at the university fast enough to gather my things and start my real life.

Tony Lee gave me two weeks to pull the magazine together. He handed me the submissions he had already received and told me that I was free to reject any I did not like. I could put out a call for others, he said.

I packed my things and took a taxi to the place where Hugh Cumberbatch QC had arranged for me to stay. The taxi driver poked his head out of the car window and whistled under his breath when he pulled up at the curb. "Is here you sure you want, mister?" I too wondered if I had made a mistake and given the driver the wrong address. Mr. Cumberbatch was not only the most brilliant lawyer on the island, but apparently the richest. His house was enormous: a huge, white, elegant wood-slatted Victorian structure with multiple windows and doors, gables and frets. I checked the letter he had sent; I had come to the right place. Obviously the cottage would not be visible from the street; it was at the back of the house. Then I saw the narrow pebbled path along the side of the wide, recently mown lawn.

The cottage was tiny but spotless, furnished simply with an old-fashioned bed with iron railings, a table and four chairs made out of pine wood, and a closet to hang my clothes. There was a window on either side of the front door, and in the back, a kitchen and bathroom separated by a narrow corridor. There were no doors to either the kitchen or the bathroom; instead, for privacy, the housekeeper had hung cloth curtains with a flowery pattern on each of the entrances. I made a note to get solid-color curtains as soon as I could. Happily, there was a door at the back of the kitchen. I found the key on the ledge over the door, unlocked it, and went outside to get a sense of my surroundings.

And what wonderful surroundings! The housekeeper had planted a small vegetable garden. It had gone to seed, though I could tell the soil was rich. It had dried up in the sun and turned powdery brown, but the slight breeze that stirred the leaves on the trees that bordered the lawn brought with it the faint odor of cow dung. Manure! The soil had been fertilized! With some water it would turn dark rich brown again. It would be easy for me to bring the garden to life. I could get new shoots of string beans that would climb along the wire mesh between the poles the housekeeper had dug into the ground. Plant cucumbers, tomatoes, and cabbage too! I could have fresh vegetables and garden salad for dinner. I stretched out my arms and did a little dance on the dirt, Zorba style. What luck! In just a few days I had gone from having no job and a place that at best I could stay for two more weeks, to a job I never would have imagined would come my way, and a little house to myself where I could grow my own vegetables in the backyard. Then I remembered it was my father who had made all this happen for me. I sobered up and stopped dancing. Before I went back inside the cottage, I made a promise to myself that I would call my father at least once a week.

As I settled in bed that night, a feeling of deep satisfaction washed over me. I was at peace with my father and a glorious and exciting future stretched before me. The Ducksworths and their troubles now seemed very far away.

16

I called Albert to give him my news. He was pleased, but he was preoccupied with working out plans with Glynis for the retirement homes and we didn't speak much about my good fortune.

"A retirement resort," he said, correcting me when I said *homes*.

"What's the difference?" I asked.

"We're not just going to house people," he said. "We'll have a clubhouse with activities—games and such—music, and dance. Bring in entertainers. Maybe put in a pool. And when we build the steps, people can go to the beach."

I reminded myself that Albert was ambitious. His father was a millionaire; Albert had dreams of being a billionaire.

They would break ground on the resort after the wedding, Albert said. I didn't mention the problem of Ducksworth's house and neither did he, though perhaps Ducksworth was on his mind when he added that he and Glynis had decided to start with the land belonging to her.

"So the deeds have been drawn up?" I asked cautiously.

"Oh, yes," he said. "Peter Ducksworth is a man of his word."

Corinne and I exchanged a couple of e-mails. She would be coming to Jamaica in early August to attend the university. *Literatures in English*, she wrote when I asked about the program she chose. *I want to know more than the British canon.* I was looking forward to seeing her again, but for the next few weeks Tony Lee kept me busy, so I didn't give much more thought to her except to respond occasionally to her messages.

Alicia was thrilled to learn I'd been offered the job as editor of a literary insert that would soon be in the *Jamaica Examiner*. "You are going to do it, of course," she declared assertively over the phone, daring me to contradict her.

I assured her I had taken the job and her poem would be published in the first issue. "You don't mean the poem on Dudus?" she inquired incredulously.

I told her how much I admired her poem, how much Tony admired it too.

"The politicians will come after me," she said. "You don't know Jamaica. Politics here can be rough, real rough."

She had made that clear in her poem, blaming the government for allowing drug lords like Dudus to control the lives of poor people. She had even intimated that some politicians were in bed with the drug dealers. I remembered another line from her poem: *The politicians have blood on their hands / They line their pockets with the bread they take from the mouths of the children.*

I offered to publish her poem anonymously. The phone went quiet for a while as she considered my offer, and then I heard a guttural laugh, an eruption that seemed to come from the center of her being, a roar between defiance and exhilaration. "Let them come for me," she said. "Nobody's going to silence me."

I promised her no one would, but I had nothing to back this up except for Tony's word as I was leaving his office: "Don't worry if people vex with the stories and poems you publish. There will be more people who are going to like them, especially if you give me poems like the one Alicia wrote. Jamaica not all bad, you know."

And he was right.

We were inundated with submissions. I have to give most of the credit to Alicia. She plastered notices on storefronts, on lampposts, on buses—everywhere she found a blank space—urging people to send their stories and poems to me. She went online, on Facebook, on Twitter. She wrote blogs, had her friends write blogs, about the literary insert that was soon to take newspapers in Jamaica to a higher level, giving the people ideas, new visions of what could be done, should be done, to improve the lives of ordinary Jamaicans. "It's story that moves people," she said during another phone call, "not dry statistics. Stories, poems connect with people emotionally, make them *feel*. It's the heart, not the head, that causes people to take to the streets, that sets off revolutions. When you feel other people's pain—and stories and poetry make you feel other people's pain—you can't just sit back and do nothing. You have to demand change."

Almost every day Alicia e-mailed me with the poems, short fiction, creative nonfiction, book and movie reviews she received. I selected the ones I liked, edited them, and sent them back to her. Her edits and comments were always insightful, and I also have to admit that most of the work Tony agreed to publish was work she had recommended.

By noon on the first Sunday the literary insert appeared, the *Jamaica Examiner* was sold out and people were complaining. They knew about the food shortages in Jamaica, the empty grocery shelves. But a paper shortage? An ink shortage? The island had reached a new low if it couldn't find paper and ink to print enough copies of the newspaper.

That night radio stations were blasting the news that at last someone in Jamaica "has balls." Over and over I heard snippets of Alicia's poem, often read to the rhythm of a reggae beat. Tony Lee told me he couldn't keep up with the calls on both his cell phone and landline from people congratulating him. He was getting text messages and e-mails by the minute telling him that this was the best thing the *Jamaica Examiner* had done in a long time. Some of the poems, stories, and essays made them laugh out loud, some made them cry, some made them furious; all were inspirational, the callers said. They didn't know Jamaica had such fantastic writers. Someone e-mailed: *Whoever that Émile Baxter is, keep him.*

Tony read that e-mail to me. "Well, do we keep him, Émile?" he asked.

There was not a shred of doubt in my mind. This was what I wanted to do for the rest of my life. It was by accident I had found myself in this place, an accident that seemed predestined, that ironically had been set in motion by my father who had scoffed at my literary ambition. I loved the work. No, I cannot even call it *work*. I would do this even if I were not paid. I was in a position to discover talented writers, to nurture them. With the literary arts insert in the newspaper, I could bring the poems, the fiction, the creative essays of these writers to the public, increase their readership. I was now one of those people who could influence the strengthening and shaping of the culture on the island. Still, my motives were not entirely altruistic. The writers would inspire me too, give me the courage to continue writing, knowing that poetry could and would change the world.

Do we keep him? Whether or not I got the teaching job in Trinidad, I made up my mind that this was where I would stay. I told Tony he could keep me on his staff for as long as he wished. I was proud to work for him. I could see the magazine growing, getting bigger. We were on the forefront of a cultural shift in Jamaica, I said. Writers like Lamming would find their readers here, in the Caribbean. They would no longer need to seek exile in countries eager to offer them time, space, and financial support that would enable them to continue writing, bring them readers who would embrace their work.

"Whoa!" He held up his hands to stop my babbling. "It's an insert in a newspaper, not a freestanding magazine. And what's this about a cultural shift?"

But I knew he saw what I saw. This was a beginning. From an insert, he could go on to publishing a magazine, perhaps even books. The advances in digital technology had already made it possible to self-publish books. He could start a publishing company, publish, distribute, market books. I could see the wheels spinning in his head even while he was trying to tamp down my enthusiasm.

He threw a party for me, a small celebration in the office. At first I worried about the other reporters. They were older men in their late forties, seasoned journalists, and I wondered whether they would resent the attention Tony was giving me. But they were more interested in politics and investigating the violent crimes and drug epidemic on the island than what they called make-believe stories. "Nice work," they said, and slapped me on the back, but clearly they thought: *Nice but unimportant work, not when people have no food to eat and no place to sleep.*

Alicia came with Michael and some of her friends from the Irie Café. The flush of my infatuation with her had simmered down so completely that I could kiss her on her cheek and feel no stirrings of desire. She and Michael seemed comfortable together. If there was the slightest twinge of regret I felt, it was fueled by envy. They seemed at ease with each other, he sometimes finishing her sentences and she his. I admired how tenderly she looked at him; how no matter where she stood in the room he found a way to be near her. Envy, yes, but mostly they gave me hope that one day I would be lucky enough to find the same happiness.

We were toasting the success of the insert with champagne Tony had poured for us in plastic cups when Corinne walked in. I knew she was already at the university. In my last e-mail to her I had promised to take her to dinner, but I hadn't kept that promise yet. It was strange to see her out of her surroundings, out of Barbados, and here in Jamaica, among my new friends, in the place where I was working.

"Don't just stand there. Give me a hug." She held out her arms to me. She was the same Corinne, with the same brightly tanned skin, same brown eyes, same thick hair worn the same way, in a single plait behind her head, but there was something new about her: her breasts, waist, hips, legs. Surely I had seen them before, but never when she was in a tight tank top and close-fitting jeans. Never when those breasts, that tiny waist flaring out to slim hips, those long legs eclipsed the face I had found so endearing. When my arms encircled her and she pressed herself against my chest, I felt my heart do a somersault and I backed away.

"So where have you been hiding this beautiful woman?" Michael came toward us, Alicia on his arm.

"A girlfriend from back home, eh?" Alicia winked at me.

"A friend," Corinne said.

I laughed off her response to hide my confusion. She was indeed a friend. So why did it distress me that she had so quickly corrected Alicia's assumption?

She was full of praise for the insert in the newspaper.

"Maybe you'll publish some of my poems too," she said.

"Send them to me," I replied, my tone as nonchalant and as causal as I thought hers was.

She was serious, though. "I don't want any favors. Publish them only if you think they are worthwhile."

"Oh, he only publishes work that is worthwhile," Alicia assured her. "I know. He asks for my opinion, but he only publishes work that *he* considers either good or shows lots of promise."

"And that is always work Alicia approves," I said, aware that there was a big grin plastered on my face that I couldn't seem to make go away. "She's impartial. She doesn't do any favors."

Corinne moved closer to me. "I came to make you keep your promise," she said.

I wrinkled my brow.

"Don't pretend you don't know." She raised her voice. "You said you'd take me to dinner."

"Then join us." Alicia touched her arm. "We're going to dinner at the Irie Café. What do you say, Émile?"

What *could* I say?

Corinne was the youngest in our group at the table in the Irie Café, but she fit right in. She was quiet at first, just listening as the talk went back and forth about conditions in Jamaica—the astronomical levels of crime and poverty, the corrupt politicians—but when Alicia mentioned Dudus, she piped up: "The question the government has to answer is why so many people were willing to die for Dudus." All eyes turned on her. The expression on her face was so earnestly serious that everyone stopped eating, waiting for her to say more.

"I think the US was in shock to see men and women

taking a bullet for Dudus," she went on. "They couldn't believe how people were prepared to sacrifice their lives so he could escape from the American police."

"You know about Dudus?" Michael asked, squinting at her.

"Doesn't everybody in the Caribbean?"

"Not white girls like you."

I came to her defense, though I thought Michael had asked his question more out of admiration for her than any kind of judgment. "Corinne's father lets squatters live on his land," I said.

"One love!" One of the men—I think it was the lawyer in the group—raised his hand in a fist.

Later, when we were alone, as I was walking with her back to her hall, Corinne asked me why I had said there were squatters. "There's only one squatter I know on Daddy's land."

I had exaggerated—no, lied. I wanted to protect her and now she was reprimanding me. "A whole family," I protested. "His wife and two children."

She looked away in the distance as if her thoughts were elsewhere, and then, turning back to me, she said: "Anyhow, it's not his land anymore."

"True," I agreed, and added, "You were brave to stand up to Glynis when you did."

She twisted her lips into a wry smile. "Left to Glynis, Barbados would become an island for tourists only. The local people would have to leave or go live in the bush. Nowhere near the beaches. It's their sea and sand, but they'd only get glimpses of it from the road."

I dropped her off at her hall. This time there was no brotherly peck on my cheek; she seemed suddenly shy. I didn't know whether to shake her hand—that seemed too formal—or hug her. But I couldn't take the chance that the persistent fluttering in my stomach would lead me to hold her more tightly than would be appropriate. Instead I said it was nice to see her again. "We'll do this another time soon," I promised.

She shifted her feet on the gravel pathway leading to the steps of her hall. "I thought you were trying to avoid me," she murmured, her eyes lowered to the ground.

"Why would I want to do that?" But the moment those words left my tongue it was suddenly clear to me. I was indeed trying to avoid her. I hadn't liked the way my heart missed a beat when she first told me she was coming to Jamaica. I had forced myself to be sensible. She was a schoolgirl; but the same reasoning that made it easier to say goodbye to her reminded me that she was a mere four years my junior. When she e-mailed me that she had arrived in Jamaica I found a thousand reasons to put off seeing her. She has to get settled first, I wrote to her in an e-mail. She needs to get to know the campus, find out about her classes, get her books, meet her professors, make new friends. Even as I wrote *make new friends*, I was conscious of thinking, *Girlfriends*, though I knew there were many young men on that campus, men who, like I was when I was there, were trolling for beautiful women. And Corinne was a beautiful woman; she was no longer just a pretty girl.

Now she was waiting for my excuse. I had none to give her except to apologize and promise to call her soon. Very soon, I said.

As she was climbing up the steps to the front door, she turned and called out to me: "I like your friends, especially Alicia. She's incredible."

17

His confidence buoyed by the public's reaction, Tony Lee decided to publish the literary arts insert every two weeks instead of once a month, which gave me little time to put together a new issue. As she had been the last few weeks, Alicia was invaluable, encouraging writers to submit their work, helping me select and edit the best submissions as well as arrange the layout. Given the current technology, it was not necessary for us to meet in person. We exchanged e-mails and had face-to-face discussions by Skype. She mentioned she had met with Corinne a couple of times, so I wasn't surprised when she sent me something that Corinne had written. It was an essay, not a poem as I had expected, just under a thousand words, but it hit the mark on the problem of access to the beaches in Barbados. *Most of them—the ones you see on the postcards, with the white sand and impossibly blue water—are inaccessible to the people who have lived here for generations,* Corinne wrote. *There are laws but the fat cats from Europe, Canada, and America have found a way to circumvent them. Not without the complicity of the government. A nod and a wink, some money exchanged, and the beaches are theirs, sold to the highest bidder.*

She drove home her point with a story, a personal one about an incident she had witnessed. On an extraordinarily hot day, she was driving down Barbados's Gold Coast with some friends—black Barbadians, she wrote—

and wanting to cool off in the sea, she stopped at one of the narrow access paths to the beach that was sandwiched between two sprawling hotels protected by high concrete walls. Her friends tried to persuade her that they could wait until they reached their destination. They weren't all that hot and uncomfortable, they told her, and anyhow the access path would be cluttered with broken branches and garbage flung there in the recent rainstorm. Corinne wrote that she suspected her friends' protestations were merely a pretext; that they knew the problems locals encountered— black locals, that is—with using the access paths. She decided to find out for herself if that was true. She was immediately greeted by one of the hotel personnel, a uniformed woman who invited her to lunch, a barbecue on the beach for the hotel guests. Of course, since she was not a guest, she would be expected to pay, but she was more than welcome to spend the day there, the woman said. "Bring your friends too." Corinne explained that her friends were parking the car. "Then when they come, just let us know how many are in your party."

But her friends were turned away. One of them—a young man, the darkest among them—had been impatient; he hadn't waited for Corinne to return. There was a row. A security guard had barred him from walking through the path. "Dis here ent no access road," the guard claimed. "Is not a public road. Is a private road, the hotel road. They uses it for deliveries."

Corinne ended her essay with the security guard's words, leaving it up to the reader to decide if the guard was speaking the truth. We published her essay in the next issue of the paper.

Albert had been excited and happy for me when I told him about my job at the *Jamaica Examiner*, but there was no joy in his voice when he called me on the Sunday Corinne's essay appeared in the insert.

"Glynis is concerned," he said. "We get the *Jamaica Examiner* here, you know."

"What Corinne wrote is the truth," I replied.

"There are ramifications."

"Ramifications like what?"

"You know what we want to do."

"And what does Corinne's essay have to do with your plans to build retirement flats?"

"This thing about the beaches. We can't have the public coming on the beach in front of the resort. People who live in the flats will want their privacy."

"You know the law, Albert," I said, sighing. Corinne had warned me that Glynis would have a strong influence on him.

"Can't you talk to Corinne?" he asked.

"The article is out. You read it yourself in the papers. It can't be pulled back."

"I know that."

There was silence. I waited.

"Listen, Émile, this project would work better if we had the whole cove," he said.

"You mean Ducksworth's house?"

I had not tried to disguise my contempt and he was taken aback by the bitterness in my voice. "We're talking about the beach, Émile," he said with exaggerated patience.

"And what about the beach?"

"Corinne seems to like you. Tell her we promise to put access paths on either side of her father's house."

"The public will come in. The riffraff. Aren't you afraid of that?"

"Don't joke with me, Émile," he said. "I really need your help."

"You mean Glynis needs my help." I wasn't ready to surrender.

"We are in this together. Don't forget we'll be married soon."

And the two shall become one flesh. I was speaking to Albert but I might as well have been speaking to Glynis too.

"You've fixed the date?"

"Valentine's Day," he said.

So predictable, so trite, I almost laughed.

"We want you to be the best man. You'll be my best man, right?" His tone was conciliatory.

"I'd be honored."

"So you'll speak to Corinne? Tell her no more articles like that one?"

"I can't make any promises."

"You have to help us, Émile. Glynis will give Mr. Ducksworth the best flat, one near the steps to the beach. He'll be able to swim in the ocean every day."

So the truth finally! All that talk about the beach was merely a cover to distract me from the real purpose of his call. It was Ducksworth's house Glynis was after, and though it was hard for me to admit it, Albert seemed already entangled in the string Corinne claimed was attached to the ring he had put on her sister's finger.

"The restaurant is a great idea, Émile. It will be good for the economy in Barbados . . ."

I was no longer listening. "I have to go," I said. "I have a pile of stories to edit."

I didn't tell Corinne about Albert's call; I didn't have to. She had received a call of her own. We had arranged to meet for lunch; I wanted to congratulate her in person for her brilliant and courageous essay. She was glad to join me, she said. She had something to tell me and needed my advice.

She was wearing the same tight jeans, but not the tank top. Instead she had on a sort of peasant blouse that hung loosely over her jeans, white with a low square neckline embroidered with red flowers. She looked like a country girl and exuded a womanly, earthy sexiness. It was all I could do not to hold her longer than the brief embrace she gave me.

"Your essay made quite a splash," I said. "Tony says his phone was ringing off the hook."

"Some of that splash went to the wrong places," she responded. She looked so downcast I didn't think this was the time to tell her about Albert's plea to me to talk to her, to let her know he believed her essay could damage her sister's future. His future.

"Let the chips fall where they may," I said. "That situation with the beaches needs to be exposed. What's the point of the law if it doesn't work?"

"I tried to explain that to Rebecca," she said.

"She called you?"

"She was all sweet and syrupy at first. *How are your classes? Don't work too hard. Any good-looking guys?* That sort of thing."

"Well, are there?"

"Are there what?"

"Have you met any good-looking guys?'

"Oh, Émile, don't be silly."

It wasn't the answer I wanted, but it was better than a yes. I was aware I was treading in dangerous waters. I was finding myself more and more attracted to her and I didn't know how to signal to her that I wanted to change our relationship from friendship to one I could no longer deny I desired.

"So tell me: how I can help you? You said you wanted my advice." I deepened my voice, determined not to show my hand until I had some sign from her.

"After that sugary nonsense, she got down to business. She said I was making Daddy miserable, just like I made him miserable on the night of Glynis's engagement. That was a lie, of course. Daddy and I made up long ago. In fact, he called me. He said I was a terrific writer. He loved the piece. He didn't think I should get involved in politics, though. I should stick to writing stories or poems, he said. But he agreed with me: it was about time people did something about how the whole island is becoming hostage to the tourist industry."

I had no doubt now that Albert and Glynis were barking up the wrong tree. If they told Peter Ducksworth about their intention to build flats for retirees, he might not object, but he would not agree to a resort, not to tourists cluttering up the beach. Certainly not to a restaurant on his land, in his house. And even if I wanted to, which I didn't, I would never be able to persuade Corinne to use her influence with her father to have him give up his beloved house.

Rebecca resorted to calling her names, Corinne said. She called her selfish, self-centered, concerned only about herself, and caring nothing for her family. "Said I was jealous of her and Glynis."

"Why would you be jealous?"

"Of Glynis's beauty. Her blond hair and blue eyes. Jealous she has a handsome husband."

"Albert?"

"No, silly. I said *husband*. I was talking about Douglas, Rebecca's pretty husband."

"Well, you are more beautiful than both your sisters."

She reared back her head. "You aren't falling for me, are you, Émile?" She wagged her fork at me.

"And if I am?"

"We'll see, we'll see."

I took hope in the way she pursed her lips and narrowed her eyes as if giving serious thought to my question, but then abruptly, in that split second, the moment evaporated and she returned to her quarrel with Rebecca. "So what do you think, Émile?" She looked up at me, her big brown eyes opened wide. "Should I stop writing essays about what's going on in Barbados?"

It was obvious she didn't need my advice. "If they are as impeccably written as the first one you sent me, I'll publish them," I said.

I had to get back to my office and she had a class. We parted with a quick hug, though I cheated. Before I released her, I tightened my arms around her. She didn't push me away.

Tony was waiting for me. He had new ideas for the insert; he wanted to include a column on letters to the editor.

I didn't think that was a good idea. I didn't want to turn the insert into a medium for gossip, a chance for people to attack someone they disliked or envied by lobbing negative criticism at their work. "I'd like to keep the insert strictly for the literary arts, for poems, fiction, and creative nonfiction," I said.

"That piece by Corinne was political," he responded.

"But it was well written too," I countered. "In some places poetic."

One of the reporters was passing by and snorted dismissively.

"Not that journalistic writing isn't good writing," I said, trying to appease the reporter who now had his eyes trained on me. "I mean, Corinne used a lot of dialogue and descriptions in her essay. And she included her personal views."

"Journalists stick to the facts," the man declared. "We keep our personal opinions to ourselves. We have to be objective, not subjective, when we report the news."

I held my tongue. I would lose an argument with him about the distinction between objectivity and subjectivity. The line of demarcation is a fine one, sometimes an invisible one. Much depends on the teller of the tale. Forget the facts of genocide committed on our chain of islands. Forget that there are hardly any Amerindians left and the black people and South Asian Indians are the progeny of enslaved Africans and indentured laborers. When English historians tell the story of their colonial empire, the English people will turn out to be heroes, discovering new territory for their queen, braving the rough seas and the wilderness on land, sacrificing their lives to improve those of the savages they encountered. *Our lives in the Caribbean.*

But the Jamaican reporter standing in front of me was almost three times my age. He expected deference from me. He had spent his working life bouncing from one newspaper to the other and had landed here, at a newspaper that at best was second to the *Jamaica Observer*, the paper with the widest circulation. He didn't need an upstart challenging his expertise on what constituted indisputable fact.

"You have a sharp eye," I said. "Nothing misses you."

He grinned and moved on, satisfied that I had been properly chastened.

* * *

I had lunch with Corinne a few more times. It was difficult for both of us to get together for dinner, she because of her studies, I because Tony was becoming more and more demanding. He had visions of doubling the circulation of the Sunday paper and was pushing me hard. He agreed to hold off on including a column on letters to the editor but only if I could prove to him that there was increasing interest in the literary arts. I went home every night with stacks of papers, submissions I had to read, select, and edit for the insert. I needed Alicia's help more than ever now, but often she was too busy with her own work at the community center in Tivoli Gardens to assist me, so I found myself having less free time than I had anticipated. Not that I minded; I loved my job.

Corinne too had taken on additional responsibilities. She e-mailed me that Alicia had asked her to tutor some kids at the center and now she was going to Tivoli Gardens for a couple of hours a week. The next time we met for lunch she was sporting a new hairstyle. Instead of a thick, single braid, she had cornrows, tiny braids flattened on the top of her head and cascading down her back and the sides of her face. I liked her thick, single braid, but she looked exotic now, like those rare birds and flowers that were distinctly Caribbean but were set apart from the other fauna and flora by their exquisite shapes and colors.

"So what do you think?" She twirled around and the braids flew across her face and neck, clashing against each other in a kaleidoscope of browns caught in the dappled sunlight streaming through the windows of the restaurant.

"It suits you," I said.

"The mother of the boy I tutor did it for me. Do you really like it?"

She was asking for my opinion again, but this time her request was more personal. She wanted to know if I liked the way she looked. But I would be patient; I would wait until I was certain before exposing my heart.

I was concerned, though, for her safety. Dudus had been extradited to the US but his minions had not left Tivoli Gardens. They were still there in their numbers.

The boy she was tutoring belonged to a good family, Corinne said when I voiced my fears. His mother and father were always in the house when she came to tutor him. No one would dare harm her; the boy's father was an important man in Tivoli Gardens.

Two weeks later everything changed. I was sitting at my desk finalizing the selections for the literary insert when the reporter who had sparred with me dropped a folder on my desk. "Thought this might interest you," he said. He was smirking as he walked away, which immediately put me on guard. Evidently he wasn't finished with our brief spat; he had another lesson to teach me.

Fearful of what I would find, I opened the folder slowly. There, inside, was a photograph of Corinne in Tivoli Gardens. She was wearing a dashiki, made out of kente cloth, in a distinctive weave of orange, red, green, blue, and yellow. Her hair was still in cornrows. I had admired her cornrows, thought she looked beautiful with her hair styled that way, but I had also been aware she was consciously making a statement about her solidarity with the people in Tivoli Gardens. But the dashiki too!

In the photograph Corinne was sitting at a desk next to a little brown boy. Behind him were his parents. On his father's head was a hand-knitted cap in the Rasta colors: red, gold, and green. Curled dreadlocks fell below his shoulders and printed across his T-shirt was the head of a lion, its teeth bared. *The lion of Judah, the national animal of Ethiopia.* At the Irie Café I had seen photographs of Selassie petting the head of a lion, Selassie cupping his hand under the mouth of a lion.

So the boy Corinne was tutoring was the son of a Rasta family! My fears intensified. The boy had dreadlocks too, though his were not yet as long as his father's. His mother's hair was covered with a white cotton turban that rose like a pyramid high on her head. She had on a white loose gown, garb from Africa. Everyone was smiling, the father, the mother, the child. Corinne was smiling too.

I ran after the reporter, who I knew better than to address by his first name. He was Mr. Miller to me, he had told me more than once. "What's this?" I asked him, controlling my tone so I sounded curious rather than flustered.

"Objective reporting," he said, reveling in his chance to gloat at my discomfort. "You recognize your girl, don't you?"

"If you mean Corinne, I see her here," I said, pointing to the picture. "What are you going to do with it?"

"Put it in the papers, that's what. We're doing a report on the work at the community center in Tivoli Gardens."

"You know that photograph can get Corinne in trouble," I said.

"Trouble?" He came closer to me. He was shorter than I was and I could see the circle of hair thinning at the top of his head. In a matter of a few years, he would be bald.

"Mr. Miller, I know I don't have to explain to you how dangerous Tivoli Gardens is."

"People live there every day. Children, women . . ."

"I know, I know, Mr. Miller. But Corinne . . ."

". . . will stand out like a sore thumb? That's what you want to say?"

"She's white."

"And she's wearing a dashiki and her hair is in cornrows. I think she knows very well what she's doing."

"Some of the people may know she's there to help, but the gangs may see her as the enemy."

"Oh ye of little faith," he said, stepping away from me and grinning triumphantly as if he had beaten me in a jousting contest.

"You're going to be responsible for what could happen to her if you print that photograph," I blurted out angrily.

"That is the difference between you and me." He was back again and now was poking me in the chest with his index finger. "We journalists write the truth; we take responsibility for giving the people the truth. You print fairy tales, make-believe."

I had to remind myself of his age; Tony Lee had told me that Mr. Miller had close to thirty years on the beat through the streets of Kingston, keeping the people of Jamaica informed about what was going on in their island. He covered crime, political corruption, drug busts, but he also covered celebrations: weddings, births, good deeds his neighbors had done. The prime minister had given him an award for his incisive coverage of the rise in crime in Jamaica.

"The stories I publish tell the truth," I said, careful not to let my voice betray my frustration. "They tell the truth about human nature, about the human condition."

He snorted. "The human condition? I know more about the human condition than you can put in your little finger. And if you are so concerned about the truth, why do you want me to hold back the photograph?"

"Because it doesn't tell the whole truth. People see this photograph and may come to a conclusion that may harm Corinne."

"And what conclusion is that?"

He knew the answer as well as I did. If that photograph was printed, Corinne could be in danger. The gangs could take her for a spy, an informant for the police. She would be a marked woman. They could kidnap her in revenge. *Kill her.*

My heart was throbbing wildly, but I wanted to wipe the smug smile off Mr. Miller's face. "She's trying to help," I said, managing to speak calmly. "Don't you see? She's tutoring that little boy. Look, his parents are smiling. They appreciate what she's doing to help their son."

"But they know she'll be going back to her nice house, in her nice neighborhood, and they'll be going back to their rundown shacks where they sometimes have electricity and water and sometimes they don't. Where the schools don't teach their children how to read and write."

"Corinne wants to teach them," I said, painfully conscious of how pathetic I was sounding.

"Then you should like the photograph," he said with a snicker. "It shows her doing just that: teaching a little black boy." His voice turned hard. "We're going to publish the photograph, Émile. Tony approves. It will be in tomorrow's newspaper."

18

I called Corinne and told her about the photograph. "Oh!" That was her only reaction. Worried that she might be unaware of the trouble the photograph could cause her, I invited her to have dinner at my place later in the evening, determined to talk to her, to get her to understand the dangers she could face.

After I left work I stopped at a restaurant nearby and got dinner for us: jerk chicken, pigeon peas and rice, fried plantains, and ginger beer. Fortunately, I had cleaned the cottage the day before and had already replaced the curtains on the doorways to the kitchen and bathroom, the ones with the flowery print, with deep-blue canvas sheets. My plan, though, was to have a carpenter install doors. Mr. Cumberbatch had written to me to say he had no plans to return before Easter. I offered to pay rent, but he declined, agreeing only to allow me to pay the electricity and water bills. I certainly was not rolling in money. Now that I had a steady income, my father had stopped depositing checks in my bank account, but I was comfortable; I didn't need much.

Corinne liked the blue canvas curtains right away. They reminded her of the sea, she said. And of course that was why I had chosen the color. I was relieved to see she had taken out her cornrows. Her hair was back in the style I liked: stray curls around the sides of her face and the rest of her hair swept back in a thick, single plait. She was wearing a dress this time, a green-and-white-striped cotton shift held up with thin straps. It showed off her smooth shoulders and tanned skin above her breasts. "You look beautiful," I said.

"Because of the hair?" She eyed me suspiciously and I quickly responded that I liked her cornrows, but I also liked the way she was wearing her hair now.

She smiled grimly and massaged her scalp. "I had to take them out," she said. "They were hurting my head."

Was that the real reason? I didn't ask.

"Can I see the photograph?"

She held out her hand and I gave it to her.

"The mother lent me the dashiki," she said, as if my silence prompted her to give me an explanation. "The father wanted the photo. He wanted to hang it on his living room wall." She sighed. "I don't know how it got to your newspaper."

"The father gave it to the reporter."

She didn't respond right away, seeming to think over what I had said, and then the tightness in her shoulders loosened and she tapped my arm lightly. "You worry too much, Émile. Of course the father gave the photograph to the newspaper. He is proud of his family, proud of his son who is reading pretty well now. I think he'll be pleased to see the picture of his family in the newspaper."

"Would your family be as pleased?"

She turned away from me. "Whose side are you on, Émile? I thought you said you were in my corner."

I didn't want to frighten her. I didn't want to say I was worried there may be people in Tivoli Gardens who would want to harm her, people who could take her for a plant, a spy for the police or a rival gang.

"Your heart is in the right place, Corinne, but you need to be careful."

"I *am* careful," she said. "That boy's father protects me."

"Your father may not think that's enough."

"It'll be my sisters who'll be furious when they see my photograph in the papers," she said.

"Your father may be angry too."

"Maybe not." I had put the computer on the floor and she was clearing away the piles of paper from the dining room table.

"Couldn't you tutor that boy somewhere else?" I asked.

"You too?" She stopped and pulled the stack of papers she had gathered from the table close to her chest. Her eyes were shadowed with so much disappointment I was forced to look away.

"It's just . . ." I began.

"Would you prefer I inconvenience him rather than myself? Would you like that small boy to spend what little money he has on bus fare to come to me? Or would you rather he walk the miles to where I am? I can take a taxi to him. That won't inconvenience me."

I felt ashamed of myself. For what I hadn't said was that I didn't want her there; I didn't want her risking her life by being in that neighborhood. And why? It was dangerous, yes, but I couldn't deny my uncharitable thoughts that she was too good, too refined to be among people who volleyed curse words at each other in casual conversation. People who easily snuffed out the lives of their neighbors. Who could easily snuff out hers.

"Corinne," I tried again, "it could be dangerous for you to be there."

"Alicia goes there and she isn't worried. She feels safe."

"You are not Alicia."

"Why? Because I'm white?"

The answer was obvious, to me as well as to her. Because she was white, because there was history between her people and the people who lived there. Because the memories of the people who lived in Tivoli Gardens were vivid, passed down from generation to generation, memories of the cruelty of slave masters whose daughters looked just like her.

"Well, I'm going to tutor that boy." She slapped down the papers in her arms with such force on my bed that parts of the manuscript I had been editing fell to the floor. She stooped down and picked up the loose pages before I could retrieve them. "Sorry," she said, her voice muted but the anger still there. Facing me, she let me know that not only was she going to tutor the boy but she would tutor any other little boys or girls who needed her help. "I'll deal with whatever fire when and if it comes. In the meanwhile, let's eat. I'm hungry."

Her mood was lighter when I brought out the food I had purchased. "Where's the pepper sauce?" she asked. "You don't expect me to eat this without pepper sauce?" I had forgotten to ask the man at the restaurant for any. She dashed into the kitchen. "The housekeeper must have kept a bottle." And sure enough, in the back corner of one of the kitchen cabinets was a bottle of homemade pepper sauce.

She was a true Caribbean girl—no one could deny her that—a woman who loved the ocean and the sand, the scent of the salt-filled sea air on a windy day, the heat rising from the hot pavement after the rain, the pulsating rhythms of calypso and steel band music. A woman who could run barefooted on hot asphalt. I had seen her put salt on a green mango, swish the pulp of acidic tamarinds in her mouth without flinching. I should have known she would want pepper sauce on her meal.

She used her fork when she ate the peas and rice, but

she set it aside when she reached for the chicken. "This is my favorite way to make chicken," she said, pulling apart the thigh from the leg with her hands.

"You make jerk chicken?" I was astounded.

"I wish," she said. "Our cook does."

Our cook does. A Caribbean woman, but I was not wrong to think she would be out of her element in Tivoli Gardens, unable to decode gestures and words, unable to detect whether there was malice intended or not under the current of seemingly harmless exchanges. She had not lived with these people; she had not gone to school with them. None of them were her friends. They were the cooks in her father's house, the maids who cleaned their toilets.

She was so relaxed now, her elbows on the table, the drippings from the chicken running down her arms, that I took the chance to probe her again about boyfriends.

"Met any interesting guys on campus?"

She stopped eating, and holding the chicken leg suspended in her hand, she looked at me as if I were an immature schoolboy, which, given my question and the motive behind it, I was at that moment. "Only you," she said.

19

I didn't have to wait long for Albert to call me, as I knew he would the moment he opened the newspaper. "Cornrows? A dashiki? In Tivoli Gardens? Has Corinne lost her mind?"

"She's doing good work," I said.

"You and I never went to Tivoli Gardens." The words whistled through his teeth. "You know that, Émile. And you know why."

"Maybe we should have. Maybe we shouldn't have remained in our ivory tower."

"What ivory tower? We were students. And we're not from Jamaica."

"Same Caribbean region. We should have cared."

"You know what I'm talking about. The crime, the drugs. For God's sake!" I could hear him pacing the room. A door opened and closed. "It's Émile," he whispered.

"Say hello for me." Glynis's voice. Then her footsteps quickening toward him. "Here. Give me the phone . . . How are you, Émile? I understand you have a big job."

"A small one."

"Editor of a literary arts magazine. That doesn't sound like a small job."

"An insert in the newspaper," I said.

"Soon it'll be a full-fledged magazine, I bet."

I laughed. "If wishes were horses . . ."

She took a deep breath. Air rushed out of her mouth

when she exhaled. "Daddy is worried." It was the end of her banter with me. Another breath, shallower this time. "That article Corinne wrote in your newspaper . . . How could she? I can't believe you let her do something like that, Émile. We were all depending on you to keep her in line."

Perhaps if she had not used those words, not said *keep her in line*, as she seemed to be keeping Albert in line, I would not have been so defensive. "Corinne is her own person," I said firmly. "She makes her own decisions."

"Well, her decisions are affecting us. They can hurt us, as they have already hurt us with that nonsense about the access paths to the beach. The engineer we hired to build the steps to the beach told us people are talking. The hoteliers. How do you think the economy in Barbados is kept afloat? Without the tourists all that blue sea and white sand would be worth nothing. Nil! And now you want vagrants on the beach."

"Not vagrants, Glynis. Just the people who live here. Who were born here."

"They wouldn't have food to eat or a roof over their heads if it wasn't for the tourists."

"Lower your voice, Glynis," I heard Albert say.

I waited for the next attack, for what she would say about the photograph of Corinne in a dashiki, her hair in cornrows, sitting next to a little black boy on his porch in Tivoli Gardens, his parents behind him in Rastafari garb . . . but nothing. Not a word about the photograph.

She continued on about the consequences of Corinne's essay on her plans to build a resort. "Who do you think cleans the beach?" she asked testily. "The hoteliers, that's who. They are the ones who pay workers to keep the beaches clean. Left to the people who live here, there'd be garbage all over that white sand you love so much."

"I've never seen a cleaner island than Barbados," I replied, getting impatient with her complaints and yet readying myself for the one I could not as easily defend.

"You are supposed to be Albert's best friend," she whined. "How could you do this to him?"

"I'll talk to him, Glynis." Albert had taken the phone away from her.

"How could you, Émile?" Glynis shouted one more time into the phone, and then her voice retreated and I heard a door slam shut.

"You know what will happen when she sees that photo of Corinne, don't you, Émile?" Albert said.

So she hasn't seen the photograph! He hasn't shown it to her!

"It'll only be a matter of time before she opens the newspaper and sees it, or someone calls and tells her about it. How do you think Mr. Ducksworth will feel?" he asked tersely. "His youngest daughter with cornrows and in a dashiki!"

"I don't think Mr. Ducksworth will be all that pissed off."

"Then you don't know him. There's not much difference as you may think between him and Glynis," he said.

But Ducksworth liked the article Corinne had written. He agreed with her; he thought that Barbados was in danger of becoming hostage to the tourist industry. And Corinne had said "Maybe not" when I told her her father might be angry when he saw the photograph. Still, *maybe not* wasn't a definitive answer; *maybe not* left open the possibility for *maybe yes*.

When Ducksworth eventually called Corinne, he gave no indication one way or the other of his position regarding the photograph, or that he had even seen it. He simply said it was time for him to find out for himself how his daughter was getting along in Jamaica. Would Émile mind if he came over to his place?

Corinne told him I had only one room and a narrow bed, barely enough space for myself. Oh, no, Ducksworth told her. He didn't intend to spend the night. He merely wanted a place where they could meet and be free to talk openly. Just for a couple of hours, he told her. He had to return on the evening flight.

Corinne was not so naive as to think her father's sudden decision to come to Jamaica was unrelated to her photograph in the newspaper. She knew that Glynis would eventually see the photograph, and when she did, she would show it to their father. Yet she hoped. "He probably wants to talk to me about being careful," she said. "He worries about me."

But a father does not board a plane to fly hundreds of miles to see his daughter for a couple of hours if all he wants to tell her is to be careful. He could tell her that on the telephone. Send her an e-mail, if he preferred. No, Ducksworth wanted a face-to-face with Corinne. He wanted to be next to her, where he could see her every reaction, look into her eyes, judge her body language, not merely her words. He had something more serious to say to her. I couldn't help but think that Glynis had filled him with her biases and that her reasons for doing so were directly related to the house and land Ducksworth had bequeathed to Corinne.

I did what I could to spruce up my place. I cleaned the kitchen, mopped the floor, put away the dishes in the cabinet, cleared the dining room table, and stuffed the newspapers and stacks of work I was editing under my bed. Then I polished my shoes and put on a clean shirt and my best long pants. At the last minute I rushed out to Mrs. Cumberbatch's garden at the front of her house and picked a bunch of ginger lilies from plants clustered together under a mango tree. I made sure to mix the colors—reds and pinks with whites—and to choose the ones that had no brown marks on the petals. I didn't have a vase, but in the kitchen I found a tall glass jar. I filled it with water, arranged the ginger lilies in it as best as I could, and put it on the table.

Corinne arrived early. I could tell she was nervous. She kept biting and releasing her bottom lip and pushing back the curls and wisps of hair that fell stubbornly around her face. She loved the flowers in the glass jar. "You are so good to me, Émile," she said. "What have I done to deserve your kindness?"

Of course it was not kindness that had sent me running out to Mrs. Cumberbatch's garden to cut the ginger lilies. It was something more. Something like love.

"Just be yourself," I said. "You have a good heart and your father knows it."

"Does he?"

"It's going to be all right, Corinne."

"I think he knows."

For the first time she expressed her fear to me directly. I told her what I had assumed. I said that Glynis had probably shown her father her photograph in the newspaper.

She sat down at the table and put her head in her hands. "He won't like it," she murmured.

"He didn't agree with Glynis about the squatter on his land." I was grasping at straws, but I couldn't bear to see her so sad. "And he won't agree with her now."

She looked up at me, her eyes moist, wide as saucers.

"There's a difference," she said. "I'm not a squatter; I'm his daughter."

She wanted me to be nearby when her father came. "Could you hide in the kitchen or the bathroom?"

The curtains would not be enough to give her father the privacy he seemed to want, I said. And I didn't want to eavesdrop on their conversation, to be put in the role of a spy.

"Not a spy," she said. "It's just that I would feel better knowing you were close."

I repeated to her that no matter what Glynis could have said, her father loved her. He would do nothing to hurt her.

"He has a temper," she said.

I shook my head, but I had seen him snarl at her, push her away when she tried to soothe him, when she reached for his hand, desperate to convince him that half did not mean she loved him less.

"He drinks." She looked past me.

"But he has never done anything to you when he drinks, has he?" I asked cautiously.

"Oh, no," she said quickly, facing me again. "He's never touched me. I mean, hit me or anything like that. But he can be mean with words when he's in that state."

I said I would wait for her in the backyard. I had added more fertilizer into the dirt, and the tomato and string bean seedlings were already beginning to sprout leaves. "I'll finish planting my vegetables."

She pointed to my freshly polished shoes. "With those on? Did you dress up like that to work in the garden?"

I saw the smile twinkling at the corners of her mouth. *For her.* I had dressed up for her.

I tugged her plait, relieved that I had amused her. "Go hide in the bathroom," I said, laughing. "I'll change."

＊ ＊ ＊

Her father arrived at one o'clock, the exact time she had arranged for him to meet her at my place. She had assured him they would be alone; she didn't tell him I'd still be there, behind the cottage. There were no windows in the back so we knew he wouldn't be able to see me, though I wouldn't be able to see him either. But I had taken the precaution of unlocking the kitchen door so I could reach her in seconds if she needed me.

I was looking out for him, peeking around the side of the cottage from time to time, when I saw him striding down the pathway. He looked like a man with a purpose, grim-faced, mouth puckered, eyes blazing, arms swinging, head jutting forward, his sand-colored hair, which had more gray in it than I recalled, askew, strands falling about his face. My worst fears were going to be realized, I thought. He had come with the intent to reprimand Corinne. Worse. But I forced myself to be sensible when *worse* entered my head. Corinne had been confident: He was often drunk, but he was never violent with her. Except with words. *What words will he say to her now?*

He was wearing knee-length shorts and a white cotton shirt that fluttered behind him as he quickened his pace, his thin legs making long strides along the pathway. Instead of sandals or more comfortable shoes, he had on black tasseled dress shoes and black and gray argyle socks. The mismatch would have been comical had I not feared his purpose. It was urgency, not carelessness, that had caused him to make this mistake, to put on dress shoes with shorts he would wear to the beach.

I heard nothing to alarm me when the front door opened and they greeted each other. Quite the opposite. "I've missed you," Ducksworth said.

"I missed you too," Corinne replied. I assumed they embraced. Then the door closed.

I pressed my ear against the back wall. Again, no sounds to alarm me. They were speaking quietly, and though I couldn't decipher their words, I took it as a good sign that no one was shouting. In any case, Ducksworth didn't look drunk to me, not with his firm, determined stride. Perhaps I had allowed my growing attachment to Corinne to fuel my fears, to see more purpose in Ducksworth's intent than the anxiety of a father who had come to give his daughter advice. It would make sense for him to warn her, given the notoriety of Tivoli Gardens. I had tried to warn her too. Tivoli Gardens was not a safe place for a young woman, not a young woman like Corinne.

I had gone back to planting my seedlings when I heard the front door slam shut with such violence the thin walls on the back of the cottage shuddered and the door hinges creaked. I ran quickly to the kitchen door and just as I opened it, the front door flung open again. I stayed still and quiet behind the canvas curtain, ready to jump out and rescue Corinne if there was an argument, or—God forbid—blows.

Ducksworth was saying something to her in a low voice, and I could only make out a sort of rumbling noise, a growl that sounded menacing to me. Then I heard him say loudly and clearly: "I meant what I said. It was not a threat." The door opened and shut again. He was gone. I could see him through the front window, arms swinging, the heels of his leather shoes pounding the pebbled path.

Corinne was in tears, her back bent down low over the table, sobbing loudly into her arms. I came over to her and rubbed her shoulders. She sank her head deeper into her arms, her sobs coming louder and more rasping. "It's okay, it's okay." I did my best to soothe her, but I didn't know what was okay, what Ducksworth could have said to her to make her so despondent.

Eventually, the words came out of her mouth, one at a time, through gasps for air. "He said I . . . was . . . no longer . . . his . . . daughter."

I let her cry some more and when her sobs died down and her shoulders were no longer rising and falling with each gasp she took, I knelt beside her and put my arms around her. She turned toward me and our lips met. I cannot say I intended to kiss her right then, though I would be lying if I didn't admit that I had played this moment over and over again in my mind. She had leaned forward and I didn't back away, but when I kissed her, all the warmth and passion I had bottled up in my heart came rushing out. It was a long, tender kiss, and when we finally parted she looked up into my eyes and asked, "Why did it take you so long?"—reproach, but happiness too, in the question.

The tears on her cheeks had not dried. I wiped them away with my fingers. "Because I am a fool," I said, and folded her hands in mine. "I loved you from the beginning."

"The beginning?"

"When you fell into the mud on the way to the racetracks."

"In the Savannah?"

"The first time I saw you," I said.

"I looked a mess. Mud on my hands and on my behind."

"You were beautiful."

"You helped me up."

"And so young." I clasped her hands more tightly in mine.

"Too young to love?"

"You were a child," I said. "I loved the child you were. I admired you. So brave, so determined."

"And now?"

I kissed her again. "Now I have fallen in love with a woman."

"Oh, Émile." She burst into tears. "What am I going to do?"

And then she told me everything her father had said.

Glynis had indeed given him the newspaper. He had seen the photograph of Corinne sitting with a Rastafari family in Tivoli Gardens. He admired her spunk, he said. He admitted he often felt guilty about his people's past in the islands, how they got rich on the backs of black people. How he got rich. It was charitable of her to want to give back. He should do more himself. She was setting a good example for white people on the island.

Their conversation went well at that point, she said, and I suppose that was also the time I couldn't hear their voices.

Then everything turned ugly when he asked her to promise him that she wouldn't go back to Tivoli Gardens.

How would she be able to help the children then? she asked.

He said he would donate money to the community center, but he insisted—no, demanded—that she not return there.

She told him she couldn't make that promise. She had already made a commitment to that boy's parents. When she first began to tutor him he could barely figure out the simplest words; now he was reading picture books. He needed her, she said.

What about her commitment to the father who had raised her, taken care of her? Who had been mother and father to her after her mother died? Ducksworth asked.

She repeated that she loved him, that she was eternally grateful for all he had done for her. He was the best father a daughter could ever have.

"Gratitude!" he scoffed. "That's all the feeling you have for me?"

"And love," she said.

He brought up an old wound she thought had healed. "Half. That's all you said you'll give me."

"All of a daughter's love for the best father in the world," she said.

"No more?"

She begged him to tell her what more she could do to prove her love for him.

"The daughter can obey her father," he said.

But he had asked her for more than she could give him. "When I was a child, it was my duty to obey you," she responded. "But I'm not a child anymore."

"You're *my* child," he said.

"I'm an adult. A woman. I'm expected to keep my word when I give it."

That was when he exploded, Corinne told me. She was no longer his daughter, he declared. Daughters obey their fathers. He would disinherit her if she continued to defy him. "Promise me you won't go back there," he said.

Once again she told him she had promised the boy. He was relying on her word.

Ducksworth opened the front door and slammed it behind him, but in seconds he returned. Tears brimmed his eyes. "I loved you best," he said. "You were closest to my heart." He stretched out his arms toward her and she rushed into his embrace. But the moment did not last. He grabbed her shoulders and pushed her away. "I was gullible." He swiped his hand across his eyes; a tear trickled down his cheek. "A fool to believe you when you swore you loved me. But I have two more daughters. They love me, they obey me. They could teach you about loyalty, about obedience. About *love*. About caring for your father's happiness, for the things that are important to him. You are no longer my daughter. I meant what I said. It was not a threat. I will disinherit you."

I tried to reassure her that her father would never disinherit her. "He was angry," I said. "People say things they don't mean when they are angry. Of all his daughters, your father wanted *you* to have his house, the most precious thing he owned, as you, of all his daughters, are the most precious to him. He won't change his mind because of this. You quarreled, that's all."

"He was sober," she said.

"But not in his right mind," I countered.

She shook her head. "He knew what he was saying."

20

Corinne continued to tutor the little boy. She called her father several times, hoping there was something she could say to make him understand that she loved him but she needed to live her own life by her own rules. He slammed down the phone the moment he heard her voice. "He won't give me a chance to explain," she told me. But there was nothing she could explain that would persuade her father to change his mind, nor, for that matter, that he could say to persuade her to change hers. He demanded she obey him as proof of her love for him and she was equally determined to keep her promise to the boy. I could no longer pretend their disagreement was a simple quarrel between a daughter and a father who was finding it difficult to accept that his child was now a grown woman no longer in need of his protection. A part of me could empathize with his disappointment. She was his youngest, his favorite child. He adored her, had raised her with love, fed her, clothed her, put a roof over her head, and he believed he deserved more in return, if not all her love then at least obedience. But I could not condone his anger, his intent on revenge

Yet I did not think Ducksworth would have been so obdurate had he not had encouragement. Surely it had crossed Glynis's mind that there was advantage for her in her father's stance against Corinne. He had announced his intention to disinherit Corinne. If he remained firm, his house and the land it stood on would be hers to be shared with a sister ever willing to please her.

Ducksworth's change of heart must have fired Glynis's ambition to turn his house into a five-star restaurant. But Glynis wanted the house now, not years later after her father died, and I wondered what guile she would use to make that happen. *I will not be put out of my house*, Ducksworth had said. *Mark this, Gopaul*. And Gopaul had recorded Ducksworth's words in his notebook.

Contrary to my fears, the article in the newspaper turned out to be a boon for Corinne. Parents in Tivoli Gardens wanted their children tutored too and students at the university volunteered to help. Alicia arranged for space in the community center and soon Corinne was tutoring not just one boy but several, as well as coordinating a small program where young boys and girls could be tutored in reading, writing, and mathematics. I was proud of her, though I cautioned her not to get distracted from her studies. "You came here to get a university degree," I said. "You can't allow yourself to lose focus."

"Are you playing father to me?" she teased.

Nothing was further from my intentions. I loved her. I wanted to be with her, and I was jealous of the time she was away from me.

She was spending weekends at my cottage now, often other days too, and we'd become quite the domestic couple, she cooking sometimes, I at other times, both of us weeding the garden together. She had added more vegetables to my small plot—cucumbers, lettuce, cabbage, sweet peppers, eggplants—and within weeks my backyard was ablaze with variegated greens, some climbing the poles I had dug in the earth, some rising on thin spines, the lettuce and cabbage beginning to unfurl like the petals of rosebuds opening. Often before the sun began to set we would bring out chairs and read, each seemingly in our own worlds, and yet there would be outbursts of delight as she read to me certain passages from her books, or I from one of the poems I received that I found especially moving. We had our Garden of Eden in my backyard and night sometimes met us there, below the canopy of the midnight-blue sky, silvery stars twinkling above us, frogs croaking, lizards slithering through the dry grass, the occasional restless birds, impatient for dawn, squawking among the tree branches, green leaves swishing back and forth in a breeze redolent of the rich scent of the earth and newly sprung vegetables, the world around us peaceful. Paradise.

I gave her the dining room table to write her papers for her classes at the university and used an old table I had found as a desk for my work at the newspaper. If she wrote more essays like the one I'd published in the insert, criticizing the hoteliers in Barbados for making it difficult for the local people to have access to the best beaches, she never gave them to me. I hadn't encouraged her to, but I hadn't dissuaded her either. I think she wanted to offer an olive branch to her father. She would keep her opinions out of the public eye, and, hopefully, he would forgive her.

I published two poems in the insert I had written for her, without naming her of course. In one of them I wrote of my unconditional love. I quoted lines from a sonnet by Shakespeare: *Love is not love / Which alters when it alteration finds, / Or bends with the remover to remove.* Was I worried we might trip and fall into the quicksand of biases and prejudices hurled at interracial relationships like ours, and find ourselves unable to resurface? Perhaps subliminally, but she was quick to reassure me.

"Nothing will ever make me remove my love for you," she swore.

I spoke to Mr. Miller. I told him what had happened as a result of his insistence on publishing Corinne's photograph in the newspaper. He was remorseful; he had adult children of his own. "Some people don't understand when it's time to let go of their children," he said. "I understand how Mr. Ducksworth could feel, but it's not right to disinherit your own flesh and blood."

Christmas was coming and I decided to spend the holidays with my father. As I said I would, I called him once every week, sometimes twice. Our conversations were still awkward and brief. He was always the one to end them, though I had a sense he was glad to hear from me and looked forward to my calls. There would be no more than two rings of the phone before he'd pick up. "Émile? Is that you, Émile?" he greeted me the first time, but by my second call, his voice was softer and he was addressing me as son. "Is that you, Émile? Is that you, son?" Each time my insides would melt, and yet I could tell by the way he hurried on to give me some complaint about Henrietta—how she overcooked his vegetables, or undercooked the meat—or about the noise coming from the street or from his neighbors, he would rather I accept his tenderness in silence than acknowledge it in any way.

The frequent heart-pounding rhythms blaring out of speakers in the cars whizzing past his house was a growing irritant to him. He wanted me to speak to the police, register a complaint for him. "Why must the whole neighborhood be disturbed by their horrible music? If you can call that music."

"Hip-hop," I said. "It has become very popular."

Life was passing him by. The "boom-boom" from the

cars, as he called the music of my generation, was a constant reminder to him that he was on his way out, that he had become a foreigner in his own land.

His cough had dissipated somewhat, though there were times when he hurried me off the phone and I felt it was because he sensed a spasm rising in his throat. When I told him I would be coming to Trinidad to spend the Christmas holidays with him, he was so overwhelmed he almost choked in a fit of coughing. After his lungs cleared, he warbled: "I look forward to it." He hesitated, and then, his voice so low I barely heard him, he added an endearment: "To seeing you again, my dear son."

I invited Corinne to come with me. I told her I could arrange for her to stay at a bed-and-breakfast near my father's house. The very next day, however, she received a letter from her father. The envelope was square and stiff like the ones used for Christmas cards. Still, she was nervous to open it. She had been trying to quiet the reverberations of her father's voice in her head declaring she was no longer his daughter, and was afraid he would say something even more hurtful than before. "He wants to make amends," I told her. "He wouldn't put anything like that in a Christmas card."

She wanted me to open the envelope for her. Her hands were shaking and beads of sweat had made a line across her forehead when she pulled it out of her backpack and handed it to me. It was an ordinary Christmas greeting card with the usual cheerful words, but her father had added a note inviting her to come home for the holidays. *This is your home,* he wrote, *until you graduate from university. I made promises to your mother. I told her I'll see our daughters through university. So your old room is still yours if you so desire to come home for Christmas.*

If you so desire . . . There was no warmth in his note, no indication that he had forgiven her, or even that he was looking forward to seeing her. He was simply fulfilling a commitment he had made to her mother.

I tried to comfort her. "See, see," I said, "your father was angry, that's all. It was just a dark cloud that has passed over."

She was too smart a young woman to be persuaded by hollow bromides. We both knew the invitation was a mere formality, a father doing what society expected of him. But she wanted to go home. She had never missed a Christmas Day with her father, she said. And she loved him; she was concerned about his welfare. "He is drinking too much," she said.

21

As I suspected, Glynis had gone with her father to the lawyer to revise his will. Albert sounded uncomfortable when he told me this on the phone. "What actually happened that day to cause Mr. Ducksworth to disinherit Corinne?" he asked me, though I was certain he had some idea of what had transpired. And indeed he did. Some idea, though a perverted one. Glynis had led him to believe that Corinne told her father she didn't love him. "What else was Mr. Ducksworth to do?" Albert said. "I mean, if Corinne disavows her father, it's only fair that he disavow her."

"I can't believe what you are saying," I said. "Would your father ever disavow you, no matter the reason? Is there anything you could do to him for him to declare you are no longer his son?"

Albert grew quiet. "My father is different," he said at last. "And I am his only child."

"Well, Glynis is wrong. Corinne never disavowed her father. She never said she didn't love him. She loves her father very much. He asked her not to go back to Tivoli Gardens and she refused to obey him."

"She shouldn't be in Tivoli Gardens," he said. "You know that, Émile. If you care about her, you should tell her so."

"She's doing good work with the children there. She's teaching them to read and write."

"Someone else can do that, surely. Why her?"

"Why *not* her?"

He had no answer for me, except to say that Glynis was concerned about Corinne's safety. "She is beside herself with worry," he said.

With some trepidation—though I needed to find a way to let him know that Glynis's motivation may not be benign—I took the chance to ask him if he thought she would be able to convince her father to move to one of the flats she planned to build.

Mr. Ducksworth was still adamant, he said. Glynis had tried to reason with him. She pointed out that soon the house would be too big for him. Corinne was at university and likely to live somewhere else after she graduated. If he took one of the flats, he could walk right out his front door and down the steps to the beach. Every day, she told him. Whenever he wanted, he could swim in the sea. Mr. Ducksworth had turned red with anger and grabbed her by her shoulders, Albert said. He yelled at her at the top of his lungs: "This is my house, and it will be where I'll stay until they cart me out!" And he warned her never to speak to him again about where he would, or should, live.

I left for Trinidad the day Corinne flew out to Barbados. My father was waiting for me and when the taxi stopped at his house, he opened the front door. I had to stifle my shock when I saw him. His caramel-colored skin was gray, his jaw slack, and bluish-black rings circled his eyes. He was a sack of bones. His pants and shirt hung on him as if there were nothing beneath them and his shoulders were the rod holding them up. I dropped my bags on the floor and stuck out my hand. (We never embraced and I didn't think he'd want me to embrace him now.) When I enclosed his hand in mine, I could feel his bones sliding against each other. He smiled and his eyes sank deeper into their sockets.

I went to the kitchen to greet Henrietta. She hugged me and whispered in my ear that I was not to say a word about my father's weight. "He's a proud man, your father."

So I avoided my father's eyes and he avoided mine. Every morning, directly after breakfast, he went to his office at the hospital and I was left alone with Henrietta until he returned for dinner. He no longer did surgeries, but he had post-op patients. I couldn't imagine any now, but there were the old-timers, Henrietta said, who wouldn't go to anyone else. In any case, she told me, my father needed to do something to keep his mind off the sickness that was eating him alive.

I suspected he had lung cancer and during the four days I spent with him, I looked for chances to talk to him about getting treatment. At breakfast I would begin to say something about his cough and he would silence me, claiming he didn't have time to talk; he had to leave for the hospital immediately. If I asked the question later, at dinnertime, he would say he was taking care of his cough. *With what? How?* I didn't know until one day, tiring of my questions, he offered this explanation: "I'm old. I don't have many years left, and all that chemotherapy and radiation do not extend a man's life for long. I'd rather have my strength and my wits about me while they last."

On Christmas Day he opened up further to me. Henrietta had made an elaborate turkey dinner and served it to us on my mother's lace tablecloth and with her special china dishes and silverware. This must have been how my father and mother celebrated Christmas together before I interrupted their happiness, and for the first time the memory seemed to put my father in a good mood, a tender mood. After dinner, he asked about my personal life. "Have you found anyone yet to settle down with?"

I told him about Corinne. He remembered Peter Ducksworth, of course. "She comes from a good family," he said. "Strong values. That's what you need in a marriage."

I didn't tell him that Ducksworth's strong values included disinheriting his daughter if she didn't obey him.

The next day I flew to Barbados to spend Boxing Day with Corinne, intending to return to Trinidad soon after the New Year. I didn't think my father would miss me. He had long stopped caring about Boxing Day, a revered holiday tradition in the English-speaking Caribbean celebrated on the day after Christmas. Some say it began because families needed time to put away the presents they received on Christmas—box them up, so to speak. Others say it's food that is put in the boxes, leftovers from the Christmas feast. Both views may be true for both traditions still hold on the islands. Boxing Day is the day we put away the presents, gather the wrappings, and throw them in the trash; it's the day domestic helpers are given a holiday and their employers dine on leftovers. Boxing Day is also the day when families and friends visit each other.

After my mother died, my father's colleagues—the doctors and some of the nurses—would bring presents for me and gifts of food and drink for my father on Boxing Day. I think they felt sorry for him, a widower alone with a young son. I understood early that my mother's family—the ones who had not emigrated to England, a sister who never married and another who had a daughter my age—would never set foot in our house. They were embittered over my mother's untimely death, blaming my father as he, unfortunately, continued to blame himself. Eventually, though,

our visitors on Boxing Day dwindled to two or three doctors who remained loyal to my father. They came without their families and left within an hour. I cannot fault
them—my father never reciprocated; he never visited their
homes and, as far as I know, never gave them gifts. So I
sensed he wouldn't mind if I left him on Boxing Day. Indeed, he would prefer to spend his day resting in his room
free from my prying eyes and my unsuccessful attempts to
inquire diplomatically about his health. Then, too, I wanted
to leave; I was anxious to be with Corinne again.

22

S he met me at the airport where the crowd was thick with returning nationals come to spend the holidays with their relatives, and tourists here for the sun and the sea after cold, snowy days in the north. Corinne took no mind of them or the locals who gawked to see a pretty young white girl throw her arms around a brown-skinned man and kiss him fully on his lips. Her peals of laughter when I lifted her up in the air and spun her around brought smiles to their faces. "They young. They don't know," I heard one woman say. "Not yet," another responded darkly. "Give them time."

She came alone. I asked her how she was getting along with her father. "We are cordial," she said. "And he avoids being in the same room with me."

"What about Glynis and Rebecca?" I asked.

"I hardly see them. They are always doing something together out of the house and they never invite me to go with them. But Albert is nice to me. He lets me use his rented car. I think it must be because you told him about us."

In fact I had done just that. I wanted to be honest with him so I called before I left for Barbados to alert him to the change in my relationship with Corinne. He was happy for me but concerned also. "You must be more worried about her than Glynis is," he said, and pleaded with me again to stop Corinne from going to Tivoli Gardens. "For her own good, Émile, and now for yours too."

I explained that there were people at the community center who looked out for her. I told him about Alicia and the group who worked with the people there. "They are doctors and lawyers and engineers and writers. They all want to make the lives of those people better, especially the children. Anyway, Corinne wants to do this, and I love her too much to interfere."

"You're a lucky man, Émile, to have a woman like Corinne," he said.

I asked him to keep my relationship with Corinne a secret. He said he had to tell Glynis—they didn't keep secrets from each other—but understood why this would not be the right time to tell Mr. Ducksworth that his daughter was practically living with me. Mr. Ducksworth was still smarting from Corinne's refusal to obey him and it wouldn't make sense, Albert said, to put salt in a raw wound. We skirted around the issue of color and race, as though it was not the salt he spoke of.

English blood ran in Ducksworth's veins, but, as he often said to me, he was a "true Trini." He liked his rum punch, callaloo, and pelau. Hot pepper in his food. Calypso, steelpan. He lived for the sun and the sea. Some of his best friends . . . He rattled off names of Trinidadians. But there was the Miranda test. Would he object to his daughter marrying a black man, having children with a black man? As a writer from my homeland put it in her fictionalized version of a romance between Miranda and an educated Caliban: *Pass it [the test] and I believe you. Fail it and all you say about the races being equal, that character, not color, is what matters, becomes theoretical.*

Corinne didn't want to take the chance her father would fail the test and we agreed that while I was at his home, I would pretend I was no more than a good friend to her. It was the Christmas holidays; we didn't want to spoil the festivities for him.

I had rented a room at a bed-and-breakfast close to the Ducksworths. Corinne dropped me off and went back to her father's house. I would see her soon for her father was hosting his annual Boxing Day party and I was invited.

Around lunchtime Albert came with Glynis to fetch me. No sooner had I slipped in the backseat of the car than Glynis brought up my relationship with Corinne. I had made the right decision not to tell her father that Corinne and I were romantically involved, she said.

"Yes," Albert agreed, "Corinne just started university. Mr. Ducksworth may think it's too soon for her to have a boyfriend."

"Not just any boyfriend. A certain kind of boyfriend," Glynis said. *No skirting around the bush for her.* "Or haven't you noticed that Émile isn't white?" She was looking directly at him, sliding her hand down her blond ponytail. Once, when a breeze parted her hair, I saw the dark roots. She caught my eye and pushed her hair back. She was wearing a turquoise cotton dress with a low scooped neckline. The color complemented her yellow hair, pale skin, and blue eyes. "Well, haven't you, Albert?"

Albert clutched the steering wheel and kept his eyes fixed on the road ahead. "And neither am I," he replied tersely.

She laughed and swiped his arm playfully. "Oh, Albert, you're Lebanese. It's not the same. Émile is black."

Albert did not have African blood in his veins, not sub-Saharan African blood. That was the point she wanted to make. His father's skin was olive brown, and his mother, who had died some years ago, was milky white and had green eyes. I remembered how Ducksworth stared at her photograph long and hard and then remarked to Mr. Glazal about his late wife's beauty. "Such wonderful green eyes," he'd said admiringly. "Just like one of my mother's relatives in London."

I thought then of Trevor's derisive remarks at the race-tracks which I had dismissed as foolish talk. But Duck-sworth must have realized, as I did, that Douglas was not much of a catch for his daughter. Perhaps it was Douglas's blue eyes and blond hair that had softened his disappoint-ment, just as it was the lightness of Albert's mother's skin and her green eyes (I struggled to tamp down the thought raising its ugly head) that made it easier for him to accept an olive-skinned son-in-law. Then, too, Albert was rich.

Glynis turned around and faced me, her elbow resting on the back of her seat. "Anyhow, Émile," she said, laugh-ter still in her eyes, "Albert told me that you're just dating. Nothing serious."

Albert doesn't keep secrets from her, but he hasn't told her the whole truth either.

"Not yet," I said, and met her eyes. I didn't want to break the agreement I had made with Corinne, yet I wanted her to know that neither she nor her family would dictate the extent of my relationship with her sister.

She clucked her tongue and gazed out of the window, the thud of the car wheels against the potholed street mag-nifying the silence that had enveloped us. Then, suddenly, she swiveled her head back to me. "You must talk some sense into him, Émile. You must. Daddy's so stubborn."

I knew, of course, she was no longer thinking of Corinne and me.

"All that space. It's not necessary. I don't see why we must wait," she whined. "It could be for a long time. Years. A decade!"

The words had slipped off her tongue accidentally. Or so I hoped. I refused to believe she would be so callous, so ungrateful, so *unnatural* a daughter as to complain about the many years still possible for her father. *A decade.* Maybe she meant it could take that long to persuade her father to move into one of the flats she intended to build. But then Albert said: "I hope Mr. Ducksworth lives a very long time."

She slunk down in her seat, clearly mortified by Albert's rebuff. "I didn't mean . . ." she mumbled. Soon, though, as Albert shifted into a lower gear for the climb up the hill to her father's house, she sat up, revived, and peered intently up the road ahead, her face wrinkled with irritation. And there they were, the people she knew would be on the other side of the hill walking heedlessly in the middle of the road, fifteen, maybe twenty of them—men, women, and children all dressed in holiday clothes, the women in jeans and T-shirts, the girls in loose print dresses, and the men, like the boys, in brightly patterned shirts hanging over light-colored pants, caps on their heads, sandals on their feet. Glynis put her hand to her mouth and groaned. "My God, Daddy's done it again!" Albert blew his horn and they scattered to either side of the road. "Wave, Albert." She reached in her handbag and pulled out a thin, silken scarf. "You too, Émile. Wave to them. They expect you to."

Albert slowed down the car and waved. "Should have taken the hill slower," he called out to one of the men. I recognized him; he was the man from Mango Trace who had given us directions to Ducksworth's house when we got lost the first time we came there. He was holding his toddler on his hip; his other arm was around his wife's waist.

"Is you!" the man shouted back, and his wife waved. "Glad you find your way. Not to worry. Is Boxing Day. Nobody get hurt anyways." He doffed his cap in Glynis's direction. "See you in the big house, Miss Ducksworth."

The crowds thickened as we approached Ducksworth's house. Many were dressed similar to those we had passed walking freely in the road on the way up, laughing and chatting merrily. More were climbing out of minivans parked precariously on the side of the grassy embankment, and more still were coming out of cars lined up one behind the other.

"Every year it's the same thing," Glynis hissed. Albert blew his horn again and the crowd parted.

Everyone waved and shouted greetings to Glynis. "Morning, Miss Ducksworth."

Glynis's lips remained frozen in a smile as she waved her silken scarf. "Must be at least a hundred of them," she grumbled.

"They obviously like your father," Albert said, waving too.

"They're freeloaders. Moochers. Come for free food and liquor. Using the excuse that it's Boxing Day."

"That's unfair, Glynis," Albert said. "Your father invited them."

"I warned him. They roam through the house and take things." She folded her scarf and put it in her handbag. I wondered if she had brought the scarf just for this occasion, to wave to the villagers as if she were their queen on her way to her castle.

"Take things like what?" The frustration in Albert's voice was unmistakable.

Glynis rubbed his forehead and said soothingly, "If I didn't know you were a brilliant man, Albert, I'd say you were soft in the head. Don't you remember I told you about my gold bracelet?"

"You could have simply misplaced it," Albert said tersely.

Glynis kissed him on the cheek. "Oh, Albert, you are so naive."

I would not have had such patience as Albert displayed then. He simply clamped his lips together and for the rest of the way to Ducksworth's house he did not speak.

There were no cars in Ducksworth's driveway. For that Ducksworth earned Glynis's praise. "At least Daddy had the sense to tell them not to park here," she said. "But look at the crowd."

People were lined along the sidewalk; others were gathered on the front steps and on the veranda. The front door was wide open and I could see even more people in the living room.

"Drive around to the back. Quickly, quickly, before they stop to talk to us. We'll go through the kitchen." Glynis was issuing orders to Albert, her tone harsh, but she was still smiling and saying hello to the people who greeted her. "At least a hundred here," she grumbled again. "It's a good thing I locked my bedroom door."

"Oh, Glynis," Albert protested, "you can't believe . . ."

But Glynis was already out of the car, storming up the back steps. Albert followed her and I was about to do the same when Corinne appeared.

It was a relief to see her pretty, welcoming face. I had felt like a prisoner in the backseat while Glynis flung barbs and Albert did his best to dodge them. I wanted to throw my arms around Corinne and kiss her, but of course I didn't. We had agreed: not in her father's house.

"Daddy's in the kitchen," Corinne said, and grasped my hand.

"Maybe we should go there to help him. Glynis is furious," I informed her.

"We had the same crowds last Boxing Day and Glynis told Daddy to cut down the numbers, but how could he? The villagers have been coming here for years. They expect Daddy to give them a party." Her father's house, she explained, originally belonged to the owner of the sugarcane estate that once thrived in the valley. It was a tradition that every Boxing Day the boss would invite the workers to the plantation house for food and drink.

"Workers? You mean slaves."

She reddened and I was immediately remorseful for my pointed accusation.

"I didn't mean—"

She stopped me. "No. No need to apologize. It's right to remember that history. Anyhow," she said, smiling, already forgiving me for my foolish remark (foolish, because she didn't deserve to be lumped with those who pretended no such brutal history had occurred on this paradisiacal land), "Daddy likes entertaining the villagers."

Still holding my hand, she led me to the back of the house. We were halfway up the steps when we heard Glynis's voice rising to a shriek: "How could you, Daddy!"

We raced up the steps and pushed open the door. Ducksworth was sitting at the kitchen table with a drink in his hand. He looked up when we came in. His eyes were watery, whether from tears or from that glassy sheen of men who drank too much, I could not tell. Rebecca and Douglas were there too, sitting next to Albert. Glynis was standing, hovering over her father. "Here comes the disobedient daughter," she said. I held Corinne's hand tightly and took her with me to the back of the room.

For a brief second Ducksworth's eyes lingered on

Corinne and then abruptly he turned away and brought his glass to his lips, swallowing down hard and grimacing as the liquor burned his throat. "They are having a good time, Glynis," he groused, resuming his quarrel with her. "Why do they bother you so much?"

"They come just to drink punch-a-crema, eat your food, and dance."

Ponche de crème, pronounced *punch-a-crema* on the islands, is our version of eggnog that came to Trinidad with the French, who had turned the island into a slave plantation after the Spanish conquistadors, preoccupied with their search for El Dorado, had neglected it. It is made with eggs, condensed milk, evaporated milk, a smidgen of nutmeg and lime zest, Angostura bitters, and rum—lots of rum. But Ducksworth was not drinking punch-a-crema. I could tell from the brown color of the liquid in his glass he was having his rum straight.

"Just once a year," he said, and drained his glass. "Can't you be more understanding? I can do this once a year. They look forward to coming here on Boxing Day."

"They trample all over the house. They go in my things."

"So lock up your things, Glynis," Ducksworth said grumpily.

"Mummy's things too."

"Then lock the bedroom door."

"They dirty the house," Glynis declared, and sniffed as if an unpleasant odor had wafted across the room.

"The maid will clean the house afterward."

"You'll have to pay the maid for extra hours."

"I can pay."

Glynis was getting flustered by Ducksworth's patronizing demeanor. "You promised. You gave me your word," she said, hoping finally to disarm him with an appeal to his sense of fair play, an appeal he had denied Corinne. "You promised you'll have half as many this year."

"And what would that number be?"

"Fifty. Fifty is more than enough."

Rebecca was biting her nails, shifting her eyes from her sister to her father. Ducksworth turned to her. "And what do you say, Rebecca? What should I do? How many should I invite?"

Rebecca glanced furtively at her sister. Glynis held her eyes and nodded encouragingly. Rebecca took a deep breath, released it, and said forcefully, "Glynis is right. They dirty the house. And . . . and . . . they break the glasses," she added, tripping over her words.

"Break the glasses? Is that all you're worried about?" Ducksworth slapped his thighs and roared with laughter. "I can buy new glasses, Rebecca. Glasses cost next to nothing." He wiped his eyes. "You and your sister worry too much. I can easily replace anything that breaks."

"Not Mummy's good china." Glynis refilled his glass from the bottle of rum on the table. "And what if your silverware is stolen?"

"Your mother's good china and silverware are safely locked up in the credenza," Ducksworth said. "Here. I have the key." He pulled out a ring of keys from his pocket and rattled it in front of her.

Glynis was unmoved. She pushed away the keys and confronted him again. "And your nice manicured lawn? What about the lawn you are so proud of? Before the day is done, they'll park their cars on it. It'll cost you a pretty penny to repair the grass. Hundreds of dollars. All those feet, trampling up and down."

Ducksworth swirled his drink, the ice cubes bouncing merrily against the sides of his glass. "So tell me, Rebecca.

How many say you? Is fifty enough?" He had stopped laughing and was peering intently at her with seemingly genuine interest in her answer.

Rebecca looked over her shoulder, assuming, I thought, that Douglas would come to her aid, but he just shook his head and turned away. I wasn't surprised. I had heard him snicker when Ducksworth laughed.

Her father had embarrassed her. *Glasses! How stupid to be complaining about broken glasses!* Rebecca pressed her fingers against her mouth and stilled the slight tremor making its way across her lips. I was certain she was about to cry, but she fooled me. "A quarter of the people you had last year," she said, her voice low but gathering strength. "Twenty-five," she added loudly. "That'll be plenty."

"Twenty-five?" Ducksworth squinted his eyes. "Your sister was more generous. She told me fifty."

"Twenty-five," Rebecca repeated, and her eyes skidded once more over to Glynis. She looked positively elated when Glynis smiled approvingly.

"Then, by God," Ducksworth banged his glass on the table, "I'll take Glynis's fifty. Fifty is twice as many as twenty-five. I'll tell the villagers fifty. I'll make a sign and put it at the entrance of the driveway. *Fifty maximum.* I'll hire a guard to count."

"Don't be silly, Daddy." Glynis took the glass out of his hand.

Ducksworth grabbed it back. "But we'll need a guard, Glynis," he said plaintively. An act, a pretense. He was having fun at their expense, and yet I sensed beneath the grin, in the twitching of his lower lip, apprehension. *Do they mean to control the way he lives his life? Will they really try to put him out of his house?*

"A guard to count! I've never heard anything more foolish," Glynis spat out angrily.

"How else will we make sure no more than fifty can come? And children?" Ducksworth shook his glass at her. "What about children? Do your fifty include the children?"

"Albert!" Glynis turned to her fiancé. "Do you hear him? Talk reason to him."

"I cannot be so partial."

"What does that mean?" she snapped.

"You are my fiancée but this is his home. He's your father."

"You take your kindness too far, Albert. Don't you see Daddy's making a fool of me? A guard! What does he need a security guard for?"

"To make sure there are no more than fifty," Ducksworth said, his tone maddeningly condescending.

"Then make it twenty-five. No . . . ten. No . . . five!" Glynis shot back.

Emboldened, Rebecca made a counteroffer: "One. That's enough."

"One?" Ducksworth wrinkled his brow.

Glynis and Rebecca exchanged glances. "Invite one family," Rebecca said, smirking.

"You are getting old, Daddy," Glynis crooned, and poured more rum in his glass. "You can't continue like this. One family. I think the villagers would understand."

"Wise to stay out of this, Corinne." For the first time since he looked up when we entered the kitchen, Ducksworth acknowledged her presence. "But I want to hear your opinion. Come closer." He beckoned her, his fingers wavering as if they were weightless as feathers blowing in a breeze. "I want to know what you think. Should I have fifty next year, or twenty-five? Or just one family as your big sisters now advise me?"

Corinne removed her hand from mine and stepped

forward tentatively. "It's your house, Daddy," she murmured. "Indeed."

"So you should invite as many people as you want."

Ducksworth's eyes shot open wide and something like surprise mingled with regret crossed his face. He had told her that her sisters could teach her about love, about caring for his happiness, for the things that were important to him, and now her sisters were telling him he should have one family over, and the daughter he had cast out was saying as many as he wanted. He seemed about to reach for Corinne's hand but suddenly a loud cheer went up from the living room, followed by hoots and wild laughter, and in the background the strains of the cuatro and the maracas. He withdrew his hand, swallowed the rest of his drink, slammed the glass on the table, and bolted out of his chair. "They're here! They're here!" he shouted out. And to the astonishment of us all, particularly me (for I was sure he was about to embrace Corinne and put an end to his foolish misunderstanding of her love for him), he rushed through the swinging kitchen doors into the living room, leaving the rest of us behind, the question unresolved as to whether or not he would do as his two older daughters demanded: entertain just one family the next Boxing Day.

23

Parang. It had come to Trinidad from Venezuela with the coco paynols, the farm workers who rowed their pirogues across the Gulf of Paria—the narrow strip of water, seven miles wide, that separated the two mainlands—in search of work on the cocoa plantations in the north of Trinidad. I recognized the peculiar strumming of the cuatro, the four-string guitar, and the swizzle-swizzle sounds of the maracas, or the chac-chac as we called it. I looked out of the kitchen window. The paranderos, the singers, were coming up the driveway; apparently the instrumentalists had already made their way into the house. I hadn't expected to hear parang in Barbados—it was the music we played in Trinidad at Christmastime—but Ducksworth was Trinidadian and he would want parang at his Boxing Day party.

In the past the singers and the instrumentalists were mostly men, their brown leather faces and dark flashing eyes bearing their history of Spanish conquest, the near-genocide of the Amerindians, the brutal enslavement of Africans. Lately, though, more and more women were joining the parang band, mostly as the singers, the men playing the cuatro, the maracas, and the tambourine. And there were more women than men among this group of paranderos heading for Ducksworth's front door. They were dressed in traditional costumes: Red tops, the men's shirts loose, the women's tight, made out of some kind of Lycra material hugging their breasts. The men wore black pants and the women flowered skirts fitted at the hips and flaring out below to their ankles, but only the women had on the wide-brimmed straw sombreros. The men, seemingly as a nod to the modern times, wore baseball caps.

"*Drink a rum and a punch-a-crema, drink a rum* . . ." We could hear Ducksworth belting out the words.

Glynis clutched Albert's arm. "Daddy! It's Daddy!" She pulled Albert with her to the living room. Corinne and I went quickly behind them. "Don't let him do this!" Glynis was rasping hoarsely in Albert's ear.

She was already too late. The crowd had parted in the corridor that led from the front door to the deck at the back of the house, and there, in the middle, flanked on both sides by cheering villagers, was Ducksworth.

I had seen Ducksworth besotted with rum, red-faced, eyes glazed, his hair in disarray, but never had I seen him so unrestrained. He was holding a large red bandanna between his hands, stretched high above his head, and was dancing a wild, unbridled dance, his thin legs like props carrying the weight of his broad torso. He stomped his feet up and down on the floor, hips jerking, the bandanna swinging from side to side to the beat of the music from the parang band that was now installed on the deck. He had undone all the buttons of his shirt, and his shorts had fallen below his belly. Thin tendrils of graying hair, some straight, some curled, were clustered in wet clumps beneath his collarbone, more stuck across his chest and over the mound of his large belly.

"Look at him!" Corinne clapped her hands and led me to an empty spot in a corner near the deck. "Look how happy he is. All year he waits for Boxing Day, for this, to dance with the parang band." And I had to admit that

Ducksworth looked deliriously happy, crazed but happy, a lopsided grin across his lips. His thinning hair was stuck to his forehead, soaked with perspiration, but he was still stomping wildly, showing no sign of slowing down.

Glynis, with Albert in tow, approached us. "You put him up to this," she said, scowling at Corinne. She tugged Albert's shirt and pushed him forward. "Stop him, Albert. She wants this. Don't let Daddy make a fool of himself in front of all these people."

The paranderos, the singers, had arrived. Ducksworth rushed out to the veranda to welcome them, his arms open wide, the grin on his lips blossoming to childlike laughter. He embraced the leader, wrapping his arms tightly around the man's chest and kissing him on both cheeks. He did the same to each of the women paranderos. They giggled, returned his kisses, and told him sweet lies: "You looking better every year, Mr. Ducksworth." "You didn't age a day from last year, Mr. Ducksworth." "You too handsome, Mr. Ducksworth."

The paranderos followed Ducksworth into the living room and immediately began singing: "*Drink a rum and a punch-a-crema, drink a rum, Mama, drink if you drinking . . .*" Soon the house was vibrating with the rhythms of parang.

Glynis let go of Albert's shirt and ran to her father. "Daddy! Stop this, now! You're making a fool of yourself."

Ducksworth pushed her away with the knot of his elbow. "*Drink a rum and a punch-a-crema, drink a rum, let we fête if we fêteing . . .*" He was singing off-key, but the paranderos didn't seem to mind. Nobody did.

Glynis stumbled back, tried to regain her footing, and stumbled once more. "People are laughing at you!" she yelled when she steadied herself.

Ducksworth ignored her and began dancing again, his

movements wilder now, twisting his body and flinging his arms in the air. Once more Glynis tried to stop him, but as Ducksworth attempted to jab her again with his elbow, she retreated, glancing sullenly back at him over her shoulder, her pale face turning redder with frustration. "Laughing at you, Daddy!" she was muttering when she reached the spot where Albert was standing.

She demanded that Albert take her father off the floor. Albert did not move, not one inch. He crossed his arms over his chest and turned away from her. Perhaps, like me, he saw no harm in Ducksworth enjoying himself, but perhaps he could no longer tolerate Glynis barking orders at him. He was not soft in the head, as Glynis seemed to imply, but he was a gentle man, a kind man who would neither cause harm nor be the cause of harm to anyone.

Unable to get Albert to obey her, Glynis sent a parting shot at her father: "You're making a spectacle of yourself, Daddy! Have you lost your mind? You're dancing like a madman. People are laughing at you."

But no one was laughing at Ducksworth. Certainly not the people from the village who had been talking about what a nice man Mr. Ducksworth was. "Is not too many of them have us in dere big house. And he bring the parang band too! Mr. Ducksworth too nice!" They swayed to the music and clapped their hands, Corinne with them. One of them, a man of about Ducksworth's age, short and wiry, graying at the temples, bald in the middle of his head, broke loose from the clutch of villagers and came forward, his dark brown face glistening, red T-shirt worn for the Christmas season soaked at the neckline, his black pants rolled up at the bottom, flip-flops on his feet. He danced toward Ducksworth and reached for one end of his bandanna. Ducksworth released it to him and now the two of

them were dancing together, the bandanna stretched between them high in the air. They waved it, stomped their
feet, shook their hips, their voices raised in raucous delight, their necks straining as they sang with the paranderos.

Ducksworth and the man were still singing and dancing, sweat pouring down the sides of their faces, when a
woman called out from the sidelines: "So what, Bob, is
man you like?" Bob dropped his end of the bandanna and
spun around. The woman flew into his arms. Suddenly
Ducksworth found himself alone. For an instant he lost his
footing. He swayed to one side and then the other, turned
full circle, stopped and steadied himself, then wiped his
brow with the bandanna. A sort of calm seemed to come
over him and a beatific smile spread across his lips. He
was looking in Corinne's direction, pointing his finger
at her.

"Oh no!" I heard Glynis gasp. But Ducksworth was already stepping toward Corinne, who was no longer clap-
ping or smiling or shaking her head to the music. She turned
toward me, a question unspoken in her open mouth. *What
should I do?* I didn't have the chance to answer; Ducksworth
was standing in front of her.

"My baby daughter," he murmured softly.

A groan like the cry of a wounded animal broke from
Glynis's throat. She flattened her hand on Albert's back
and pushed him forward. "Don't let Daddy do this," she
urged him frantically. Without a word, Albert loosened
her fingers from his back and moved away.

"Dance with your father?" Ducksworth stretched out
his hand to Corinne. She looked over to me again, the same
question in her eyes, but this time she didn't seem to need
my answer. She took her father's hand and Ducksworth
slid his palm along hers until only the tops of their fingers

touched. And they danced and danced, arms extended, bodies far apart but fingers intertwined.

The parang players were delighted. They quickened the rhythm of the cuatro, the beat of the tambourine. The chac-chac men turned and twirled the maracas; the singers flounced their skirts and shook their hips. *Sa, sa, yeh . . .*

The people from the village, sated from food and drink, yelled out encouragement. "Dance your dance, white man! Shake those white hips! You must have black blood in you, Mr. Ducksworth!" They were trying to make him feel special, of course. Ducksworth was no dancer—his movements were sometimes out of sync with the music—but they loved that he reveled in the parang, that he let his two thin legs sway and swivel his body, that he waved the bandanna he held in his other hand. Mostly, though, their eyes were glued to Corinne. A true Caribbean girl, Corinne danced with her hips more than with her feet, her whole body responding beat for beat to the rhythm of the cuatro. "And she pretty for so," the women whispered to each other.

Rebecca was standing close to her husband. She was grinning, a sort of vacuous grin, the corners of her mouth twitching nervously. Glynis grabbed her hand. I could not hear what they were saying to each other. Whatever it was, Rebecca was vehemently objecting, and Douglas, seeming to determine it was unwise to take sides in what was obviously a family dispute, or perhaps yielding to Glynis—for that was how it seemed to me when he shook his head disapprovingly at Rebecca—walked toward the bar to refresh his drink. The tug-of-war between the two sisters went on for a few seconds and then Glynis, using the full force of her strength this time, drew Rebecca to her so that their faces were almost touching, and pointed to their father who had now clasped Corinne's hand in his and was twirling her around faster and faster.

Corinne seemed nervous, unsure of how to react. I made a step toward her but she waved me away. The man with the cuatro began strumming the strings faster; the tambourine man and the chac-chac man quickened their beat. If Corinne wanted to, she could let go of her father's hand. She was younger and stronger. But if she let go of his hand, Ducksworth might stumble and fall. She seemed to realize that and held on to him even more tightly.

Glynis finally managed to push Rebecca out from the huddle of the cheering villagers, almost causing her to careen into her father. "Daddy!" Rebecca grasped Ducksworth's arm and tried to separate him from Corinne. Ducksworth shoved her away. "Daddy!" Rebecca shouted out loudly. Glynis had apparently worked her up and it seemed to me she wanted to prove to her older sister she was not a weakling; she was not afraid of her father. "Daddy, what are you doing?"

The paranderos looked at each other, puzzled by this strange scene in front of them: one Ducksworth daughter pulling her father away from another Ducksworth daughter. They didn't know how to respond to their host's increasingly bizarre movements. He was spinning one daughter like a top and shoving away another. The men playing the cuatro slowed down, the voices of the singers trailed, the chac-chac men held their maracas still. Suddenly the room was silent, the stillness broken with the soft rhythmic beat of the waves unfurling against the shore beneath us.

"What are you doing?" Rebecca's question sliced through the room like the blade of a machete.

"Doing? Doing?" Ducksworth looked lost, confused.

"Doing with *her*!" Rebecca pointed to Corinne.

"Her?"

"Yes, *her*. Corinne. What were you doing with her?"

"Corinne, my daughter," Ducksworth murmured softly. He was still holding Corinne's hand.

"Your disobedient daughter," Rebecca retorted.

"Disobedient daughter?"

"Yes. She. Corinne."

Ducksworth was squinting now, turning his head from Corinne to Rebecca and back again.

"Don't you remember? The photograph. Tivoli Gardens."

"Tivoli Gardens?" Ducksworth frowned and removed his hand from Corinne's.

"After all you did for her."

"My beloved daughter?"

It seemed to me Ducksworth's question was a cry of disbelief. *Not his beloved daughter; she would never hurt him.* But Glynis, who had pushed Rebecca into leading the attack, was not about to take the chance that Ducksworth would doubt Rebecca, that he would change his mind and forgive Corinne. The house, the land, the five-star restaurant, all her dreams seemed to be riding on the memory Rebecca had been trying to revive. She came close to her father and wrapped her fingers around his wrist. "She chose them over you," she sang into his ear. "You told her not to go and she went."

"Went?"

"To that Rastaman's house. She refused to do what you asked her to do."

"Refused?" Ducksworth looked bewildered. "You refused, Corinne?"

Glynis chimed in before Corinne could answer: "She disobeyed you."

"Yes, she disobeyed you," Rebecca echoed her sister.

A glimmer of light flickered in Ducksworth's eyes. "Wouldn't stop going," he murmured unsteadily.

"*Didn't* stop going," Glynis said forcefully.

The glimmer of light in Ducksworth's eyes grew brighter, his memory gradually returning. "Refused to obey . . ."

"Yes. And she still goes there now."

I felt the hair on the back of my neck stand up as Glynis's voice, oily and seductive, slid through the portals of her father's brain, fueling his memory.

"Disobedient daughter. Refused . . ." Ducksworth placed his hand on his chest and grimaced as if a sharp pain had shot through his heart.

"Ungrateful daughter," Glynis rejoined. "After all you gave her." She would not spare him. "And this is how she repaid you. With ingratitude."

"After all I . . . She . . . she . . ." Ducksworth was breathing heavily, both hands clasped over his chest on the left side, on the side where I imagined his heart was beating rapidly. He shook his finger at Corinne. "You! You wouldn't listen. Wouldn't obey!"

Corinne backed away. Her eyes were red, tears dripping down into her mouth.

"Come," Glynis cooed and held her father's hand firmly. "Come sit with us on the deck."

"Just one thing I asked of you. One thing." Ducksworth had not taken his eyes away from Corinne. "After all these years of giving and giving. *Loving.*"

"Don't, Daddy. I love—"

"Half! That's what you said."

"I've always loved you."

"Leave her!" Glynis's voice rose above Corinne's desperate plea. "She's not worth your love." And still mumbling, "Disobedient daughter . . . ungrateful daughter . . .

half," Ducksworth let Glynis lead him to the deck and ease him into his favorite chair near the railing overlooking the astonishing sea.

Tears were rolling in long lines down Corinne's cheeks. I went to her and put my arm around her. I didn't care who saw us, or what they thought. I brought her with me to the back of the house, to the maid's quarter. The maid had the day off so I knew the room would be empty.

Half an hour later, Albert knocked on the door. He had come to tell me that the paranderos had left and so had the villagers. Douglas and Rebecca had gone home too, and after he helped Glynis clean up the place, he'd be going back to his hotel. "It would be best," he said, "to take Corinne for a drive until all this blows over."

Then, just seconds after we left the house, we heard a bloodcurdling scream.

24

To this day I do not know who was to blame, if anyone at all. Before the police inspector could ask, Glynis said, her lips trembling in grief or fear—it was difficult to tell which: "It was Bob. Bob threw my father over the railing."

She had not seen Bob do this. In fact, she was not even on the deck at the time Ducksworth was supposedly thrown over the railing. Her father was hungry and she had gone to the kitchen to get something for him to eat, leaving Bob with him on the deck. She was about to warm up a pastelle when she heard Bob's footsteps along the corridor. He was walking fast, she said, as if he were in a hurry. Like he was running away from something. She popped her head out of the kitchen and called out to him. He did not answer her. Ten minutes later, she went back to the deck with the pastelle for her father. He wasn't there. Then she saw him and she screamed.

"And where was Mr. Glazal at this time?" the inspector asked.

"My fiancé was in the kitchen helping me clean up. Boxing Day. We had a lot of dishes to wash."

"Too many." Albert came forward. "I didn't . . ." He glanced at Glynis. "We didn't want to leave all of them for the maid."

"And did you hear anything, Mr. Glazal?"

"I heard when my fiancée screamed. I thought she was

hurt. I ran out to help her." Albert put his arm around Glynis.

"It was Bob. I know it was Bob." Glynis drew closer to Albert.

But what would be Bob's motive? Glynis had no answer to that question. Then too Corinne and I had seen Bob at the bottom of the driveway when we were walking toward the car. He was with the woman he had been dancing with, the woman who had pulled him away from Ducksworth. For a poor black man who had supposedly thrown a rich white man over the railing of his deck, Bob seemed incredibly relaxed and unconcerned. He was jostling with the woman playfully, laughing and whispering in her ear when we heard Glynis scream. He let go of her immediately and rushed up to the house. A man who had just committed murder would not likely rush to the scene of the crime; he would run away as fast as he could.

The sun had not yet descended so there was still some light, enough for us to see Ducksworth lying in a pool of blood between lumps of rocks at the bottom of the slope that dropped precipitously from the deck. Branches, lopped off the trees when he crashed into them, lay crisscrossed over his body, the leaves scattered on his broad torso and thin legs. I could tell immediately from the way his body was folded up like a broken doll—his head twisted to one side, one leg bent at the knee and lying lifeless over the thigh of his other leg which had long, purplish gashes across it—that he was dead. The blood that had oozed from his mouth and nose had begun to congeal and form a dark trail in the dirt.

Bob had been ordered by Glynis to sit in a corner of the deck. Over and over he repeated that he had nothing to do with Mr. Ducksworth falling over the railing. He wasn't there. Mr. Ducksworth was alive and breathing and sitting in his deck chair the last time he saw him. He didn't hear Miss Glynis call out his name when he was leaving. Yes, maybe he was in a hurry, but his girlfriend was waiting for him. She was still mad that his first dance was with Mr. Ducksworth instead of with her, and she would be madder if he stayed too long talking to Mr. Ducksworth.

A few minutes later his girlfriend came up to the house and she corroborated his story. "Is true what he say." She put her arms around him protectively. "He was with me all that time."

Douglas and Rebecca arrived soon after the police inspector. "Don't you move!" Douglas yelled at poor Bob who was cowering in the corner, whimpering and pleading with anyone who would listen that "swear to God" he never touched Mr. Ducksworth.

"Bob did it," Glynis repeated. "He's lying."

Corinne pressed her face into my chest. "Why would she say that?" she murmured. "She has no proof."

"She's confused," I said. "The shock. She'll change her story when her head clears."

But would she? I couldn't be certain. By Bob's account, Ducksworth was alive when he left the house. It would be her word against his. Would I be called as a witness to say I had seen Bob at the bottom of the hill talking to his girlfriend? Would the police inspector take my word against Glynis's?

The police inspector was listening carefully to Glynis, scribbling down notes on his notepad. He asked Bob to repeat his statement and showed no emotion when what Bob said contradicted Glynis's accusation. Then, with his assistant at his side, the inspector went to the spot on the deck where Ducksworth had tumbled to his death. The railing was broken, twisted forward over the slope that ran down to the sea. The inspector knelt down, examined it, got up, passed his hand over the top of the railing, frowned, and said something to his assistant we could not hear. They talked for a while, their voices low, and then the inspector turned to Glynis. "Mr. Ducksworth was a big man, yes?"

"Strong," she said, blowing her nose in the tissue Albert had given her.

"But big too?"

"I was always telling him he needed to lose weight," Rebecca offered. She was leaning against Douglas who had his arm around her waist.

"Oh, Rebecca, you say such stupid things. Why would you say that at a time like this when poor Daddy . . ." Glynis dissolved into another burst of tears. Albert hugged her closely to his chest and stroked her hair.

"It explains things," the police inspector said.

"What things?" Glynis removed Albert's hand from her hair.

"Was Mr. Ducksworth drinking?"

"It was Boxing Day, inspector!" Douglas stepped forward.

"How many drinks did he have?"

"Everybody was drinking," Glynis said.

"But how many drinks did Mr. Ducksworth have?"

"Punch-a-crema and rum punch," Glynis said. "Right, Rebecca?"

But I had not seen Ducksworth drinking punch-a-crema. The liquid in his glass was brown; it was rum.

The inspector turned to his assistant, who was busy taking down notes. "Got that. Punch-a-crema and rum punch."

"Everybody drinks punch-a-crema and rum punch on Boxing Day," Rebecca said.

"And the number of drinks?"

"We didn't count," Glynis said.

"Four glasses of rum. Straight, no chaser." All eyes were fixed on Corinne when she spoke. I had managed to persuade her to move away from the edge of the deck where her father lay partially buried under the branches and leaves on the rocks below, but she was still staring in that direction, her eyes dull, her hands icy cold.

"How many did you say, Miss Ducksworth?" the inspector pressed her.

Corinne repeated the number.

"She's lying!" Glynis shouted.

The police inspector approached Corinne. "You're certain of that, miss?"

"I counted," she said.

"So he was drunk?"

"I couldn't stop him from drinking," Corinne said softly. "Glynis would not have let me. She served him."

"She got him all riled up," Glynis spat out. "Dancing with him. She knew he was angry with her. She was taunting him."

"Now, now, Glynis." Albert pulled her more closely toward him. "Don't say things you don't mean."

"This milky kindness of yours, Albert . . ." Glynis's eyes flashed angrily.

"She's had a shock, inspector," Albert said. "You understand that, don't you? She doesn't mean what she's saying. Mr. Ducksworth—"

"Look, I understand these things," the inspector interrupted. "You don't have to say more. Nobody here to blame. We just need to get all the details. My assistant and I examined the railing. Just a cursory look for the time being, but I think when the engineers come they will agree with our findings."

"Findings? What findings?" Glynis disentangled herself from Albert's arms.

"That railing was painted not too long ago, not so?" the inspector asked.

"Daddy painted it a few months ago," Rebecca said.

"He covered up where it was split," the inspector said. "Come, take a look."

I went with them to the edge of the deck. Even to the unprofessional eye it was obvious that the wood on the top beam of the railing had rotted and split. At the place where Ducksworth had apparently fallen, the nails that had held the broken pieces together were loose and rusty. It was the very spot where I had been about to lean over that first day I came to Ducksworth's house and he cautioned me to step back. He said he had just had the railing repaired and painted.

"Mr. Ducksworth leaned too far over the railing," the police inspector said. "And if he was drunk, it seems he was unable to gauge when the wood cracked under his weight. It gave way and he tumbled down. It was an accident."

Corinne didn't want to stay in the house, not that night, so after the coroner had taken Peter Ducksworth's body to the mortuary, she went with me when I left for the B&B where I was staying. I had just driven to the bottom of the driveway when we saw Bob sitting alone at the side of the road, his head bent over his arms. I pulled over and got out of the car. Bob stood up and his legs wobbled under him. I thought he was about to fall so I hurried over and placed my hand firmly on his arm and steadied him.

"I didn't do it, Mr. Baxter. I didn't. I swear," he said, shaking his head vigorously.

"Not to worry. It's all settled and done. The police inspector believes it was an accident."

He passed his hand across his forehead. "Miss Glynis . . ."

"What about Miss Glynis?" Corinne had stepped out of the car and was standing next to me.

Bob glanced nervously from her to me. "Tell her," I said.

With his eyes still on me, he mumbled, "Is not right she blame me."

"You know why she blamed you, Bob?" Corinne asked quietly. "Anything you want to tell us? Miss Glynis said she was in the kitchen and left you with my father."

"That was before," Bob said.

"Before what?"

"Before she start quarreling with him. I don't tell the police inspector about the quarrel. Is better I only tell him I rushing to see my Esther."

"But there was a quarrel. Right, Bob?" I asked him.

"You get in trouble if you tell on white people," he said. He glanced apprehensively at Corinne.

"Don't worry," she said, "I won't cause you any trouble. But I want to know what my sister said to my father."

Bob lowered his eyes and circled the dirt at his feet with the tip of his shoe.

"It's okay. You can tell her," I said. "She's a friend. My friend."

Bob kept his eyes focused on the ground, digging his feet deeper in the dirt.

"It's okay," I repeated. "You can trust her."

He looked up at me. "She speaking low-low," he said.

"Low?"

"So nobody hear her. But I hear her."

"And what did you hear?"

"I hear her when she come close to Mr. Ducksworth face and tell him he stubborn. She call him a stubborn old man. Mr. Ducksworth look sad and he say he like his house. He want to stay here. She say something about nice flats and he say his house nicer. He don't want to leave. Then she talk about steps. He say he don't want steps. He say he have friends. They take him in a boat to the beach whenever he ask them. She get vex, real vex. She say he always holding her back. Everything she want to do, he say no, but everything Miss Corinne say she want to do, he say yes."

Corinne put a fist to her mouth and stifled a cry.

"Sorry. Sorry, miss." Bob looked helplessly across to me, hoping, I supposed, I could do something to stop the tears beginning to well in Corinne's eyes.

"It's all right, Bob. It's all right." Corinne drew in her breath and pushed back her tears. "I'm glad you told me this."

"Is true, miss," he offered eagerly. "I see how he dance with you. He did love you a lot, miss."

"And what happened next?" Corinne asked him gently.

"She stop quarreling and ask Mr. Ducksworth if he hungry. He say yes. And when she go to the kitchen I take my chance and run out the house. Like I say, I don't want to be there when white people quarrel. I don't mean you, miss. You are a nice white lady. Mr. Ducksworth, God rest his soul, was a nice white man. I sorry to see him go like that."

25

At the funeral I couldn't help thinking how every-thing had tied up nicely and neatly for Glynis. Ducksworth had changed his will and now she and Rebecca were owners of the big house and the land around it. There was no further obstacle preventing them from building the resort of their dreams with a five-star restaurant between their two strips of land. I could not stop the questions nagging at me, though. Why was Glynis so quick to place the blame on poor Bob? She knew about the crack in the railing. But didn't she say it had been re-paired? I had moved away because Duckworth had warned me the paint was still wet, not because I didn't believe her.

Was it guilt then that made Glynis point her finger at Bob? It could not be denied that she had led her father to a chair that was close to the spot where the railing was weak.

And I couldn't forget the argument earlier that day. It was their future property she and Rebecca wanted to pro-tect when they tried to force Ducksworth to decrease the number of villagers at his annual Boxing Day party. The villagers would destroy the house, trample through their rooms, steal their things, they claimed. A gold bracelet had been stolen the previous year. And Ducksworth's manicured lawn? He'd have to reseed it.

One family. That was all they would allow their father. When they inherited his house they wanted its condition pristine, unsullied by dirt clumped into the bottoms of shoes trampling through the rooms.

Ingratitude, thou marble-hearted fiend.

Glynis had accused Corinne of ingratitude, but it was she and Rebecca who were ungrateful. I had not experienced the warmth of a parent's love when I was a child, but my father had fed me, clothed me, sheltered me, educated me, and for this consideration I was grateful. Ducksworth had done infinitely more for his three daughters. Even if it was true he loved Corinne more than her sisters, he didn't deserve their ingratitude.

The night Ducksworth revealed his decision to distribute his property among his daughters he had stunned us when he shouted out that he was not a doddering old man. He was virile, he said. Was he thinking of Shakespeare's old king, the one in the play I had studied at university? I had suggested as much to Albert.

Lear's two older daughters put him out of his castle. He would have died in the woods, bereft of shelter and food, if Edgar hadn't helped him. One daughter poisoned another in a jealous rage over her lover's attention to her sister, but not before both daughters had gone to war against their youngest sister. The folly of old age, hubris, betrayal, abuse of an elderly father, adultery, madness, torture, war, murder, all that and more in Shakespeare's play; and in the end, the dead—Lear and his three daughters—the stage enshrouded in grief, weighted with their bodies.

Glynis was self-centered, but not evil. She would not have pushed her father to his death on the rocks below, but she had quarreled with him; she had left him alone on the deck, drunk, agitated. Ten minutes is a long time. That was the length of time she admitted she was in the kitchen after she had seen Bob running out of the house. A man in her father's state would not be in full possession of his limbs, even less his reason.

What if he had got sick from all that rum he consumed? What if his judgment were so impaired, his brain so cloudy, all memory of the recent repairs on the railings so erased, he had leaned over too far and his enormous torso, like a ballast, had dragged him down? She could be accused of negligence, disregard for her father's welfare, but not patricide.

Or what if Ducksworth had had a heart attack? I had seen him clasp his hand to his chest, his face contorted in pain when Glynis forced him to look back to that dark place he could not forget. His beloved Corinne had disobeyed him; the daughter who was his joy would give him only half her love. The viselike grip of a heart attack would have disoriented him, made him lose control of his limbs.

Still, Glynis could not be blamed because her father's heart was weak. Yet she had blamed Bob, and now that Bob was in the clear, she had her daggers aimed at Corinne. It was Corinne who had so upset her father that he got sick to the stomach and, leaning too far over the railing to vomit his insides, fell to his death. That was her current version of what had occurred.

In the church, at the funeral Mass, Glynis and Rebecca sat in the front pew with Douglas and his parents; Corinne, Albert, and I took the pew behind them. Mr. Glazal, who had come as soon as he heard the news, was puzzled by this seating arrangement. He thought the sisters, all of them Ducksworth's daughters, should sit together.

Albert made up an excuse that seemed to placate him. He said that the daughters were grieving, each in her own way. Rebecca wanted to be next to her husband and Glynis was afraid that Corinne, who had not stopped crying, could cause her to break down too. She was the eldest and had to give the eulogy. She needed to keep a steady voice, so she sat apart from Corinne. And it was good that she did, though it was not Corinne's weeping but an outburst from Rebecca that caused her to break down.

Glynis was recounting a picnic at the beach that could have ended tragically. She had swum out too far in the sea and was drowning. Rebecca, who had seen her fighting for her life, called out to their father. Mr. Ducksworth was sitting on a beach chair reading his newspaper. He was fully dressed: long pants, shirt, loosened tie, socks, shoes. That morning he had gone to town to attend to some official business and had promised his daughters to take them to the beach after lunch. He was late and the girls were impatient when he finally arrived home, so he didn't stop to change his clothes and drove them to their favorite beach dressed as he was.

Glynis recalled that when a gigantic wave washed over her, she was certain she had reached the end, and then she felt her father's arms lifting her up. "He could have drowned too," she said. "His clothes were weighing him down. I think he still had on his shoes when he rescued me." Rebecca began to cry, loud sobs that so affected the mourners in the church that I saw several women reach for their handkerchiefs. Glynis began sobbing loudly too. All Ducksworth's daughters were wreathed in grief, tears pooling in translucent beads on their chins.

At the luncheon at the house after the funeral they all seemed calmer, but Mr. Glazal continued to detect a level of tension in the room. He was a perceptive man and he confided in me that he had not missed the angry glances Glynis had directed at Corinne. Twice he had seen Rebecca turn her back on Corinne. Something had happened, he said. What was it? He pressed me to tell him. Were they angry because Corinne now owned the house, the bigger part of their father's estate? he asked.

It was obvious Albert hadn't told him that Ducksworth had changed his will, but it was not my place to inform him.

But why hadn't Albert told him? It seemed to me that if Mr. Glazal was going to be a major investor in the resort, he should be pleased to know that the land connecting the two fingers jutting into the sea would be shared between the two sisters, one of whom would soon be married to his son. Did Albert's reluctance to tell his father the "good news" have anything to do with that long silence that followed my question when I asked whether his father would ever disavow him? He was certain, as I was, that his father would never do that, would never disinherit him, no matter the reason. Did he fear that his father would sense there was something wrong, if not downright unnatural, about a father leaving his youngest daughter homeless, to fend for herself in a male-dominated world? Something worrisome, underhanded even, about Glynis and Rebecca being the sole beneficiaries of their father's property?

I was fishing around in my head for an answer to give him that was not a lie, and yet would not betray my friend, when Glynis joined us and relieved me of this burden. After some gestures of grief—and I admit to being cynical, for it seemed to me that it was the prospect of owning her father's house that made her voice resonate with excitement even as she was wiping away her tears—Glynis declared: "Poor Daddy. He loved that view from his deck so much. Now he'll never see it again."

"Well," Mr. Glazal said sympathetically, "one continues to live through one's children. Mr. Ducksworth may not be here in body, but he's here in spirit. Every time Corinne sits on the deck and looks out at that wondrous view of the sky and the sea, your father will be looking at it too."

"Oh, you don't know? Albert didn't tell you?" Glynis made a show of drying her eyes with her handkerchief. "It won't be Corinne looking out at that view. It will be Albert and me." And she gave Mr. Glazal her version of what had transpired between Mr. Ducksworth and Corinne, the same version she had given to Albert: Corinne had told her father she didn't love him.

Mr. Glazal was flabbergasted and fell into a fit of coughing. Luckily, one of the waiters Glynis had hired was passing by and gave him a glass of water, which he drank in three swift gulps.

"The air-conditioning in planes always affects my sinuses," Glynis said, seeming to make no connection between his sudden gasps for air and the story she was relating to him. And motioning to the waiter to give Mr. Glazal another glass of water, she continued to prattle on: "So you see, Mr. Glazal, what's mine will soon be Albert's as well."

Mr. Glazal pulled me aside before he left for the airport, and with the same look of bewilderment in his eyes as when Glynis told him that Ducksworth had disinherited his youngest daughter, he asked: "So what's going to happen to Corinne now? Where will she live, the poor girl?"

I told him I was in love with Corinne. She could live with me.

"And marry you?"

"I haven't asked her, but I plan to."

He rubbed his chin and grimaced. "The world is changing," he said. "In my day . . ."

"In your day a white woman did not marry a black man."

"Nor a Lebanese man marry out of his culture," he said gruffly.

It was the first time I had heard him express any concern about his son's marriage. "And that troubles you?" I asked.

"Love," he said after a long pause. "I suppose it is love. Love breaks down barriers."

I said I was happy for Albert. He had found the woman he wanted to spend the rest of his life with.

"And they are in love?" A question odd for a father who appeared to have approved of the marriage.

"Yes, they are in love."

But I wasn't confident this was true, at least not as far as Glynis was concerned.

26

Everything went more quickly than I had anticipated. Two days after the funeral, Glynis announced that Douglas and Rebecca would be living with her in her father's house. "It's ours now anyway," Glynis said.

Glynis had invited me for afternoon tea at the house. I was supposed to leave the day after the funeral, but Albert had asked me to stay until the end of the week. The will was going to be read then, he said, and he thought I would be a comfort to Corinne when she heard the bad news. I reminded him that Corinne already knew her father had disinherited her. Still, Albert insisted. It's one thing to know your father has left you out of his will and another to have to read the actual words and see his signature at the end, he said. So I agreed to stay. Thanks to technology Tony Lee and I could Skype each other, and when I was finished editing the entries for the insert, I could easily e-mail them back to him.

Glynis's brusque announcement about the new living arrangements seemed to startle Albert and he tried to restrain her from saying more about her grand plans. "Don't you think you should wait for the reading of the will before you make any decisions?" he said to her.

They were sitting together on one of the yellow cushioned couches in the living room. I was struck again by how different they were. The physical differences were obvious, of course: she bottle-blond, pale; Albert swarthy and dark-haired. It was the more substantive differences that worried me, differences in temperament, in values. I hoped for Albert's sake she loved him and tried hard to suppress my doubts, the suspicion that it was his father's willingness to bankroll her plan to build a resort for rich American seniors that made him so attractive to her.

Like Glynis and Albert, Douglas and Rebecca were dressed casually in jeans and T-shirts. I was wearing the pants to my suit and a white long-sleeved shirt. Douglas remarked on my pants, perhaps hoping to squash the squabble evidently beginning to brew between Albert and Glynis. "You're a formal sort of guy, eh, Émile?" he said, pushing back his thick mane of golden hair and smirking. "Where are your jeans?"

I had come for a funeral; I had not thought I'd need jeans. "I didn't bring them," I said.

The maid placed a platter of scones, a steaming pot of tea, cups, saucers, spoons, a sugar bowl, and creamer on the coffee table between us. "And why is that?" Glynis reached for the teapot.

"Why didn't I bring jeans?"

"No, silly, I meant Albert. Why do you think I should wait for the reading of the will, Albert?"

Albert glanced at me as if expecting I would intervene and support him. But this was not my business. He was the one who would soon be married to the part owner of the house. When I continued to remain silent, he said solemnly, "As a courtesy."

"To whom?" Glynis responded stiffly, and poured herself a cup of tea.

"To your sister. To Corinne. If Douglas and Rebecca move in, where will she stay?"

"She should have thought of that when she disobeyed

Daddy." Glynis blew the steam from the top of her cup and brought it to her lips.

"Yes," Rebecca echoed her, "you should have thought of that, Corinne." She was practically swaggering with her newfound confidence, tossing her shoulders like an impudent schoolgirl.

"I'm going back to my room at the university," Corinne said, her quiet dignity forcing Rebecca to retreat.

"And after that?" Glynis balanced her cup in one hand, the saucer in the other. "You can't come back here, you know. When your semester ends, you'll have to go somewhere else."

Albert reached for Glynis's hand. "Didn't Mr. Ducksworth say he promised your mother—"

"Promised her what?" Glynis snapped, and shook him off.

"You know, Glynis. You heard him. I was there. He said he promised your mother to see their daughters through university."

"And he left money to pay for Corinne's tuition and boarding," she said impatiently. "I'm not denying her that."

"It's only fair to let Corinne keep her old room, Glynis. At least until she graduates."

I felt embarrassed for Albert. He sounded weak, humiliated by Glynis's brazen display of hostility toward him.

"And what about our plans, Albert? The restaurant in Daddy's house? I mean in my and Rebecca's house?"

"Yes, our plans," Douglas jumped in. He was literally quivering with excitement. And why not? No longer would he be at the beck-and-call of parents. He'd be an entrepreneur, a businessman, a partner in a resort with a five-star restaurant. He put his arm around Rebecca's waist. I had never seen him so affectionate with her nor so excited. "We want to start building the resort as soon as we can," he declared pompously.

Rebecca slid closer to him. "Douglas is right. Why should we wait until the end of Corinne's semester? We want to move in now. Right, Douglas?"

She was claiming him. They were one, she and Douglas, a team, husband and wife. *Right, Douglas?* But she was looking at Glynis and I got the distinct impression that the inference behind the question was intended for her older sister rather than for Douglas.

The golden boy kissed his wife on her cheek. Glynis pursed her lips and stared at them. Douglas pulled Rebecca nearer to his side.

"I'll stay with Émile." Corinne spoke softly but with decisiveness.

Glynis twisted her head sharply away from Rebecca and Douglas and faced her. "With Émile?"

"If he'll have me," Corinne added shyly.

Glynis strained her head forward, her eyes pinned on mine. "What's this, Émile?"

"Corinne is welcome to stay with me," I said.

"Live with you as boyfriend and girlfriend?" Glynis was still glaring at me.

"Or more if she's willing."

Slowly, deliberately, Glynis set her cup and saucer on the table. "You do realize she has nothing, don't you, Émile?" She narrowed her eyes. "Daddy has left her with nothing. Her university fees, but nothing else. No land, no house."

"She is herself a dowry," I said quietly.

My calm manner seemed to inflame her. She sprang to her feet, but the object of her ire was not me; it was

Corinne. "Daddy protected you," she hissed. "But he's not here now. Do what you want, but before you go back to your place at the university, pack your things. Everything! Douglas and Rebecca will be moving into the house when you leave."

"Glynis!" Albert stood up. "You don't mean what you are saying."

"Every word," she shot back, and walked out of the room, leaving my friend looking sheepish and helpless.

It was just after five o'clock when Corinne and I arrived at my small bed-and-breakfast. The sun was already beginning to throw off that somnolent gaze typical of late afternoons in the tropics before it would make its final exit in a fiery blaze across the horizon. Now its light was diffuse, hazy, as if it were exhausted, spent from the day's work blasting down its powerful rays to heat the earth and spread its golden sheen across green-leaved trees and sky-blue sea, not just today, but 365 days, year after year, no short winter hours to bring relief. We were exhausted too, drained from Glynis's rancor, her threats that we had no doubt she meant to make good. I couldn't say Glynis had put her father out of his house, but I was certain that eventually she would have found a way. She wanted a five-star restaurant for her resort. Her father's house with its magnificent view of the sea on the top of the hill was where she dreamed the restaurant would be. The only obstacle now was the apple of her father's eye, but she could, and would, put her out.

On the drive to my place Corinne and I were both silent, wrapped in our own thoughts. *Or more if she's willing*, I had said. But I wanted Glynis to know she had not boxed Corinne in. Corinne would not be homeless; she would have a place to stay even if her sisters had thrown her out of her father's house.

"Were you proposing marriage?"

We had just settled down for dinner when Corinne asked that question. Her head was lowered over her wineglass so I couldn't see the expression on her face. "One day," I said, taking the chance that her question was not an idle one. "If you'll have me."

"One day? Not now?"

"After you get your degree."

"And in the meantime we'll live in sin?"

I removed the wineglass from her hand and put it down on the table. "Today," I said, and brought her hands to my lips. "I would marry you today. But . . ."

"But what?"

"I don't want you to have regrets."

"You think I'm too young. Is that it?"

"I think you should go back to the university, and when you graduate, if you still want me, we'll marry."

"I'll still want you," she said with a finality that made my heart race with happiness.

"I'll be in Jamaica," I said. "I won't leave."

"And when Mr. Cumberbatch QC returns?"

"One step at a time," I said.

We kissed. "*She is herself a dowry*," she murmured in my ear. "Oh, Émile, you have no idea how much those words mean to me."

27

Corinne and I were already in the reception area of the lawyer's office when Glynis and Rebecca walked in, followed by Albert and Douglas, the sisters in business suits, the men in jackets and ties. Glynis was holding a large brown envelope. I saw the lettering on the front only partially but enough to make out the words: *The Last* . . . She had been named executor, or, rather, executrix, as Rebecca had been quick to inform Corinne the previous night.

Glynis was bubbling over with excitement when she came over to where Corinne and I were sitting on the black leather divan near the door to the office. "So I see you found a place to sleep last night," she said with false gaiety. "Not too soon to be leaving, right? How many days before you go back to the university?"

Corinne did not answer her.

"Well, Albert has a soft heart. He persuaded me to give you a week. But, of course, I can ship your things to Jamaica if you haven't finished packing by then."

Corinne kept her lips tightly shut.

"A week is generous, don't you think?"

When Corinne still didn't respond, Glynis came closer to her. "Poor Daddy," she said, her voice saccharine sweet. "He was always boasting how strong-willed you are. He didn't think you'd use that strong will to disobey him."

I had witnessed Ducksworth's boast the very first day

I met Corinne. My father was astounded by her refusal to take the handkerchief her father had offered her, more astounded when Corinne wiped her hands on her shorts smearing the mud all over it. *She has her own mind*, Ducksworth had said, beaming with pride.

Corinne's hand shook. I covered it with mine and held it still.

The door to the lawyer's office opened and we were saved from more of Glynis's taunts. "Come." She signaled Albert. "Let's go. This shouldn't take long." And she walked past the secretary into the lawyer's office.

The lawyer was Mr. Gopaul, as I had expected. He stood up behind his desk when we entered and Glynis put down the envelope she was holding. "Well, we are all here, Mr. Gopaul, and we all know what's in the will, so there's no need for formalities." She pushed the envelope across his desk. "The question we most want answered is how long it will take to execute Daddy's wishes."

"Sit, sit." Mr. Gopaul indicated the three plush leather armchairs in front of his desk. "These are for you, the daughters. I asked my secretary to bring in three more chairs. You men won't mind folding chairs, will you?" He turned to Albert, Douglas, and me and pointed to the row of metal chairs behind the armchairs. "Sorry they are not as nice. Hope you won't be too uncomfortable."

"No need to apologize," Albert said. "These chairs are fine. We're just here as extras. The ladies wanted us to come."

Glynis took the middle armchair. "Good, good," Mr. Gopaul said, and rolled his hands over each other. "The executrix between the sisters, the daughter in charge." There was not a trace of irony in his voice. And why should there have been? Glynis was indeed in charge.

Mr. Gopaul sat down on the chair behind his desk and called out to his secretary, "Bring us a pot of coffee. And five cups. You drink coffee, don't you?" he asked us all. "Coffee in the morning, tea in the afternoon, not so?"

"Always tea for me," Glynis said.

"So tea for Miss Ducksworth," Mr. Gopaul instructed his secretary.

"For Rebecca and Albert too," Glynis said.

"And for Corinne?"

Corinne shook her head. "I won't need anything."

"And neither will I," I said directly to the secretary.

"So it's one coffee and three teas. No need for a pot." The secretary left. "Everyone comfortable?"

"Mr. Gopaul," Glynis began, "we are appreciative of your concern for our comfort, but we are anxious . . ."

"Yes, yes. The will." Mr. Gopaul rifled through the stack of papers on his desk.

"I have it." Glynis slid to the edge of her seat and pointed to the envelope she had put on his desk.

Mr. Gopaul placed his wide palm on top of his papers and held them still. "I can see that," he said. His eyes fell on Glynis and rose again.

"It's Daddy's official will," Glynis said.

Mr. Gopaul coughed.

"How Daddy wanted his property distributed."

Mr. Gopaul removed his glasses and wiped them with a handkerchief he had fished out of his breast pocket. "A will is a serious document," he said, his eyes lowered on his hands. "A legal document—"

"That's why Daddy engaged you as his lawyer," Glynis interrupted. "You are the best," she added gratuitously.

Mr. Gopaul seemed unimpressed by the compliment. "A will represents the wishes of the deceased," he went on. "And as your father's lawyer, I have a responsibility to make sure it's properly executed."

"And that's what we want you to do. I . . . All of us."

"A will speaks for the dead as if he were able to speak himself." Mr. Gopaul continued to wipe the lenses of his glasses with studious attention. "That's why it's called a will. But we have to consider the state of mind of the deceased when he made his will."

"Yes, yes," Glynis said. Mr. Gopaul's ceremonious disquisition on the purpose of a will was clearly unnerving her, but he appeared to belong to the old school where the trappings of the legal profession were assiduously observed. I wouldn't have been surprised to learn he was among the lawyers who protested the recent changes in sartorial decorum that no longer required them to wear the traditional gown and stiff white wig at court when they argued a case before a judge. Glynis would need to be patient. Mr. Gopaul would lay out the rules; he would make certain there would be no cause for objections once the will was probated.

"Ah, the tea." The secretary had returned. "And coffee for me."

"Mr. Gopaul." Glynis pushed aside the teacup the secretary had placed in front of her. "We know Daddy was of sound mind when he wrote his will."

"Dictated to me," Mr. Gopaul said emphatically. "You can leave us now," he said to his secretary. He shoved his handkerchief back in his pocket, put on his glasses, and stirred his coffee.

Glynis picked up the envelope and pulled out the papers. "This is Daddy's will," she said, her voice unraveling. "He gave it to me." She clamped her fingers on one end of the papers and shook them apart. They fluttered open like a lady's fan.

"But it is not the official will," Mr. Gopaul said firmly.

"I was there when he signed it, Mr. Gopaul."

The lawyer put down his spoon and hunched forward on his desk, raising his bushy eyebrows. "But you were not there when he came back, Miss Ducksworth." He held her eyes.

"When he came back?" A thin lock of hair had strayed over Glynis's forehead. She did not push it back.

"Mr. Ducksworth came back a week later. He said he had been impetuous. He had acted out of anger. He was not in the state of mind to make decisions about his will. His daughter had refused—"

"Yes," Glynis interjected harshly. "He was a good father to her, but she refused to do the one thing he asked her to do."

"He said he overreacted." Mr. Gopaul sat back in his chair. "He was afraid. Tivoli Gardens is a dangerous place." He sighed; his chest rose and then dropped down like a heavy weight on his stomach.

"She knew that, but she defied him. She was always defying him."

"But he loved her," Mr. Gopaul said.

Rebecca snorted.

Mr. Gopaul sat up. "Mr. Ducksworth loved all his daughters," he said, peering intently at Rebecca. "He told me he was wrong to strike out at Corinne. She had been kind to him. She was the one who made sure he took his medicines, ate the right food—"

"Took advantage of him in his dotage." Rebecca reared forward.

Glynis restrained her. "Let Mr. Gopaul continue," she said.

Corinne began to cry and Mr. Gopaul pulled open a drawer at the side of his desk and took out a box of tissues. "Here." He passed the box over to her. Corinne took out a tissue and dried her eyes. "Your father loved you very much," he said softly.

Glynis curled her lips. "What did Daddy do when he came back?"

"He reverted," Mr. Gopaul said without emotion.

"Reverted?"

"To his original will."

Glynis bounded out of her chair. "That couldn't be! Daddy would not do that. He promised . . ."

"He said it was always his intention to give you and Rebecca the land to the left and right of his house and to give Corinne the house where he hoped to live out his days. He didn't think his days would come to an end so soon." Mr. Gopaul looked over at Corinne and added gently, "I think he wanted to apologize to you. He didn't get the time."

"Pride," I muttered under my breath.

Mr. Gopaul glanced at me. "Ego," he said. "Mr. Ducksworth admitted it was his ego that propelled him to do what he regretted the moment he put the last stroke of his signature on his will, removing Corinne from inheriting his house. He was being selfish, he told me. Corinne was moving away from him, claiming her own life, her independence. He didn't like it, but his daughter . . ." He paused and faced Glynis. "*All* his daughters, he said, had a right to live their own lives, make their own decisions. But it was more than ego with him. Mr. Ducksworth confessed to me that he was stupidly holding on to a grudge."

"She hurt him with her sanctimonious mumbo jumbo." Glynis's tone was acidic. "Telling him she would give him only half her love."

"I was there," Mr. Gopaul observed dryly.

"I didn't love him less," Corinne murmured. "But I

would have to share my love for him with my husband."

"Lucky husband." Mr. Gopaul's eyes swept over me. The moment was brief—the next second he was reaching for his papers—and I blushed, except with my dark skin he would not have known; my face and neck felt hot and I couldn't stop a wide smile from making its way across my lips.

"Stop this!" Rebecca stood up. "You have it all wrong. She never loved Daddy. And he never would have—"

"I have his most recent will here." Mr. Gopaul pushed a sheaf of papers across his desk toward Glynis. "You can examine it. You'll find it was properly witnessed and signed. The date, you will observe, is one week after the date of the will you are holding." He withdrew his hand. "Read it. You can have this copy. I'll make sure your sisters each have a copy."

Glynis put down the papers in her hand and picked up the ones Mr. Gopaul had given to her. She scanned the pages from top to bottom. "I don't know these witnesses," she said, waving the last page at Mr. Gopaul.

"You don't have to know them," the lawyer responded calmly. "But I can assure you they are respected citizens. I trust you'd know I wouldn't compromise my reputation or the reputation of my office with false witnesses."

"She did this!" Rebecca shook her finger at Corinne. "Dancing with Daddy. Acting innocent!"

"And this is his final will?" asked Glynis.

I had to hand it to her. She had total control of her voice. She did not stutter; she did not whimper.

"Yes, it is his final will," Mr. Gopaul said.

"So there's no use?"

"It's Mr. Ducksworth's last word on how he wanted his property to be divided."

"The date?" Glynis was studying the last page of will again.

"It's one week after . . ."

"One week after . . ." Glynis murmured, her finger on the line Mr. Gopaul had indicated. "Come," she said, and turned to Rebecca. "There's nothing we can do."

"It's Mr. Ducksworth's final wishes," Mr. Gopaul repeated.

Glynis was already at the door. "Let's go. There's no more to say." She motioned to Albert and they all followed her, Rebecca whimpering, Albert and Douglas gallantly behind.

They were huddled together in the reception room when I came out of Mr. Gopaul's office, leaving Corinne behind to discuss the details of her father's will. Albert was not with them but would soon reappear with glasses of ice water for Glynis and Rebecca.

They didn't seem to notice me as I stood nearby, behind a column, waiting for Corinne, or if they did, they didn't care that I could hear their conversation. I heard only snippets: Douglas trying to console Glynis and his wife, Glynis hanging on to his every word, and in the end, by the time Albert returned, Glynis was already so revived, her enthusiasm so restored, that she called out loudly to him, "Let's go out for lunch at that new restaurant in town."

These are the snippets I overheard:

Glynis: I told him not to invite her for Christmas
Rebecca: She wheedled her way back in his good graces. Dancing with him!
Garbled words. Corinne's name stood out.
Douglas: Wasn't it he who asked her?
Rebecca: He was drunk.
Glynis (*bitterly, tone subdued*): Besotted, but it makes no difference. Daddy had already changed his will.

Silence.

Douglas *(piping up merrily):* We can still make a go of it.

Glynis: I don't see how.

Douglas: Mr. Glazal has not withdrawn his money, has he?

I pressed my ear closer to the wall.

Glynis: Albert says his father will back us.

Douglas: Can you be sure?

Glynis: He agreed to invest in the retirement flats. He won't let down his only son. Albert's happiness means everything to Mr. Glazal.

More garbled words, but I didn't dare get any closer.

Rebecca: The flats, yes, but it won't be the same without the restaurant.

Douglas: There's a bright side.

Glynis: How could there be? Corinne has ruined us.

Douglas: We can have a ferry.

Glynis: A ferry?

Douglas: Shuttling between the two sides.

Douglas explaining, his words tumbling over each other, difficult to decipher.

Glynis: And that would work?

Douglas: People would come from all over the island.

More hushed whisperings.

Glynis: A party ferry! Yes, that's it! We could put the restaurant on the ferry. We could have music. Lights on the ferry. Dancing! Who needs to walk up the hill to the restaurant?

Rebecca: Yeah! Who needs to get all sweaty walking up a hill?

28

When she returned from lunch, Glynis announced she wasn't going to spend another
day, another minute in a house that wasn't
hers. She had friends who would welcome her. She seemed
more hurt than angry and Corinne was sympathetic. She
told Glynis it wasn't necessary for her to leave. After all,
soon she would be going back to the university in Jamaica.
Glynis could remain in the house as long as she wanted.
"Stay," Corinne urged her. And I think as a way of salvag-
ing Glynis's pride, Corinne added: "Someone has to look
after the house."

It was a mistake. Glynis lashed out at her: "Did it just
occur to you that someone has to look after the house? That
the people in the village will destroy the house if it's left
vacant? They'll ransack it. You'll have a shell of a house
when you return. But you were too busy bending Daddy's
ear with your lies to think about that."

"I did no such thing," Corinne said softly.

"Daddy would never have changed his will. You did it,
you with your pretend innocence, your cunning. Sly like a
fox."

Sly like a fox. Corinne's exact words to describe Glynis.
How easily people find relief by transferring their own
guilt to someone else. Glynis was the sly one, accompany-
ing her father to the lawyer to make sure he carried out his
threat. I couldn't be silent; I couldn't stay on the sidelines

while Corinne squirmed under Glynis's false accusations.

"I think you're wrong," I said. "Mr. Ducksworth made his own decision. I think he wanted to be fair."

"Fair?" Glynis pounced on me. "What's fair about Daddy giving Corinne the largest part of his estate? She's the youngest."

"Maybe that's why. Maybe because you and Rebecca are settled. Rebecca's married and you are about to get married. Maybe he wanted to give Corinne some security."

"Maybe because she is the only one he truly loved." Her voice cracked, her face flushed deep red, and her bottom lip quivered. For the first time I glimpsed the child she had been, fighting for her space in the knot of daughters clamoring for their father's love. She was the eldest; she was expected to yield, to subordinate her wishes, her needs, to those of her siblings. Corinne was the baby; Corinne was the one needing her father's attention, not Glynis. She had consoled herself with Rebecca, systematically cultivating her sister's admiration and dependence on her. *Give me a child until he is seven years old and he is mine for life.* Rebecca was young when their mother died. Glynis had time to shape her into a mirror reflection of herself. But Rebecca's adoration was not enough; it couldn't fill that yawning hole in her heart.

Ducksworth insisted he didn't want to be the cause of discord among his daughters. Yet he was the one who lit the match, showing preference for one over the others, sparking the future strife among them. He had saved her from drowning, but nothing had changed, Glynis told Albert, who confided in me, trusting I would not judge his future wife too harshly. Corinne was their father's joy and when she broke his heart he grieved, day after day, as if he had no other daughters to console him.

Perhaps I was too hard on Glynis. I knew the pain of longing for a father's attention, his love. I could empathize with her. "Your father loved all his daughters," I said tenderly. "He loved you very much even if he didn't always show it."

The scathing look she gave me, chin upturned, eyes narrowed, the muscles on her brow drawn together in a tight bunch, silenced me. "How would you know?" she sneered.

I had overstepped my boundary. She had momentarily exposed her vulnerability and I should have been sensitive enough to hold my tongue. When she spoke again, she was the old Glynis I knew: "And you? You plan to move in with Corinne? Because if you think you and Corinne will turn this place into another Tivoli Gardens and bring your Rasta friends with their dreadlocks, smoking weed and whooping it up with that reggae music, you better think again. This is Barbados, not Jamaica. Or haven't you noticed? We are civil here. We don't have their riffraff, or their crime, or their vicious murders." She brought her finger close to my face. "I have friends, Douglas's parents have friends. High up in the government. We'll be watching."

She turned her back on me and strode to her room. To pack her things and leave, she said angrily.

Corinne went to her room too. She wanted to be alone for a while, and as I stood on the deck looking out at the still, calm, radiantly blue sea, I had to acknowledge that Glynis was right. Barbados was not Jamaica with its high crime and devastating poverty. I had never seen a dreadlocked Rasta smoking weed in the streets or anywhere else in Barbados. I had read the reports on the island's literacy rates. Ninety-seven percent of the population could read and write. And that was a UN estimate. Some claimed the literacy rate in Barbados was even higher. If Corinne turned her house into a community center, it would surely not be like the one in Tivoli Gardens. There would be music, art, dance, theater, poetry, literature. The notion of such a place was extremely pleasing to me.

29

Ducksworth had put aside a little money in his will for the maintenance of the house and Mr. Gopaul said he would hire some people who would make sure it would be protected and any damage immediately repaired. So two days later I flew back to Jamaica with Corinne and once she was settled in her hall at the university and had returned to her classes, I went to Trinidad to see my father. He looked more gaunt than he had been when I left him just days earlier and his cough had grown worse; now he seemed to be fighting for breath. Henrietta had moved in. She said she found herself spending more time in my father's house than in her own home. She and Trevor quarreled about that, but it was hard for her to leave the old man. "What if he drown in his spit?" she said.

She had then managed to persuade my father to allow Trevor to move in with her, which was remarkable. I never would have predicted that my father, a recluse, or almost a recluse, would have permitted not just his housekeeper, but her husband too (common-law husband, as he often reminded me), to sleep under the same roof as he. I attributed his change of heart to the extent of his illness. I thought perhaps I should give up my job in Jamaica and stay in Trinidad to take care of him, but he would not hear of it. "My conscience is already burdened by my obstinacy, my unmanly grief," he said. "I cannot bear more."

It was the most he could manage in the way of apologizing for ignoring me when I was a child, for shuttering himself in his rooms grieving for my mother, but it was enough and I was grateful for that acknowledgment. I had waited years for some sign from him that he was aware of how his coldness had affected me. I was an adult now; I did not have the same needs I had as a child. I had accepted him for who he was, and yet it felt good to know he regretted his actions. "Enjoy your life while you are still young," he said. "Time moves too quickly."

And so I agreed to return to my job in Jamaica after the weekend, comforted by the knowledge that Henrietta and Trevor would take good care of him.

Albert was also in Trinidad. He had come to see his father, to discuss with him the change in Ducksworth's will. Glynis, he said, was anxious to have his father's reassurance, for without Mr. Glazal's involvement, it would be almost impossible to persuade investors to put their money in the project she and Douglas envisioned.

Albert said he liked Douglas's idea of a ferry, though by the time Glynis told him about it, Douglas had expanded the plan. It was not to be merely a floating restaurant but rather a floating nightclub with music, dancing, and a fully stocked bar. And not just for the seniors at the resort, but for tourists coming off the cruise ships and for prosperous locals as well.

Albert predicted the project would be successful even without the big house. Obviously it would be more successful if the house belonged to Glynis and Rebecca, but all's well that ends well, he said. He would not have been happy knowing their business was thriving because Corinne had been disinherited.

The day before I left for Jamaica, Albert called. He needed to talk to me, he said. Could I meet with him early the next morning, somewhere we could speak in private?

He chose one of the public benches that surrounded the Savannah, one next to a coconut vendor, his horse-drawn cart piled with green coconuts. Albert arrived before I did and had secured a bench shaded by one of the large saman trees the French Creole and English slave owners planted to protect their estate homes from the broiling sun. See a saman tree in Trinidad and you know where there were Africans beaten and tortured.

"Americans are now discovering that coconut water contains powerful antioxidants," he said, handing me a coconut. He had bought two; the vendor had sliced them open at the top and inserted straws in the soft jelly. "Now they're packaging it up like orange juice."

"Still the businessman," I teased, sucking up the coconut juice through my straw.

"My father's looking into it," he said. "He's thinking of buying a coconut estate."

He was toying with me. Dry goods, he'd told me a long time ago, were what his family was good at selling. Some people got caught up in trends and they lost everything, he had said. Still, I didn't miss the fine lines of tension gathering along his temples. He was worried, but I would have to wait until he was ready to tell me why we had to meet in a safe place, why our conversation needed to be private. In the meanwhile I tried to distract him.

"The breeze feels good here, coming off the mountains," I said, pointing to the blue haze of the northern range behind us. "And the girls are not too hard on the eyes, either."

Two groups of young women had passed us by, lithe in their Lycra outfits, tight tops outlining their breasts, sports shorts showing off backsides firmly rounded, legs lean and sculpted. He hadn't noticed the first group and so I drew his attention to the second.

"Where?" He swiveled his head from back to front.

"I know you'll be getting married soon, but you must still have eyes," I joked, draining my coconut and discarding it in the bin nearby.

"And what about you? I thought you were in love," he responded, putting his coconut in the bin too.

I could see the beginnings of a smile on his lips and took my chance. "So what's on your mind so early in the morning?" I poked him playfully in the rib with my elbow.

"Glynis," he said. "I've disappointed her."

He had told his father what Ducksworth had done. I listened in silence as he filled in the details, alternating between hope and despair, three times telling me that Glynis loved him, each time sounding less and less confident. He crossed and uncrossed his legs, bit his lips, scanned the pavement, shifted his eyes in a vacant gaze to the Savannah behind us, patched with dried dirt and tough knots of grass. At one point he paused, his attention seemingly swayed by the cricket match in the field beyond us. He remarked on the skill of the bowler and just when I was about to agree with him, he turned back to me, his eyes pathetically dull, and asked: "Do you think she loves me?"

What was I to say but that I thought she did, relieved that my brain had sent the right verb to my tongue. I had not said, *I believe she does*; I said, "I *think* she does."

Here is what he told me:

His father had found it difficult to sleep the night he returned from Ducksworth's funeral. He tossed and turned in his bed, perplexed by Ducksworth's decision to disinherit his daughter. He could not believe Corinne would say outright to her father that she didn't love him. So early the next morning, Mr. Glazal called Albert. "Mr. Ducksworth must have done something terrible to his daughter for her to treat him that way," he said. "What did he do?" And having the correct version of what Corinne had said because I had apprised him of it, Albert told his father that Corinne had never told her father that she didn't love him. Mr. Ducksworth wanted her to stop teaching the children at Tivoli Gardens and she said she would not. She had given them her word.

"So she disobeyed her father?" Mr. Glazal asked his son.

"She said she had a responsibility to the children and their parents. They were depending on her."

Mr. Glazal pondered Corinne's response for a while and then asked Albert if he knew how a mother bird was certain she had done her job well. The answer was obvious and Albert told him so.

"Well, then," Mr. Glazal said, "Mr. Ducksworth should have been proud to know he raised an independent daughter. Corinne is doing the right thing helping those poor people."

So when Albert returned to Trinidad after the reading of the most recent will, he told his father that Mr. Ducksworth may indeed have been proud of Corinne, for he had changed his will again and left his house and the land around it to her.

Mr. Glazal was elated. "They blinded me, those two sisters," he said. "All those protestations of love for their father. I thought Mr. Ducksworth was lucky to have daughters who loved him so much. Still, I couldn't remain blinded when Glynis told me that Corinne was left out of her father's will. Corinne loved her father too. I am glad in the end that Mr. Ducksworth did the right thing. You make your own bed, Albert, but I don't have to lie in it." And dismissing his son's pleas to him to reconsider, Mr. Glazal withdrew his offer to invest in Glynis's dream.

I wanted to applaud when Albert told me this, but I restrained myself.

"Glynis was upset, naturally. She said it was over," Albert murmured darkly.

"Just like that?" I did not disguise my disdain and Albert was quick to admonish me.

"Oh, not the way you're thinking," he said, guessing my intent. "She meant her dream of a fancy resort. Beautiful flats, bright blue umbrellas on the beach, white lounge chairs with striped blue cushions, people sunning themselves on the sand on pretty colored towels, a ferry shuttling back and forth between the tips of the cove. Parties, wine, expensive liquor, good food, a five-star restaurant with André Lambert as head chef. She had the picture fully drawn out in her head." He sighed. "Now her dream is completely shattered."

I couldn't help thinking her dream should have been a future with Albert.

"I've disappointed her," he repeated.

"It was your father's decision, not yours."

"She thinks I could have done more to persuade him. I did my best. My father wouldn't budge."

"Have you told Rebecca and Douglas?"

"Glynis and I are meeting Rebecca and Douglas for brunch tomorrow," he said. "Glynis has already told Rebecca, but Rebecca is afraid to tell Douglas. He has his heart set on the project. It's his ticket out of his parents' house."

And to the dollars dangling before his eyes.

"He could get a real job," I said, "instead of piddling around his parents' house."

"He's not piddling. He's fixing up the house for them."

I didn't bring up Mr. Glazal's analogy of the mother bird, though I was much tempted to do so.

"It's just that he was depending on my father," Albert said. "And now my father has withdrawn his help."

"He'll get over it. Men like Douglas always have another trick up their sleeves."

Albert looked hard at me. "Why do you dislike him so much?"

"He doesn't think much of us," I said.

"You mean *me*. He does not think much of *me*. That's what you really wanted to say, isn't it? It was a bad war," he said bitterly, pressing his fingers to his lips and releasing them to add sadly, "done for the wrong reasons. So many young people died, so many maimed for life. And they never found the purported WMDs."

"But you are not to blame," I protested.

"My family comes from Lebanon. The Lebanese are Arabs. That's all the evidence Douglas seems to need. It's hard to overcome prejudices especially when they are so hardwired as Douglas's are. His brother suffered from PTSD when he came back from the war. He drowned in an accident. Or was it suicide?" He shook his head. "It doesn't matter which. He died. That was all that mattered to Douglas. And he wouldn't have died if he hadn't been in Iraq."

"So there you are," I said. "The war was in Iraq, not in Lebanon."

"Muslims killed him."

"You are not a Muslim. And anyhow, most Muslims are peaceful people."

"It doesn't matter. I am an Arab."

"You are Trinidadian."

"Of Arab descent."

"Don't let Douglas's warped views infect you," I said. "He's not a nice man."

"He's still grieving for his brother. I make a convenient scapegoat."

His eyes were so pained it was hard to keep facing him. I had a four-hour stopover in Barbados on my flight to Jamaica. I could be with him when he broke the news to Douglas at brunch the next day. I could be his support, the person he could depend on, who would stand by him no matter what. Glynis should be that person, and perhaps she would defend him, but I couldn't take the chance. Rebecca was her sister. Blood, as Ducksworth once reminded us, is thicker than water.

"Would you like me to be there with you when you tell Douglas?" I asked.

His face lit up like a child's on Christmas Day. "You'll do that? You'll do that for me?"

"What are friends for?"

"I will owe you one."

"You will owe me nothing," I said, and slapped him on the back.

30

I n my fairly young life I had been to two wakes, one on the eve of the burial of a school friend, the other for my aunt, my mother's spinster sister. My friend was just a boy, nine years old. He had drowned in an undertow that had pulled him far out into the sea. There was loud wailing and pitiful screams at his wake. "Why him? He was so young. Lord, Lord!" His parents were inconsolable. At times his father had to hold up his mother when she crumbled to her knees; at times it was his mother who cradled his father's head on her breasts. His siblings were crying too, their arms locked around each other. My aunt's wake was quite different. My aunt had never married; she had no children; what few friends she had sat in stony silence around her coffin, neither looking at each other nor at my aunt's body laid out in her best going-to-church-on-Sunday dress. I thought of my aunt's wake when I saw Rebecca, Douglas, Albert, and Glynis, sitting stiffly in a dark corner of the restaurant, the couples paired off opposite each other.

Though I could not hear a word Albert was saying, I could tell he was apologizing. He was tracing his finger around the rim of his water glass, his eyes cast down as if to avoid looking across at Douglas and Rebecca, or over to Glynis. Rebecca, as I guessed immediately, had already given Douglas the bad news. But Albert need not have been concerned about avoiding the sisters' eyes. Both Glynis and Rebecca were staring with fixed intensity at their folded hands. Only Douglas faced him, eyes cold and hard as marble, lips firmly locked.

Douglas saw me first and bounded up. "Oh, there you are!" He held out his hand, but before I could grasp it, he sneered, "The Arab's friend."

I looked over at Albert. His face was gray.

"Albert's friend," I said, refusing Douglas's hand. I pulled out a chair and sat down next to my friend.

Douglas seemed not to have taken offense at my refusal to shake his hand. He returned to his seat and refilled his wine glass. "I suppose you already know what your friend's been telling us," he said, stretching out his long legs. "I warned Glynis not to trust him." He sniffed the wine in his glass with a grating air of superiority, swirled it, took a sip, swirled it again, and swallowed.

"You trusted him enough to want his father's money," I said, pinning my eyes on his.

He blinked and pulled in his legs. "They're all the same," he muttered. "It runs in the blood. You can't depend on them. They never keep their word."

And so the accusations began, the vitriol, he accusing, I responding, Albert trying to stop me, saying, "It's no use. He thinks the way he thinks. Nothing you say is going to change his mind." But I had to say something when Douglas claimed Albert belonged to a clan of terrorists.

"Albert is a Trinidadian," I said firmly, but I kept my voice low, determined not to lose my temper.

"His family is from Lebanon," Douglas struck back. "They—all of them—are up to their eyeballs in blood. My brother's blood!" he spat out through clenched teeth, his face lobster red.

My friend had a soft heart. Douglas was still grieving

over his brother's death, Albert had told me more than once. He had to be patient with him; Douglas could say things he didn't really mean.

I was certain that at any moment Rebecca would put an end to her husband's ravings, or that Glynis would come to her fiancé's defense, but neither sister said a word.

Rebecca began to cry; big fat tears rolled down her cheeks. Glynis stretched her arm across the table and handed her a napkin. "This is not the place to carry on like that, Albert," she said. Then, noticing my raised eyebrows, she quickly added, "You too, Douglas. You're upsetting Rebecca."

For the umpteenth time Albert attempted to explain his father's position: he had withdrawn his offer because Mr. Ducksworth had withdrawn his.

This time it seemed Glynis could no longer bear to hear him make excuses for his father. She twisted her body violently around toward him. "You can't be such a fool, Albert! Can't you see? Can't you get it into your brain that Corinne tricked Daddy? If she hadn't filled his head with lies, Daddy would never have changed his will and your father would have been willing to give us the money. How many times must I tell you this?"

"Don't, Glynis." Albert put his hand on her arm and squeezed it gently. "You have no proof that Corinne did such a thing. She was in Jamaica."

Glynis batted away his hand. "I'm going. I'm leaving now. Rebecca is not well. I'm taking her home." She stood up. "Coming, Douglas?"

Douglas pushed back his chair and rose. "Remember what I told you, Glynis? They cannot be trusted."

Had she and Douglas talked about Mr. Glazal this way?

Albert made a half-hearted attempt to join them, but

then, as if it suddenly struck him that Glynis had not defended him, that she had asked Douglas to leave with her and had ignored him, he sat back down.

They were gone and for a long time we didn't speak; I was giving Albert the space I thought he needed to collect his thoughts. At one point he grunted, and alarmed, I looked up. He had a clownish smile plastered across his face, but his eyes were incredibly sad. I moved forward in my chair as if to say something to him—what, I did not know, hoping only that when I began to speak, something comforting would come out of my mouth. But he held up a finger and stopped me, so I retreated.

My plane to Jamaica was leaving in two hours. I had to get to the airport soon. I glanced at my watch and he noticed.

"Don't worry," he said. "I'll get you to your plane on time."

I tried once again to comfort him. "You'll work this out with Glynis," I said.

He shook his head. "I don't think this marriage will work."

It was a statement. He did not ask for my opinion or my approval.

31

I had empathized with Glynis. With Rebecca too. It must have been almost impossible for them to block out the trills in their father's voice so present in his endearments meant for Corinne alone. *My joy. The apple of my eye.* Still, what might have begun as sibling jealousy soon became greed to possess all that their father would bequeath to Corinne. Greed, though, is one of the seven deadly sins and is said to bring its own karma. Payback, we say on my island. If that is true, then Glynis and Rebecca have had their payback, Rebecca the less deserving, for she was a follower, the one who latched onto her sister's dreams because she had none of her own.

In the beginning, times were good for Douglas and Rebecca. Douglas found a buyer for the strip of land Ducksworth had left for his daughter, but soon the money was swallowed up, for Douglas was a man who believed he was entitled to the good life. Hadn't the Creator made him handsome, tall, muscular, fair-haired, a Caribbean Douglas Fairbanks? His friends thought so too and enticed him into spending on luxuries—a fancy car that he crashed in a drunken stupor on the highway after a night of riotous partying, and a mortgage on a house that he couldn't repay. Rebecca found herself barely managing to put food on their table and married to a man more attached to the bottle than he ever was to her.

For Glynis there was the loss of the one thing she ever

truly wanted. It was her childhood dream, Albert said, but it was greed that motivated her to stalk him. Perhaps I'm being unfair, yet I was always suspicious of their whirlwind romance. Albert was rich, but he was dark, olive-skinned, a Trinidadian of Lebanese heritage, not the kind of man a woman from the Caribbean who had deliberately sought to preserve her English roots, protecting her fair skin, changing the color of her hair to English blond, would have ordinarily chosen. Albert was a cautious man and it had seemed to me much out of character for him to make the commitment of a lifetime to a woman he had known for a mere few weeks. But even a cautious man is easy prey for a beautiful woman who is intent on capturing him.

It was greed, too, I am convinced, that led Glynis to show her father that photograph of Corinne in Tivoli Gardens, her greed that wouldn't allow him a moment's peace until he changed his will. For though Ducksworth had declared openly to Corinne that he would disinherit her, I never thought he meant to do it, and neither did Glynis. Which was why Glynis made certain to accompany her father to the lawyer's office to witness his signature on the transference of the deed for the house to her and Rebecca after he died.

In the end Rebecca discovered that Glynis was having an affair with Douglas, had been having an affair for months, though for Albert's sake, I hope not when he and Glynis were engaged. Rebecca summoned the courage I didn't think she had and returned to Trinidad, the place of her birth where she had spent happy days. Predictably, Glynis soon got tired of Douglas's drinking and his free-wheeling spending and left him too. I heard she immigrated to America. She will be all right. Women like Glynis can always rely on their beauty to capture the hearts of men willing to pay mightily for the chance to marry them.

It took Albert a while to get over his broken heart, but he has renewed his romance with the girl he was dating in Trinidad before he met Glynis. She shares his values and ambition. If they marry, I am certain he will have a happy life with her.

My father died peacefully not long after I parted from him on New Year's Day. I wasn't there when he died, but Henrietta said she was holding his hand until he took his last breath.

There was more than I thought in his estate: his house and some stocks, which he left to me, and a pretty hefty savings account at the bank which he left to Henrietta.

I had said to Corinne one step at a time, but I couldn't wait the years it would take for her to complete her degree. In September she transferred to the Barbados campus of the University of the West Indies and by the end of the year, we married. Tony Lee pulled a few strings for me and I got a teaching job at a small private school in Bridgetown. He had to hire a new person to edit the literary insert, but I agreed to review the editor's selections for a small fee. I sold the house my father left me and with the money, Corinne and I were able to refurbish that miraculous house overlooking the sea that her father had bequeathed to her.

In a way our lives have not changed. The house we live in is bigger; we are not cramped in a tiny cottage, but our days and nights follow the same rhythm. While Corinne writes her papers and studies for her exams, I sit at a desk next to her and prepare for the classes I teach or I edit the submissions for the literary insert. I have even written a number of poems and hope to have a collection published one day.

I never found out what had happened in my father's

past that caused him to give me a copy of the film *The Battle of Algiers*. Perhaps he was thinking of the story of Émile Fornier, my mother's French relative, but now I understand fully his intent and the values he wished to impart to me. *Know the price people are willing to pay for freedom*, he once said. I am fortunate to have a wife who has the courage to stand up for her convictions.

After she graduates, Corinne intends to convert the main part of the house into an arts center where artists can exhibit their work and writers can give readings. We plan to sponsor forums and discussions on all forms of the arts at our place—Corinne has insisted that I drop "her" and refer to this place as "our house." In exchange I insisted that we name our forum Corinne's Salon.

Glynis has not developed the land her father left for her. My hope is that Albert will make her an offer she'll find difficult to refuse and will build a vacation home on the land and we will be neighbors.

Now when I stand on the veranda and look out at that dazzling blue sea, the future shimmers before me full of wondrous possibilities.